DOCTOR WHO

CASUALTIES OF WAR
STEVE EMMERSON

Published by BBC Worldwide Ltd,
Woodlands, 80 Wood Lane
London W12 0TT

First published 2000
Copyright © Steve Emmerson 2000
The moral right of the author has been asserted

Original series broadcast on the BBC
Format © BBC 1963
Doctor Who and TARDIS are trademarks of the BBC

ISBN 0 563 53805 8
Imaging by Black Sheep, copyright © BBC 2000

Printed and bound in Great Britain by Mackays of
Chatham
Cover printed by Belmont Press Ltd, Northampton

For Shirley and Ben

Prologue

19 March 1918

The cries in the night were terrible things. They echoed with an eerie hollowness, amplified by the luxuriously spacious rooms that made up Hawkswick Hall.

Corporal John Sykes lay awake, fully dressed in khaki kit, listening to the shrieks. Every night, the same torment. Every morning he woke with the same dark bags under his eyes. He wondered which was better sometimes; this nightmare world, or the one in the trenches. Both were filled with dead men. Except the dead men here still screamed.

Sometimes he even considered making a request for an early board. Get himself back to the front. Get himself over the top to find a final release from this hell. But Sykes had a wife and a baby. He found Lily's face in his dreams, her eyes swelling with tears as he boarded the train. And most nights he woke with his pillow soaking wet. There were many kinds of wounds, he'd learned. And the worst of them weren't visible at all.

Lifting his watch into the moonlight, Sykes saw that it was almost 0100 hours. He should be in the land of Nod now, being plundered by the Germans and murdered in his sleep. Reliving the horrors like everybody else in this godforsaken place. But instead he was waiting for Collins so they could pursue their crazy scheme of getting into the good doctor's secret room in the cellar. Now the time had arrived, Sykes was beginning to have doubts. If Dr Banham wanted to vanish into a locked room every night when he thought nobody was watching, who were they to pry? Even if Collins insisted that Banham was up to no bloody good down there, and even if he *had* heard screams coming from the room, which Sykes doubted anyway, surely it was the man's own personal business?

There was a light knock at the door, and it swept open to reveal Lance Corporal Collins's shadowy face peering at him. Sykes swung his legs off the bed and waved Collins in.

'Did you get it?' Sykes whispered.

Collins waved a large key through the air between them, a Cheshire Cat grin slapped across his scarred face.

'You ready?' Collins asked.

He reminded Sykes of a kid on a night-time raid on the apple orchard. Except that most kids Sykes knew hadn't had half their heads blown off in the mud of Ypres.

'Yeh. Come on.'

They left the room together and ventured silently into the large corridor that was the first-floor landing. It never failed to amaze Sykes that people could live like this. This landing alone was as long and wide as his street back home. The rooms off to each side were bigger than the entire houses most of these men would normally live in. And this was the home of a single family. There must be more servants than family in a house this size. Sykes wondered what the lord of this particular manor was doing in the War. Very doubtful that he was on the front line, knee deep in shit and splashed guts, shoving shells into mortars one after another faster than you could shoot the bloody things off. That wasn't a job for the gentry. Oh no. He was probably sitting with others of his kind round a secret smoky table. Sipping bourbon. Deciding which battalion was to be sacrificed tomorrow for another two feet of advance, just for the Hun to reclaim it the day after with more slaughter and more dead Allies lost to the mud of no-man's-land –

'Shh.' Collins stopped abruptly and they both listened.

'What?'

'Thought I heard somebody sneaking about.'

'*Us!*'

'No. Listen.'

Sure enough, Sykes heard it as well. Shuffling in the dark downstairs. They crept to the banister and cautiously looked over. At first the hall was empty. Then they saw a solitary figure darting silently about, nipping from one shadow to another. The man wore pyjamas, standard issue, but had nothing on his feet. He crouched low by the door to the drawing room, listening to the silence inside, then glared fearfully at the surrounding emptiness. Suddenly he was scuttling like a spider, then he was gone.

'Just Richardson,' Sykes whispered. 'Poor sod.'

'Don't think Banham's sludge therapy's gonna do much for 'im, d'you?'

'Don't think anything short of a bullet's going to be much help to Richardson,' Sykes agreed solemnly.

Some of these men would be better face down in the mud than returned to Blighty. Some of them were such hopeless cases they'd never see civilisation again. Dead or Mad. Hobson's.

'Come on,' Sykes hissed, making a move to descend the stairs.

They advanced in complete silence until they reached the door to the basement. There they stopped, eyes flashing white in the black. The house had taken on an expectant, brittle silence. A stillness between the screams of terror. Sykes became aware of the scent of perspiration mixed with stale cigarette smoke coming from Collins. The air was cold but Sykes felt hot and anxious. Satisfied that nobody had heard their movements, he grasped the door handle and they plunged into the impenetrable blackness of the basement. The door sliced shut, and the narrow wedge of pale light extinguished.

'Did you bring a torch?' Collins breathed.

'No. You?'

'Did I buggery.'

'Got any matches?'

There was the sound of fumbling, followed by a sharp scratch and a puff of light. Collins's features looked to Sykes even more horrific with their shifting shadows, like dark things, alive, crawling across his pitted face. The man's eyes were sulphurous yellow. The match reeked like spent artillery. Sykes found himself shivering, unable to shake the ghosts of the trenches.

'Gi's a kiss,' Collins said.

Both men burst into a brief fit of laughter, before Collins led the way with the match.

The basement steps were narrow and built of creaking wood. They groaned under the weight of the two men, until Sykes and Collins reached the solid floor.

The air was thick with a damp, musty smell. Sykes recognised it from the yard at the back of his house, where the privy stood only four strides from the back door and the brick walls were gooey with bright-green mould. As they moved with care through the dark, Sykes found himself thinking again of Lily. He wondered what she was doing now. He wondered if she was thinking about him. If little Annie was being good. Most probably howling the house down, starving, cold and lice-ridden. Sykes wished he could be there with them. Wished he were lying with Lily, keeping warm in their bed rather than sneaking about like a big kid.

'D'you wanna wait here?' Collins asked, striking up a second match.

'Why?'

'Keep an eye out for Banham. Probably due for his visit any time.'

'Why don't *you* wait here, and *I'll* go have a look?'

'After all the trouble I went to to get *this*?' Collins waved the key. 'No chance.'

'I could order you –'

Collins laughed, his bad breath cascading in a cloud that engulfed Sykes.

'Don't try to pull rank on me, Sykesy. We're in civvies now, remember.'

'I'm still one stripe up on you, Joey, whether we're in Blighty or Berles.'

'Well I got the key, so that puts me one up on you, way I sees it.'

Sykes surrendered. 'Go on then. Hurry up. It's bloody cold standing about down here.'

Striking another match, Collins moved off into the dark, humming as he went 'It's a long way to Tipperary'. Sykes picked up the tune, his foot tapping irresistibly, his mind flooded with images of long blistering marches through the bleak French countryside.

From his position on the corner, Sykes could see back the way they had come, though he could make out no detail. Just black shadows with ashen apparitions skulking in the corners. He could see Collins twenty yards away, hunched by the door to Banham's room, toying with the key in the lock. Probably wouldn't work after all this arsing about.

A loud click echoed down the corridor and Sykes saw Collins give a brief thumbs-up before vanishing into the room. The basement was now completely black. Sykes resumed his rendition of 'Tipperary', humming to himself while he waited.

They'd find nothing in there. Probably full of photos of naked Victorian ladies. Maybe one of those 'What the Butler Saw' machines. Behind the professional mask Banham was probably a seething mass of unexpressed lechery. After all, who psychoanalyses the psychoanalysers? The man's mind was probably corrupted with years' worth of his patients' filth and debauchery. Probably poisoned with the unholy nightmares of –

Collins's scream knocked Sykes out of his reverie. He lurched down the corridor towards the door.

'Joey?'

His voice came as a desperate rasp, coarse with ragged breath. No answer. The bastard was having him on.

'Joey!'

Silence.

Sykes discovered the door slightly ajar. He grasped the handle and pushed fearfully. There was no light inside the room. No glow from Collins's match.

'Joe? Stop pissing about, Joe.'

Scuff of motion. Shadow curled. Sykes saw a shape detach itself from the gloom and approach. For a second he thought it was Collins. Then he felt the cold steel muzzle on his forehead. For the merest moment he thought he saw eyeless sockets gazing at him from the dark. A skeletal face with torn flesh hanging from the jaw. He thought he smelled the stench of rotting human bodies. The reek of the trench. It filled his nostrils and made his stomach lurch. His heart blasted like a steam hammer and he wanted to wake up screaming.

Then the pistol exploded and he never woke again.

Chapter One

19 August 1918

Emma Braithwaite was coming to the end of her twelve-hour shift when Private Corey started yelling the place down. She burst into his room to find Corey jamming himself deliriously into the corner by the window. His arms were drawn up around his head, flapping furiously as if something were attacking him. His eyes were wide and full of terrors, his face red and streaked with spittle. Emma rushed to soothe him, kneeling and talking calmly, trying to subdue the infectious hysteria.

'Hey, Daniel. It's all right. It's all right. Calm down. It's only me.'

But her words had no effect. He glared beyond her into the room, still waving frantically and screaming at the top of his voice. She realised with a start he was trying to speak, but the words were garbled nonsense, high-pitched and shattered into unintelligible pieces.

'Daniel. It's *me*. Emma…'

His breath burst from him in a series of out-of-control explosions. His eyes were everywhere except meeting hers as he swiped at the air in front of him. Emma shuffled forward on her knees, trying to avoid his lashing hands. At last, she could stand it no longer. She grabbed them and pulled them down, holding him tight until she found his eyes finally settling on hers.

They were wild eyes still, but at least the screaming stopped.

'It's all right. It's only me.'

Corey trembled feverishly in her grasp. His face poured perspiration. Gradually his breathing steadied, and she risked letting go of his arms. The tension seemed to dissipate into the floor beneath him, and at last he gave a final, shuddering breath, before trying to raise himself from the corner. She helped him on to his bed and he sat there quivering.

She saw this every night in forty men or more. Nightmare visions brought home from the trenches and the battles in the mud. Horrors she could barely imagine before she took the Voluntary Aid Detachment to Hawkswick Hall. They were things forged in the furnace of war, and they stalked the men wherever they went. Even into the most private places of sleep.

Emma had taken the job after they got the telegram. Her brother had died at Cambrai. During the same week, the conscription age was increased and her poor father, forty-nine and never raised a hand to anyone in his life, was called to France. She saw *The Battle of the Somme* at the Odeon in Leeds, and was shocked more than anything by the gargantuan instruments of war, blasting death and carnage into the air at the Germans. Shocked because she knew she wasn't seeing the equally monstrous machines of the Germans, throwing death back. Bombs as big as men. Confident young beaux in their thousands marching off to fight. She watched their black-and-white strutting about, chests thrust proudly out, faces full of confident grins. Then the field of dead heroes.

If her brother and father could face those horrors, then so could she.

Emma gazed out of the window. Corey's room faced east, and the sky was a remarkably bruised-looking black-blue-green colour, as the sun prepared to make its entrance upon the world. She turned and watched Corey's face in silence until she thought he might be ready to talk.

Daniel Corey reminded her of her brother. Same alignment of mischievous features. Snub nose. Big dark eyes. She'd taken to Corey the first time she'd laid eyes on him. And in his more settled moments she was sure he'd taken to her.

'Bad dreams still?'

Corey looked embarrassed.

'Nothing to be ashamed of.'

He said nothing.

'Not a man in here doesn't have bad dreams,' she reminded him.

Corey's tremors began to cease. At last he seemed ready to talk. She grasped hold of his hand to encourage him, and found it warm and damp with sweat.

'The trenches again?'

He shook his head. For a second she was certain he was going to burst into tears. Then he got hold of himself and spoke in a calm monotone, as if detaching himself from what he was about to say. When he spoke, he didn't look her in the eye. Just gazed out of the window into the unfamiliar sky.

'I don't dream about the war any more.'

'Then what was it?'

He was silent for a second, uncertain. Then he confided in her. Looked her straight in the eye and told her the truth.

'He was here. In this room,' he said, struggling to keep his voice level. 'It was the Devil.'

Constable Albert Briggs scratched his head in puzzlement, while Bill Cromby scrambled into the hole. Cromby tramped up and down a bit, then returned to stare up at Briggs with a blank look slapped across his clumsy, knobbly features.

'What yer reckon, then, Bert?' The big farmer's voice rumbled out of him like a train leaving a station.

Briggs didn't know *what* to reckon. In his sixty-four years, he'd never seen anything like it. 'It wasn't here yesterday?' he checked again.

Cromby shook his head positively. 'Not so much as a shovel mark last night when I come past.'

The land had been excavated to a drop of at least four foot, the removed earth piled each side of the furrow making the chasm as deep as a man. Even Cromby could hardly see over the top of the mounds of muck, and he stood six foot three in his socks. Briggs estimated there was a week's work here for two men. Two bloody grafters at that. The field was a good hundred and fifty yards in width. And the rest. He shook his head dolefully.

'Some bloody queer stuff happening these last few months,' he said, scrambling down to join Cromby in the hole. The ground was glazed with dew, the sun just burning its way over the horizon to Briggs's back. As he landed with an undignified thud in the sticky dirt, he wiped the mud from his hands down his trousers.

'What yer make of all this, then?' Cromby asked.

'I don't know,' Briggs admitted.

'Suppose it's better than dead cows and sheep,' Cromby said.

'No more this morning, then?'

'Dunno. I was just on me way up to Stony Bank. When I saw this, I thought I better get you straight down 'ere.'

Briggs scratched his head again. It was a habit formed of long bewilderment. He'd done it more and more this last summer, as the strange occurrences around the village had gradually escalated into something appalling. Now Constable Albert Briggs was thoroughly out of his depth. In all his years in the service, he'd never encountered anything like this peculiar train of events. It all seemed far outside his role as village bobby.

'I think this war's sending us all bloody loony,' he commented, more to himself than to Cromby.

'We need some 'elp,' Cromby announced. 'What's 'appening wi' them ministry folk?'

Briggs gave a dismissive shrug. 'I wrote them three times now. Suppose they've got enough on their plates. More interested in dead *men* than dead cattle. You can see their point.'

'Can't feed nobody if we ain't got no livestock,' Cromby reminded him.

'Yeh, well. Said they'd send somebody when they'd *got* somebody.'

'Which is never.'

'Which is, likely as not, when this bloody war's over.'

'This war's *never* going to be over, Bert. You know that. This ain't war, it's slaughter. My cattle's treated better than them bloody men.'

'Don't go spouting that rubbish down the village, Bill Cromby.'

'What they gonna do? 'Ave me shot at dawn?'

'Probably could do. All these new rules and regulations.'

'Well I'm not afraid to speak my mind, Bert. You know that. If I've got summat to say, I'll bloody well say it, whoever's –'

Shadow engulfed them. Briggs looked up to find a dark shape standing high on a mound above them, silhouetted against the pure new brilliance of the sky. The rising sun framed the figure in a seething halo, making it impossible for Briggs to discern any detail. For a second, he thought the man was an apparition. Briggs glanced back at Cromby, and briefly glimpsed the stranger's shadow cast behind them, stretching way back down the chasm. A shadow far too huge for a man.

The surreal moment was broken when the man spoke.

'Good morning.' He greeted them with a cheerful voice that came out of his darkness like a pleasant breeze.

'Morning,' Briggs responded automatically, but he couldn't disguise the suspicion in the word. After recent events, the sudden appearance of a stranger from nowhere didn't particularly inspire a lot of confidence.

As Briggs reached up to clamber back out of the hole, he saw a slim, pale hand offered in front of him. A city hand, Briggs noted. Not the hand of one used to the rigours of country life. Briggs grasped hold and found himself being hauled with surprising ease from the crevice. Then the man bent and helped Cromby out as if the giant farmer weighed just a sack o' spuds.

The stranger regarded them both from out of his clean-shaven metropolitan face. He was smartly dressed in attire suited to the office rather than the country, Briggs thought. Probably well used to sitting behind a desk by the look of him. He was a young man, at least compared with Briggs and Cromby. But then most men were young compared with Briggs and Cromby.

'You the bloke from the Ministry?' Cromby barged in bluntly.

'You're expecting me?' the man said, eyebrows raised in surprise.

'Only four bloody months ago –'

Seeing Cromby was about to embark on his bull-in-a-china-shop routine, Briggs quickly thrust out his hand. The Man from the Ministry grasped it warmly.

'Constable Albert Briggs, sir. I was the one put in the request. I know you've probably got more important things on your plate at the moment, but things here was just getting a bit out of hand.'

The Ministry Man shook Briggs's hand with a confident and very friendly grip.

He searched Briggs's face with an enthusiastic interest. 'Out of hand, you say?'

'I put all the details in my last report. Sent it with my letter.'

The Ministry Man opened his arms and cocked his head in a dismissive gesture.

'I'm afraid they sent me without a full briefing,' he admitted a little bashfully. He glanced into the chasm behind Briggs, then Briggs found a pair of wide blue eyes watching him with childlike inquisitiveness. 'Perhaps you could enlighten me.'

'Down the station house, sir. I can tell you all about it there.'

Briggs gave Cromby a furtive, nervous glance. Cromby appeared about to explode.

'What about *this*?' He indicated the churned field.

Briggs turned back to the Ministry Man. 'Bill Cromby, sir. This's his field. Don't see what we can do about this just now,' he said. 'Do you?'

The Ministry Man gazed into the fissure, lost in thought.

'Appeared overnight,' Cromby announced. 'Out of nowhere.

When I come past last night, not a mark on the field. Now look!'

'Has this happened before?' the Ministry Man asked. He hunched in the dirt by the edge of the fissure with a complete disregard for his smart city trousers.

'Nothing like this,' Briggs informed him.

'No sign of dirt on the road,' the man mused. 'You'd think they'd have made something of a mess getting a big job like this done overnight, wouldn't you?'

Briggs gazed about. True enough: although there was an enormous trough, there was not a trace to suggest that anybody had been around to dig it. Not a single muddy footprint on the road surface, except those left by Briggs and Cromby. Until the Ministry Man pointed it out, he hadn't noticed. Seemed to know what he was about, this bloke. Briggs felt a tinge of relief, as if a great weight had been lifted off his weary shoulders.

'What d'yer think it is?' Cromby demanded.

'Isn't that obvious?' the Ministry Man asked.

Briggs and Cromby both looked blank.

'It's a trench,' he told them.

'*A trench?*' echoed Cromby.

'That's what I'd describe it as,' the Ministry Man affirmed. He stood up and turned to Briggs. 'Wouldn't you agree?'

Briggs looked troubled. 'Well, I suppose it is. But who'd build a trench here in Hawkswick?'

'No training bases nearby?'

'No. This is cultivated land.'

The Ministry Man stood and gazed into the field.

'You know what I find most fascinating of all?' he asked Briggs abruptly.

'What's that, sir?'

'Those marks over there.'

'Marks, sir?'

'You haven't seen them?'

13

'I'm afraid not, sir.'

'Come on,' he said, leading Briggs and Cromby around the edge of the trench and down into the field.

Finally, Briggs found his missing footprints. The field was full of them. As if an entire battalion had been stomping about in size tens. Briggs watched as the Ministry Man deposited more prints of his own among those in the field. He turned amid the sea of churned mud, swinging open his arms in a wide arc like a showman.

'There, you see,' the Ministry Man said.

'Bloody dozens of 'em,' Cromby said, echoing Briggs's thoughts.

'But look over there,' the Ministry Man urged.

They followed his finger into the near distance and saw that the footprints simply faded. As if the men had grown weightless as they moved away from the trench.

'What the bloody 'ell –' Cromby began, before his words trailed off into a bemused silence.

'What do you make of that?' Briggs asked. The sound of his voice was a small and troubled thing dropped into the cool morning air.

But the Ministry Man appeared as baffled as they were. He proceeded to pick his way further through the dirt.

Briggs shook his head. 'This is mad.'

'The world is mad, just now,' the Ministry Man declared.

'Too true,' Cromby agreed. 'Bloody Germans most probably gassed us wi' madness bombs.'

The Ministry Man bent and plucked a small piece of card out of the dirt, examining it closely.

'Very curious,' he muttered.

'What's that?' Briggs asked.

'A torn piece of cigarette packet.'

'Nowt curious about a cig packet,' Cromby huffed.

'This one's French,' the Ministry Man said.

'That bloody nuthouse!' Cromby burst. 'They go for walks round 'ere. Chuck their rubbish all over the place. Ought to 'ave known. Put two an' two together. They're bloody crackers, that lot. It'll be them 'at's made this bloody mess.'

'The nuthouse?' The Ministry Man's interest was aroused.

Briggs took him by the arm and urged him back out of the field. 'You haven't seen *anything* of my reports, have you?' he asked.

'No. Sorry.'

'Well in that case we got a lot to talk about.'

Briggs led the Ministry Man off down the lane. As Cromby watched them go it looked to him like Briggs, although ostensibly holding the man's arm to lead him back to the village, was actually leaning on the man for support. Events over the past few months had been too much for the poor old constable, and Cromby had seen the strain spreading through him like a disease. Now here was this young man, keen and sharp, inspiring confidence, bringing with him all the authority of the Ministry itself. Cromby listened for a moment to their fading conversation.

'It'll be better if we can talk in the privacy of the station house, Mr… I don't think I got your name.'

'You didn't,' the stranger confirmed. 'People call me the Doctor.'

'*Doctor?* You're a medical man, then?'

'Among many things, it seems.'

'Ah… Right…'

As the two men strode out of earshot, Cromby turned and began the long, slow trudge to Stony Bank to check on his animals. The stress recently had grown too much for them all to bear. He'd lost nearly a quarter of his livestock in the last four months. This couldn't go on. Cromby wasn't going to have it. Oh no. He'd have a not-so-quiet word of his own with this Doctor from the Ministry.

* * *

15

While Briggs fussed over the teapot, the Doctor sat and scrutinised the small, dimly lit kitchen that was the hub of the constable's station house. The window above the sink was tiny, admitting precious little daylight, and the oil lamps glimmered a dull, musk-scented yellow. The effect was to shroud the Doctor and Briggs in a kind of warm umbrage.

Briggs glanced across to see the Doctor consumed in shadow by the range. There was the glint of his eyes but little else to suggest that he was there at all. Again, Briggs had the spine-tingling idea that the man might be a phantom. In his forty years as village constable, one thing Briggs had developed was a keen sense of what people were all about. It was a skill honed from years of dealing with petty villains. This Ministry Man, though, was something else. Maybe because he was from the city, Briggs thought. That alien world he'd never visited. Maybe all the people there were impossible to read, with their complex motives and secret agendas. One thing Briggs did know: for all his years' experience, this man's eyes were full of something he could not for the life of him put his finger on.

But Briggs had known instantly, of course, that this was an Important Bloke. As soon as he saw the clothes. The dark-green velvet jacket, winged collar and silk cravat. Obviously a man of the Victorian school: cultured, educated, and unwilling to yield his pretentious dress code even in times of war. While everybody in England wore dishevelled grey and black, here was a man of stature and elegance. But there was something of the bohemian about him, as well. He wore his hair unfashionably long, so that it framed his strong features with dark, reckless curls.

Briggs removed the soggy used tealeaves, pouring them on the draining board to form a neat little dark-brown mountain. He heaped fresh leaves into the pot, deciding not to stick to his old habit of leaving some of the old ones in there for added body.

'I know it's probably not as clean and tidy as it should be,' Briggs announced, self-consciously. 'Only I'm on me own now, you see, since I lost my Effie back in '14. Flu.'

'Not at all,' the Doctor said. 'It's a nice place you have here, Constable. Very cosy.'

'Aye, that it is. Course, probably not half as posh as your own place, eh, sir?'

The Doctor remained silent. He was sitting back on the little wooden chair, his features lost in darkness, so Briggs found it hard to interpret his reaction. Briggs felt a bit embarrassed. Probably not a good thing to get personal, asking questions of a gentleman in wartime. Probably lost his home to the war effort, if his garments were anything to go by. Probably a mansion like the Hall, turned into a hospital or some such.

'There you go.' Briggs rattled the teapot and two mismatched mugs on to the little table and plonked himself on the tiny wooden seat opposite the Doctor. He merrily sloshed tea into both mugs, asking the Doctor if he took sugar and milk.

The Doctor sat forward in his seat, delivering himself from inside the gloom. 'I don't suppose you have lemon?'

Briggs smiled. 'We haven't seen a lemon in this village for months. I think the blockades stopped them coming in. Samuel Hudson – he runs the shop – can't get most things these days.'

The Doctor peered at his cup of tea thoughtfully. 'Just a dash of milk, please. I don't take sugar.'

'Course. Suppose everybody's tastes change in war.' Briggs sploshed milk into both mugs. 'I used to have *six* sugars in this cup. Now I don't have none at all. In January, when they rationed sugar, I think that was probably the biggest thing that made me realise how serious this war really is. Got no children, you see. Me and Effie *had* little 'uns, but they all died young. Not one of them got to five, God rest their poor little souls.'

Briggs sipped his tea, and the Doctor listened indulgently from inside the shadow.

17

'So I got nobody in the fighting. Nobody to worry about. It's a good thing, really, the way the world's going these days. I think it's something of a blessing not to have anybody to worry about. Don't you agree?'

Briggs saw the other man's eyes become distant. He was lost for a moment in some secret memory, his face pensive. Maybe he had boys, Briggs thought. He looked as though he might just about be old enough to have idealistic sons. Young ones, but maybe just old enough to get themselves to the front in these dark days of a desperate country.

'Course, *was* a day when I had very little to worry about in this job. Rural bobbying's a bit of a doddle, truth be known. Not like them city lads, all that crime and violence. All them strikes and marches and civil unrest. The only disturbance we get here is the occasional drunken brawl, and I know all the brawlers by their first names anyway. Nah, it's a good life tucked away here in the middle of nowhere. Or it *was*, before all this weird stuff started happening, that is.'

The Doctor sipped his tea, and Briggs found two piercing blue eyes watching him expectantly.

'All started last March,' he explained. 'People began hearing things in the night. Noises. Somebody scurrying about. Then we lost a few dogs.'

'Dogs?'

'Aye. Old Jack Mundy's dog went first. Faithful old thing, it was. Never left his side. Got up one morning and it'd just gone. Then there was a spate of pets going missing. Charlie Skaggs lost four whippets and six ferrets all in one night. Bloody good rabbiting stock.'

The Doctor sat forward in his seat and rubbed his chin abstractedly. 'And none of these animals were ever found?'

'None. Vanished into the blue. Then, back in, oh, May it was, Bill Cromby had his first sheep killed. Right mess. Just torn apart. Poor thing was spread all over Top Field.' Briggs saw the scene. He and Cromby had walked up together and the carnage had hit Briggs like a slap in the face. He took a deep breath and pushed the memory from his mind. 'Went quiet for a week or so, then more sheep killed. Same thing. Bits of them found all over the place. Course, Bill went out with his gun. Said it was a beast or a big dog. We had a traveller in the village in '13. Spanish. He had this bloody big dancing bear. Bill thought it might've escaped. Gone wild. You know – out on the moors. He never caught anything, though. The killings kept on happening, but poor Bill was never in the right place at the right time. He lost cattle, sheep, pigs. Lost count how many. It's all in the files.'

Briggs shuffled off his seat and removed a large file from the shelf beside the range. He opened the file and peered myopically at the documents inside. Then simply handed the Doctor the whole lot to see for himself.

'Now barely a week goes by before he loses more livestock.'

The Doctor pulled out the top sheet and scanned it briefly.

'I see he blames the residents at Hawkswick Hall,' he said. It wasn't a statement of fact. He was asking Briggs to elaborate.

'Bill Cromby blames everybody. He blamed that Spaniard's bear, then he said it was a tiger on the moors, then he told me it was the bloody *Germans*. Said they'd invaded and they were living rough in Scarrs Woods. Even had me up there searching for their campsite. Never found nothing, o' course. There aren't no Germans round here.' He shook his head sagely at the Doctor.

The Doctor fingered inquisitively through more of the papers. 'So Bill thought the soldiers at this hospital might be responsible?'

'Aye. Not just Bill Cromby.' Briggs sipped his tea in reflective mood. 'I had reports from other people, too. Started about the same time as the sheep killings. Charlie Skaggs says he saw soldiers on manoeuvres in the night. Swears blind they were all badly injured. Some of them had half their faces missing. Charlie's not one for the drink. Needs his wits about him when he's out poaching. And he's got eyes like a hawk. I trust his word if he says he saw something. Then Betty Thistlewaite told me she saw a dead man in her garden.'

The papers stopped rustling abruptly. 'A *dead* man?'

'So she says. She keeps a couple of pigs down her yard. Woke up to them squealing, early hours. Took her shotgun down and says she saw him plain as day in the moonlight. She says he had skeleton hands. Just bones. And he didn't have no eyes. Just empty sockets.'

'Sounds like a dead man,' the Doctor agreed. 'What happened?'

'Vanished in front of her eyes, he did. Trouble is, Betty's one for the gin.' He tipped an imaginary glass in front of his lips once or twice for effect. 'She calls it "having a nip for me old arthritis". Probably got alcohol poisoning in her arthritis by now. I think she saw just what she'd heard others say *they'd* seen. Probably a vagabond looking for a place to kip down. Probably took one look at Betty Thistlewaite with her big old gun and did a runner. She's not a pretty sight with or without a two-bore.'

A murky smile passed through the Doctor's cheeks. He closed the file on his knees and rested his arms across it. 'So with all these reports about wounded soldiers terrorising the countryside, you took your suspicions to Hawkswick Hall?'

'Aye. Bill Cromby came in ranting and raving one morning after he found two more dead cows. We went to see Dr Banham up there, but I was satisfied that his people weren't responsible.'

'Satisfied?'

Briggs nodded vigorously. 'Poor sods. They've all had their fill of the war. The last thing they're gonna do is go out in the middle of the night killing defenceless animals.'

'This is a hospital for war wounded?'

'Wounded. Yeh. Not all of them have limbs missing or shrapnel buried in them, though. Some of them have more serious stuff.'

Briggs tapped his forehead meaningfully. 'Not all there.'

'And this Dr Banham?'

'Oh, he's all there all right. Got a fine head on him, he has. Does them blokes the world o' good, he does. Gets them back on their feet.'

Finishing his drink, the Doctor placed his mug on the table with a grim look.

'So,' he said at last, 'the question is, Constable Briggs, who do *you* think is responsible for all these strange happenings?'

Briggs gave him his most serious look. That trench today had clinched it for him. Those footprints disappearing into nowhere like that. No sign of mud on the road. Although he was facing a man from the Ministry and obviously a learned man as well, without a trace of embarrassment Briggs told the Doctor exactly what he thought.

'I think,' he said, 'it's ghosts.'

Despite the beautiful morning, Mary Minett wasn't surprised to see Bill Cromby stalking down the sunny Main Street with a fierce scowl on his face. Bill Cromby's face contained a scowl at the best of times. The man could be something of a human hurricane. Full of sound and fury. And sometimes he left a trail of wreckage and shivering people. But Mary also knew the real Cromby. The man inside the storm. She met him in the street and awarded him her heartiest smile.

'Good morning, Mr Cromby.'

Grinding to a halt, Cromby touched his cap.

'Mary.'

'Is this a social call, Bill?'

'Business.' Cromby growled, obviously itching to be on his way.

Mary sustained the sweet smile. 'I take it you're going to visit our venerable Constable Briggs.'

'Aye.'

21

The smile evaporated, and Mary allowed the concern she felt to show through. 'More livestock?'

'Only 'Arold the bloody Younger.'

Mary forgave the scowl. 'Harold the Bloody Younger' was Cromby's prize bull. In all probability, entirely irreplaceable. She searched the big man's rough features and discovered a devastating wrath. His fists were clenched and his usually red face was a sort of deep crimson around the edges. He looked as though his head might explode at any minute.

'There's summat got to be done about this,' he seethed. 'I'm going to 'ave a word with that bloke from the Ministry.'

Mary's face brightened. 'There's a man here from London?'

'Aye. He's wi' Bert.'

'In that case, Mr Cromby, I think we'll pay a visit together.'

And off they marched side by side, both intent, for different reasons, on meeting this Man from the Ministry.

Hoisting the water pail from under the sink, Briggs poured more water into the kettle. His poor old arms were beginning to protest lately at the fetching and carrying from the village standpipe. But, since he had his bath only once a week, it wasn't such an onerous task.

'More tea, Doctor?'

'No... thank you...'

He found the Doctor standing in front of the range, rifling distractedly through his pockets. Finally, he found what he was looking for. A small piece of paper with something printed on it that Briggs couldn't see. The Doctor raised the paper for Briggs to take.

'But I'd be very grateful if you could arrange to do something else for me.'

Taking the paper in his wet fingers, Briggs squinted at it in the light from the window. It was a baggage ticket from Grimston Station.

The Doctor remained standing, patting himself abstractedly as if he'd lost something else. He seemed mildly distressed, his face creased with what looked like unaccustomed frown lines.

'That,' he said, his mind obviously elsewhere, 'is a rather large blue box that I'd like you to have picked up for me, if you don't mind.'

He opened his jacket and poked about inside, delving into his pockets, becoming more agitated by the second.

'I don't have any transport –' Briggs began.

'There must be somebody around here with a cart,' the Doctor snapped without looking up.

'I'll have a word with Zachary Smith. He'll have something. How big is this box?'

'Two point seven metres tall, a little over one point two square.'

'Eh?'

The Doctor suddenly produced a key that he regarded with evident relief. The frenzy evaporated out of him and he gave Briggs a huge grin.

'I'm sorry,' he apologised with a look of fierce, genuine compassion. He returned the key to the pocket he'd found it in, then stepped around the table into the small space of the kitchen and spread his arms wide, looked at the gap he'd made and said, 'Four feet wide.' He stretched up with one hand, but hit the ceiling before he was at full reach. 'Eight feet tall. Or thereabouts.'

'What on Earth would that be?'

'My box!'

'Your box, sir?'

'That's right. My… travelling case, if you like.'

Realisation dawned. 'Oh I see, sir. A wardrobe, so to speak.'

'That's it exactly.' The Doctor grinned, ecstatic at Briggs's perspicacity. 'You'll probably need a pair of strapping young men to load it on to the cart,' he warned.

Briggs laughed. 'Don't have none of *those* in the village, sir.'

The Doctor looked blank, momentarily puzzled. Then came to his senses.

'No. Of course not. Perhaps a couple of land girls. It's not really *that* heavy, actually.'

'I'm sure we'll be able to get it up here for you, sir.'

The Doctor was heading for the door, apparently ready to leave. He seemed to be on edge, wanting to be somewhere else. He reached for the handle but looked back at Briggs.

'And could you put it in your lock-up? Keep it safe for me?'

'The lock-up, sir? Won't you be wanting your stuff out of it?'

The Doctor shook his head, and for a brief moment looked lost in thought. 'Not yet,' he decided, suddenly animated again. 'It'll be fine in the lock-up.'

He swung open the door but Briggs called him back.

'Where are you going, sir?'

'To have a look around.'

'But you don't know the village, sir. Hold on. I'll come with you.'

Mary Minett's first contact with the Man from the Ministry was an intimate one. She was about to knock at Briggs's station house, when the door was flung open and she met with a dashing figure about to sweep out. He was interrupted by Briggs, but continued to leave while looking back into the kitchen. Then he was suddenly pressed against her, hands raised in abject apology, eyes wide with surprise.

She caught scent of a strangely odourless man. No sweat, but no aftershave either. His eyes were the most profound blue she'd ever seen. For a moment the world simply stopped turning, she could swear. The birds silenced, and she was trapped like a fly in pure, clear amber, unable to move or take her eyes from his.

'I am sorry,' the man said, and the world resumed on its course through the universe.

24

He backed off hastily, and Mary awarded him the prettiest smile she could muster.

'You must be the mysterious Doctor,' she told him.

Hands still raised, as if in surrender, he glanced down at himself and then she found those eyes again piercing hers. Intense, playful. The shock in his expression had resolved itself into something sharp and commanding.

'I suppose I must.'

His voice was soft for a man. Mary had grown used to the gravel-pit larynx of men like Cromby. She hadn't heard the voice of the city for years, apart from the all too brief and infrequent meetings with her father.

'I believe the accepted phrase is,' the Doctor said, '"I'm afraid you have me at a disadvantage".'

She held out her hand and the Doctor shook it.

'Mary Minett,' she introduced herself brightly. 'Village midwife, nurse, sometimes even veterinary reserve.'

The Doctor nodded appreciatively and smiled warmly at her.

'Very pleased to meet you, Mrs Minett.'

'*Miss.*'

She was certain his pleasant smile amplified at that. Mary grinned back at him, feeling the sun shine even more intensely on her back, until the romance of their tryst was shattered by Bill Cromby.

'I want a word wi' you,' he barked.

'Mr Cromby.' The Doctor greeted him warmly, and it was instantly as if Mary had never existed. 'Don't tell me you've had more animals destroyed.'

Even in the golden morning sunshine, Cromby's face was dark and forbidding.

'Only me prize breeding bull,' he announced with a kind of deadpan theatrical flair that only the Bill Crombys of this world could demonstrate.

The Doctor appeared genuinely upset. He stepped past Mary and grasped Cromby by the arm, leading the big man back the way he had come. As they went she heard him say, 'I want to look at this for myself. See if we can't get to the bottom of all this.'

With a glance back at Briggs in his dark kitchen, Mary bustled after them. She almost had to run to keep up with the two men, and her long skirts didn't make the march any easier. She found herself beside the Doctor, then one or two steps behind, growing increasingly agitated by his abrupt lack of interest in her. With the sun in her eyes, and the alacrity of their pace, she was entirely unprepared for the Doctor's unexpected halt in front of her. For the second time in two minutes she found herself pressed up against him – and this time it was her turn to raise her hands in embarrassed apology.

The Doctor stood there gazing right into her face, as if he were reading her every single thought and feeling.

'Mary Minett,' he said eventually. 'That is such an attractive little name.'

Then he smiled, turned on his heel, and was gone.

Mary and Cromby stood at the gate and watched the Doctor as he crouched in the middle of the field. He'd remained motionless for a full minute at least, and Mary was beginning to wonder if he'd hurt his back. Perhaps that was his reason for not being involved directly in the war effort in France or the Eastern Front.

'Since you're here,' Cromby growled, 'I want you to look at me 'orses.'

'Of course. What's wrong with them?'

'Spooked to buggery.'

Mary scanned Cromby's features but he refused to look her in the eye, preferring to gaze at the Doctor's distant ministrations.

'What d'you think has unsettled them?'

Cromby heaved a gargantuan shrug. 'Damned if I know.'

'D'you think it has something to do with this?'

'Wouldn't be surprised. They've been edgy on an' off for a bit now. This mornin' I can't get 'em calmed.' He removed his cap to scratch the back of his head, then nodded in the direction of the field. 'Looks like the Doctor's done,' he announced.

Mary found the Doctor waving them over and they set off across the field, doing their best to avoid the sprayed visceral remains of poor Harold the Bloody Younger. Mary had seen this devastation before. Being the village's only authority on medical matters of any kind, she had been dragged out here at many a sunrise by Briggs and Cromby to identify the means of destruction. She had done what she could to help, which unfortunately amounted to infuriatingly little, and eventually they had stopped asking her advice.

The Doctor was pointing at a bare patch in the field. It was a rough circle, about three feet in diameter, Mary guessed, and it looked like the ground had been churned.

'Any idea what might have made this?' he asked Cromby.

From the look on his face, Cromby had no idea at all.

Realising the Doctor was watching her questioningly, Mary could only offer a shrug. The Doctor sighed, sending fingers rummaging through his thick dark curls while he stared about the field.

'There's another one over there,' he informed them.

'I did see one o' these before,' Cromby said suddenly. 'We lost a couple o' sheep last month; there was one o' these marks in that field.'

'Did you find them at the site of every killing?'

'Not that we noticed.'

'Very odd,' the Doctor said, more to himself than to them. He stalked about in frustration, muttering continuously. 'Very odd indeed. Very, very, very so.'

'It's possible the animals chewed the ground bare,' Mary

suggested. 'They can do that if there's a rich patch. Perhaps where fertiliser has been dropped.'

'No no no no no,' the Doctor said, still gazing about as if he were looking for something specific.

Then he had hold of her arm and she found herself hunching with him beside a clump of glistening red and white animal tissue on the edge of the dirt circle. He poked at the outer rim of the dirt where it met the grass.

'You see that?'

But all Mary saw was dirt and grass. Then the Doctor's face, urging her on. She looked again.

'I'm very sorry, Doctor. I don't see what you're getting at.'

'The ground rises here, around the edge. It's only very slight, but it's definitely a raised ridge. This earth hasn't been masticated or dug. Whatever did this came *up, out of the soil*.'

'You think summat come out o' the ground?' Cromby said, his voice thick with scepticism.

The Doctor foraged in the grass and Mary saw a yellow stain – thick, sticky clay that the Doctor kneaded thoughtfully between his fingers.

'This is a cultivated field?' he asked Cromby.

'Fallow this year,' Cromby told him.

'What depth do you think you'd find this stuff?'

Cromby peered with piggy eyes at the Doctor's fingers. 'Fair depth,' he said. 'Maybe three or four foot.'

'I think something came out of the ground here,' the Doctor announced. 'And it rose from a depth of around three to four feet.'

Even while the Doctor talked, Mary was shaking her head in disbelief. 'I can't imagine what could possibly do that,' she admitted. 'Except perhaps a giant mole. D'you think we could have a new breed of moles?'

'Moles armed with high explosives?' the Doctor asked, fiercely serious.

'I don't understand.'

The Doctor scooped up the large piece of meat and waved it in front of her.

'See this?'

'Yes,' Mary said, mainly seeing the fatty, blood-gorged residue flapping on the Doctor's hands.

The Doctor pointed out a chunk of bone sticking out of the end of the meat.

'This cartilage was *torn*. You can see the ragged edges there, look.'

Mary glanced as briefly as possible at what he was demonstrating. Then the hunk of meat spun in his grasp and he showed her the shank.

'No teeth marks,' he announced finally. 'No claw marks. This animal wasn't ripped apart by a beast, or even a man with a butcher's blade. I'm afraid our dear departed Harold the Younger was *blown* to bits.'

'An explosion?' Mary said, incredulously.

'Don't talk bloody daft,' Cromby said.

The Doctor stood and handed him the hunk of meat. 'And what's even *more* strange,' he said, 'is that there are no scorch marks whatsoever.'

He began to march back towards the gate.

'Ey,' Cromby shouted after him, 'where yer goin' now?'

'To visit some people who have experience with explosives.'

Mary made a move to follow, but Cromby grasped her sleeve as she passed.

'Me 'orses,' he reminded her. There was a pleading in his voice.

She watched the Doctor striding purposefully towards the gate, feeling astonishingly agitated to see him go. He was resolute, determined, as if he'd been struck by a sudden rationale that would explain everything. Mary was not one to stand on the sidelines to watch things get untangled by others. If this enigma

29

was to be solved, she wanted to be there at the heart of the matter. But Cromby was right. The man needed his horses. She felt the tension in her shoulders intensify as she was tugged in two directions at once.

'Come on, then, Bill,' she said at last, 'let's go take a good look at them, shall we?'

When she looked back, the Doctor was gone.

Chapter Two

Standing at his bedroom window, Private Daniel Corey looked out on to the radiant new day that touched the grounds of Hawkswick Hall. Dew-covered lawns descended in a gentle fall from the gravel platform in front of the house. In the mid-distance the stoic oak, beech, ash, chestnut, silver birch and frail elders dotted the landscape and reminded Corey of advancing troops, ripe for the picking-off from his well entrenched vantage-point. A single sweep from his Vickers, 250 rounds in half a minute, would wipe out their advance, cut them down and leave the grounds barren and empty again. Easy.

The machines of war. They made killing the touching of levers.

Even this early in the morning there were men milling about, taking their constitutionals, breathing the clear fresh air of this sweet and pleasant land. Trying to forget the stench of cordite and the sting of mustard gas that stuck in their throats.

Corey watched the black-and-white-smocked shape of a nurse supporting a man with only one leg. He leaned heavily on her, not yet adjusted to the new dynamics of his movement. They stumbled and the soldier fell awkwardly against the nurse, raising his free hand in embarrassment, toppling further as he did so, and finally collapsing to the gravel with the crunch of a discarded sack of coal. The nurse lifted him back to his feet and Corey heard the sound of their voices but not the words. She was placating, he was angry and ashamed. And then Corey saw them heading back into the house below.

'Why d'you put up with us mad sods?' he'd asked Emma once when they were alone.

Her sweet face broke into that heart-warming smile, dark eyes whimsical.

31

'It was either this or the munitions factory,' she told him. 'And I didn't fancy being a canary.'

'Canary?'

'Their faces turn yellow, working with the TNT.'

'You'd look quite nice in yellow,' he told her.

She laughed even more at that, and he felt like grabbing hold of her and kissing her then. He remembered the flush of excitement as the thought crossed his mind. They were close enough to touch, their smiling eyes only inches apart; he smelled her scent and sensed the soft warmth of her body. So close. But he stopped himself. She didn't want the attentions of some battered war loon. He was a man who had failed, who'd snapped under pressure when others went on. She didn't want that sort of man.

The moment passed, and her laugh ended not with a hug but a whimper. He avoided her eyes, annoyed at his own naivety, and she left quickly afterwards. She'd probably read his mind, he thought. Probably needed a quick getaway. Disengage in the face of the enemy.

He pushed the memory down inside, along with all the rest of them.

In the far distance, Corey saw a figure. He clambered over a stile and walked purposefully in the direction of the Hall. He was a small dark speck, but Corey sensed that he was more significant than his stature suggested. The figure moved quickly through the grounds, gaining on the house with a relentless velocity. Corey saw him greet two soldiers strolling down by the river. He had a brief conversation with them, and they pointed to the house. He left them with a wave and his march continued.

As he grew closer and his features gradually emerged from ambiguity, Corey saw that he was a man of average height, his appearance oddly out of date, as if he'd been snatched out of time twenty years ago. And his hair was unusually long, blowing around his head in a dark storm as he walked.

As he approached, Corey saw the man adopt a pleasant, disarming expression. He struck up a conversation with a nurse whom Corey couldn't see below. Their voices were muffled, but Corey could just make out mention of Dr Banham. The nurse led the man into the house below.

For all his odd appearance, the man was obviously an official. If he was here to see Dr Banham, then Corey wanted to know what they were talking about. There were things going on at Hawkswick Hall that needed getting to the bottom of, and Corey felt this visitor might just be the answer. Grabbing his cap, he stuffed it under his arm and marched from the room.

Clara Walker also thought the stranger's appearance rather unusual. She supposed that might be the new fashion in the city these days. She wouldn't know, having been stuck here in the middle of nowhere now for nearly eight months. The man was ushered into Clara's anteroom by one of the VAD nurses, and, giving the nurse a parting smile, he swept across the room to greet Clara.

'Good morning,' he said, maintaining the smile like a salesman. 'I'd like to speak to Dr Banham, if I may, please.'

Clara found the man curiously interesting. Good-looking, certainly. But with an air of authority that reminded Clara of her old boss, the rich owner of a firm of solicitors down in Romford. That sort of confidence came of a casual familiarity with power.

'May I ask who's calling?'

'I'm from the Ministry,' the man told her; then, almost as an afterthought, he added, 'of Health.'

'If you'd like to take a seat, I'll see if Dr Banham can see you,' Clara told him.

Knocking at the impressive polished oak door, Clara listened for Banham's command from inside. She entered the oak-panelled office to find Banham sitting behind his huge desk, gazing at her over the top of his glasses as he poised mid-sentence over a report he was writing.

Even in his seat, Banham was a tall, imposing man. Mid-thirties. He habitually wore a tweed suit, which Clara thought did nothing to complement his impressive shape. Although he wore spectacles, they served to emphasise his dark good looks. He had jet-black hair without a trace of grey or recession, and his eyes were a deep brown which looked almost black. At fifteen years his junior, Clara still found herself lost in daydreams about the man.

'Yes, Clara?' Banham asked sharply.

'A gentleman to see you, Dr Banham.'

'One of the patients?'

'No. He's a man from the Ministry of Health, sir.'

A storm entered Banham's face. He stood and ushered her out of the office.

Shuffling unimportant papers from one place to another, Clara watched from her desk as Banham regarded the Man from the Ministry with a kind of overbearing distrust.

'We weren't expecting any visit from the Ministry,' he told the man flatly, without bothering to introduce himself.

'Dr Banham?' the man asked.

'Yes.'

The Man from the Ministry held out his hand and Banham grasped it despite himself.

'A great pleasure to meet you, sir. I've heard so much about the good work you do here at Hawkswick Hall.'

Banham seemed to warm to this approach, although he still watched the Ministry Man with some degree of suspicion.

'I wondered if we might have a quiet chat, sir.'

'About?'

The Ministry Man appeared uncertain. He glanced over to find Clara averting her gaze with some considerable self-consciousness.

'I've been sent up from London to help investigate certain…
occurrences in the village.'

Banham faltered. In a change of tack, he ushered the Ministry
Man into the privacy of his office. Taking up position behind his
desk, he found the Ministry Man standing opposite and they faced
one another for a moment without a word.

'Please, take a seat,' the man said, throwing himself into the
small leather seat in front of the desk.

Banham sat stiffly and regarded the man warily…

'What can I do to help you, Mr…?'

'Doctor.'

'You're a doctor?'

'That's my title.'

'Of?'

'Many things, I suspect.'

'Curious credentials.'

'I'm a very curious man.'

Banham regarded the Doctor in silence while the clock on the
mantel launched huge seconds across the room. They echoed
from the wood panelling with an impressively hollow sound.

'You say you're from the Ministry of Health?'

'A slight deception,' the Doctor admitted. 'I'm actually here in
response to reports about certain… crimes in the village.'

'Crimes? You mean these supernatural hallucinations suffered
by country folk who have been living on the knife edge of full-
scale world war for four years now?'

'I see you're rather sceptical…'

'I'm a man of science, Doctor, not of fantasy. Amongst its
innumerable special new departments, does this government
now have a Ministry of Hauntings?'

The Doctor smiled in quiet amusement. 'It doesn't, I'm glad to
say. But what it *does* have is a coalition inner cabinet who take
very seriously repeated reports of slaughter in their own back

yard by means of high explosives.'

'High explosives?'

The Doctor flashed open the fingers of both hands in unison.

'*Ka-booooom!*'

Banham fell silent. His face was impossible to read, like a man of stone. The silence stretched for half a minute before he spoke again. Then his voice was softer, friendlier.

'Would you like a cup of coffee, Doctor?'

The Doctor nodded appreciatively and Banham stepped back to the door, where he poked his head out to ask Clara to do the honours. When he returned he clasped his hands together on the giant desk between them, and regarded the Doctor with a piercing look.

'So you've come to see if you can discover the source of these explosives?'

'I'm following my leads.'

'Well I'm afraid you're on a mistaken trail, my dear Mr Holmes.'

'But since I'm here, my dear Dr Banham, might I please ask if these men have access to such materials?'

Banham was shaking his head. 'There is a substantial munitions factory in Grimston. I suggest you try there.'

'But I'm *here*,' the Doctor repeated, quiet but firm.

Banham sat back in his chair and it creaked slightly under his weight. 'We have no explosive materials at this establishment, Doctor, I can assure you.'

'Guns? Ammunition?'

'A very small amount. They're under constant lock and key.'

'Who has a key?'

'Myself.'

'And?'

'And no one.' Banham stood and walked to the window. He gazed out at the bright new day and the sun brought his large physique into sharp relief. The gold albert that spanned his tweed waistcoat glistened in the sunlight.

'I handle these matters personally,' he informed the Doctor.

'Very commendable,' the Doctor commended.

'I run a tight operation here, Doctor. We're in the midst of a war. Efficiency and order are paramount, I'm sure you'll agree. Rest assured, the men here do not have access to their weapons until they are perfectly fit to return to the front with them. When they are ready to shoot Germans, they get their guns. Until I'm one hundred per cent satisfied about their mental health, they live a sheltered, protected life here.'

There came a knock at the door, and it opened to admit Clara with a heavy-looking tray. The Doctor rushed over to take it from her.

'Thank you,' he said.

She left with a fleeting smile and the Doctor placed the tray on the edge of Banham's desk.

'Shall I be mother?'

Banham nodded and the Doctor proceeded to pour two cups of coffee from a jug. As he prepared the cups, he spoke in a tone that suggested polite conversation.

'I've had reports of badly injured soldiers seen in the village after dark,' he told Banham. 'Could these men get out at night?'

The Doctor pushed the tray over to one side of the table and Banham came over and dashed milk into his cup before scooping it up and returning to the window with it.

'This is a hospital, Doctor, not a prison. If a man were dangerous, he wouldn't be here in the first place. These men have been deeply scarred by their war experiences. Their sleep patterns are often severely disrupted. I've found it helps some of them to work through their psychoses if they are actively encouraged to leave the hospital at night. It is quite possible that they might reach the village, but they are certainly not armed, and certainly not dangerous.'

'It's fair to say you have a reasonably relaxed regime here, then?'

'As far as an individual's personal freedom goes, yes. As for the gun store, *no*.'

The Doctor sipped his coffee meditatively. 'How can you be entirely certain that these men are not dangerous if they are so... disturbed?'

'If you went to your physician with a broken leg, he would very quickly recognise it as such and apply the appropriate remedy to mend it. If you presented symptoms of some malady that he was unaccustomed to seeing, he might refer you to a specialist. There are different specialities in health treatment. I happen to specialise in men's minds. I *know*!'

The Doctor looked Banham straight in the eye. 'I've discovered a considerable weight of evidence to suggest you may be wrong, Dr Banham.'

'The word of rural bumpkins.'

'This morning I saw for myself a trench that had been constructed overnight. I estimate that to get that job done overnight in August, which gives you, say, five hours of relative cover of darkness, you would need something like thirty to forty men on the job. How many patients do you have at this institution, Dr Banham?'

Banham smiled at the Doctor over his coffee. He took a sip before returning the cup to the tray on the edge of the desk and giving the Doctor a sweeping gesture towards the door.

'Perhaps since you have some difficulty in believing me,' he said, his tone still even and amicable, 'you might find it easier to believe the men themselves...'

The stables were thick with the scent of straw and, when Mary Minett entered, it took her a while to acclimatise from the bright sunshine outside. Apparently immune to such adjustment, Bill Cromby stomped headlong into the darkness. Following the sound of his clomping boots more than anything, Mary stumbled after him.

There was nothing of the stench of horse muck she might find on some farms. Cromby was a diligent man when it came to his animals. He understood that to get the best *from* them, you needed to do your best *for* them.

Finally able to actually see what she was doing, Mary followed Cromby into one of the bays to find two of his four mammoth shires looking extremely doubtful. They regarded her warily out of great brown eyes, tugging their tethers and snorting as she reached up to one of them with a slow, gentle caress.

'There now,' Mary whispered in her sensual tones.

The horse seemed to calm slightly, and Cromby watched and listened transfixed as Mary crooned in her honey-sweet voice.

'Come on. Let's take a look at you, shall we?'

The horse allowed her to lay her hands on its neck, and from there she traced a complex path around its body and down its legs, finally ruffling the fetlocks and checking the shoes. She reached up and opened the mouth delicately, examining the teeth, gums and tongue while the horse simply stood with no sign of its earlier surliness. The inspection ended with Mary holding the horse's head in both hands and pulling it down to her own level. She gazed into the brute eyes, remaining perfectly still for long, silent moments, until she gently let go and the horse heaved a vast sigh of hot breath.

Mary repeated this procedure with the other three horses, before she turned to Cromby.

'There's nothing *physically* wrong with them. They're all in excellent health, Bill. But inside their heads… Well, that's a different matter.' She gave the back of her neck a rub before telling him the next bit. 'I think they saw something last night.'

'*Saw* summat?'

Mary shrugged. 'That's what I'd guess.'

'Saw what?'

'I'm not a mind-reader, Bill. I don't know *what* they saw. But I do know they saw something that scared the hell out of them. Maybe there's a big dog loose.'

Cromby led her back down the building and out into the sunlight.

'No dog,' he said, nodding at the farmhouse with confident finality. 'My two would a' let me know if there was another dog round 'ere.'

As she stepped out, Cromby closed the stable door, then spent a long time gazing at it with an anxious scowl.

'I'm sure they'll be all right now,' Mary said, trying to reassure him.

He came out of his reverie and nodded agreement, but still seemed reluctant to move.

'Let me know if you have any more trouble, won't you?'

'That I will,' he said, and finally managed to drag himself away from the door.

He walked her to the gate and they stood together with the sound of far-off chickens clucking and flapping behind the house. There was thrush song and sunshine and Mary fancied that on days like today she could easily forget there was a war on.

''Ow much do I owe yer, then?' Cromby demanded suddenly.

Mary shook her head. 'You owe me nothing, Mr Cromby.'

'I like to pay me way,' he reminded her uncomfortably.

'I know,' she told him. 'But there was nothing wrong with them in the first place, so I can't charge you anything, can I?'

Cromby took off his cap to scratch his bald head. 'Well, if y're sure…'

'Course I'm sure. Forget it. Really.'

Abruptly Cromby thrust out his hand at her. She took it and he shook her arm vigorously.

'Y're a good woman, Mary Minett,' he announced, before turning

40

his back on her and stomping off across the yard towards the fields.

Mary watched him go, his great boots clomping on the dry earth, sending up swirls of orange-coloured dust around his ankles that chased him like strange small spectres snapping at his heels.

'Y're not a bad bloke yerself, William Cromby,' Mary muttered in deep mock dialect as she opened the gate and left the Cromby farm, massaging her arm as she went.

'Captain Miles Thomas,' Banham said quietly as he led the Doctor down the vast corridor that was the first-floor landing. 'Found one of his men blasted following two days of bombardment by the Germans. Simply "packed up" one night in the middle of the strafe. Became totally unresponsive. They had to stretcher him out. Of course, this would have been the effect of an accumulation of events, not just the two-day bombardment. He was awarded the Military Cross, so he must have seen some real action in his time.'

Banham knocked gently at the door, and opened it up to reveal a sun-filled room with beige-painted walls and a large window facing out on to rolling countryside. The sky was wispy with traces of frail cloud, but it was euphoria blue without a hint of rain.

Sitting on the edge of the bed, Captain Miles Thomas MC stared out of the window. As Banham ushered the Doctor quietly in, Thomas turned and they found a haunted man gazing at them. Thomas was in his early thirties, a slim man with slumped, defeated shoulders. He had dark eyes that might be intense if they weren't so distracted. Jowls shadowy with bristles and hair wild with uncombed tufts, he smiled when he saw Banham.

'Good morning, Dr Banham,' Thomas said, a bit brighter than his looks suggested. 'This is an unusual time for a visit. I'm not due for a mud bath now, am I?'

41

Banham grinned warmly at the man on the bed. 'Not now, no. This is just a social call.' He indicated the Doctor at his side. 'This is a doctor from the Ministry. He's doing an inspection.'

Thomas jumped up and stood to attention in his dressing gown and slippers. He gave the Doctor a stiff salute before his face cracked and he relaxed, apparently pleased with his small joke. He stuck out his hand and the Doctor shook it amicably.

'I hope you find us all in order, Doctor,' he said. 'I'm afraid the slippers don't come up with much of a shine, however much spit an' polish you rub on 'em.'

'Oh, this isn't a formal visit,' the Doctor assured him, waving at the bed. 'Please don't let me disturb you.'

'It's a bit late for that,' Thomas grinned. 'I'm afraid I'm already rather *disturbed*.' He fell back on to the bed, slapping his forehead repeatedly with his fist. 'Otherwise I wouldn't be here.'

The Doctor stepped across the room and plonked himself on the low windowsill. 'I'm sure that's not true,' he quibbled mildly. 'A man who can put his problems in proportion and regard them with a sense of humour is a man without any real problems at all.'

Thomas sat up on the bed. 'I'll admit I can smile about it now,' he said, 'but, believe me, you're looking at a true-blue loon, Doctor. Full-blown loco, I can assure you.'

The Doctor appeared pensive, the clear blue sky behind him completely at odds with the shadows that passed through his face. 'We can all sail those seas,' he said at last. 'It doesn't mean to say we're any less a man, does it?'

'Some of the men here might disagree with you,' Thomas told him.

'Some of the men here,' Banham interceded, his voice booming, 'can be very wrong in their opinions.'

Banham pulled up a seat and sat beside the bed. He looked far too large for the seat, as if he really needed something of a giant plush leather chair instead, but he sat there with his hands clasped loosely, looking quite relaxed.

Thomas regarded the Doctor with a glint in his eye. 'Listen to the voice of wisdom, Doctor. This is the man who knows.'

'So it seems,' the Doctor said.

'And I suppose that's why you're here, is it? To see one of Dr Banham's success stories for yourself? Is the government considering diverting funds from this remarkable institution?'

'That's not why I'm here,' the Doctor told him.

'Well if you're here to find out what they need on the Western Front, Ministry Man, I can tell you that all right.' Thomas's face was suddenly red. 'They need more food and a whole lot more rum. And they need armour-plated uniforms. And earmuffs. And what they really need, if you'd like to take this back to your precious Ministry, is an end to this war and this slaughter and this inhuman *hell*...'

He stared hotly at the Doctor, not for a second allowing his savage gaze to falter. The Doctor looked back evenly. When he spoke his voice was soft and it spilled into the room like a lotion for anger.

'Nobody can bring this war to an end just like that,' he announced. 'This is a situation where basal human instincts have been allowed full reign. This war was probably inevitable. Human nature. There's nothing I can do to change that.'

Thomas gazed momentarily out of the window into the sunny day, before continuing evenly.

'I apologise, Doctor,' he said. 'I'm not quite finished with my therapy yet. I seem to still have bouts of fury directed against the killing. I'm positive that, by the time Dr Banham has finished with me, I'll be perfectly ready to return to destroying Hun filth.'

'By the time my therapy is completed,' Banham said, 'you'll be perfectly ready to return to your old self, whatever that state was.'

Thomas sighed a lingering breath which seemed to empty him completely of the fury. He rubbed his face and the Doctor discovered a different man watching him from the bed.

'I was a *captain*,' he said. 'A bloody good captain. Until I snapped. Then I was a useless lump of meat. Worse than useless – I was a *liability*. You don't let your men see you crack up. Officer material is tougher than that. It's shellproof stuff, is officer.' He stroked his chin with the quiet scrape of bristles, and the haunted look reasserted itself. 'Only – the toughest armour plating's going to crack if you hit it hard enough and long enough with the right artillery. I suppose I just got sick of the slaughter.'

A long, heavy silence hung over the bright room, until Thomas abruptly jumped up, marched over to the wardrobe and tugged out his uniform. He laid it out neatly on the bed, brushing nonexistent bits of fluff and rubbing the brass buttons with his fist. Finally, he turned to the Doctor.

'I think I'd like to get dressed now, if you don't mind.'

'Of course,' the Doctor said, lifting himself off the windowsill and heading for the door. On his way, he grasped Thomas's hand again.

'Thank you for being so frank with me,' he said. 'It was very helpful. I appreciate it.'

'Don't mention it,' Thomas said. 'I love a good rant and rave. That's why I'm here.'

Bloody queer! thought Bill Cromby.

After feeding the chickens and collecting the eggs, he'd returned to the stables. He opened the door and slipped inside, only to sense the horses on edge again. At the sound of the door, they began to snort and stamp in their bays. There was the worrying sound of wooden slats being walloped, and Cromby shambled over to check on them.

He discovered all the horses with wide, fearful eyes. Tethered with their backs to the walkway, they fidgeted edgily as Cromby tried to see what the trouble was. Risking a pounding from their mighty hind legs, Cromby bolted between the two horses in the first bay. He reached up and grasped the rein, endeavouring to stroke the horse's muzzle. The horse pushed back, throwing its head about as if trying to get away.

'Ey,' Cromby growled. 'Come on. What's up wi' yer?'

He saw they hadn't touched the hay from this morning, and wondered if it'd been contaminated with something. It seemed perfectly all right. Smelled lovely and fresh. Cromby set to work removing it from the rack and piling it in the corner near the door. Then he took the fork to get new stuff. As he leaned into the stack, which was stored in the last bay, that's when he noticed it. It had been covered by the hay before, but now he could just see it poking out of the edge of the stack. Churned earth. Just like the stuff the Doctor found in the field this morning. And even in the dim light of the stable, he could see that the edges were raised as if something had risen out of the ground.

What Cromby didn't see was the dark figure watching him from the hayloft. It hunched, at home in the dark, gelatinous fluid glistening on its ragged face. The thing wore an army uniform caked in dried mud. The eyes were empty holes, shadow lost in shadow. The head was half covered in tufts of matted hair, the other half being a large bare wound that stretched around its scalp. It sat motionless and silent, with not even the sound of laboured breathing, as Cromby carefully inspected the floor of the bay below.

'*Bloody queer!*'

Cromby scooped up the new hay and stuffed the racks with it, before marching for the door. As he was about to leave he thought he sensed something behind him. He turned to scan the hayloft but found only darkness. The horses were still jittery. Cromby gritted his teeth in frustration, and clattered the door shut.

The stables were plunged into thick shadow. In the still gloom, with the nervous rustling of horses, things moved.

* * *

Banham and the Doctor made their way out from the dark wood panels of the house to the brilliant open space of the gardens. A nurse helping a man whose eyes were bandaged met them. She held the man's arm firmly, warning him to watch the step, and he stumbled up it with an annoyed scowl. The Doctor held open the door while the nurse led the man into the house.

'Thomas is typical of the men we cater for here,' Banham explained in subdued, confidential tones. 'He remains extremely angry, but for the most part that rage is directed at himself.'

They walked together across the front of the house, the Doctor pausing to gaze out across the pictorial landscape dotted with nurses and soldiers. A small flock of sparrows wheeled through the sky in vortical formation and the Doctor stood mesmerised by the spectacle. Banham, realising he'd temporarily lost the Doctor, stopped and watched the man gazing entirely lost for a full few seconds before returning to Earth.

Without taking his eyes from the sky after the birds had returned to their trees, the Doctor said, 'Go on, I'm still listening.'

'Much of his hostility,' Banham continued, 'is directed at the continuing carnage.'

The Doctor dragged his gaze back from the wild blue yonder, and met Banham a few paces on, his feet crunching a quick-march in the gravel.

'He would not go out at night killing livestock,' Banham assured the Doctor. 'It's much more likely he might try to harm *himself*.'

The Doctor spoke conversationally as they walked together around the front of the house. 'Captain Thomas mentioned a mud bath. Is that some sort of therapy, by any chance?'

Banham huffed. 'Mud bath. Sludge therapy. They all have their own epithet for it. All variations on a theme.'

'Sounds interesting.' The Doctor suddenly ducked and Banham found him examining a small flower pushing out of the gravel. 'And rather dirty.'

'But it works,' Banham said, his irritation at the Doctor's continual distractions becoming evident in the hardening of his voice.

Suddenly the Doctor had gone from one extreme to the other, and Banham found the man's eyes afire with renewed fascination. 'I don't suppose you could elaborate?'

'Come on,' Banham said, marching off with the Doctor at his heel.

The Doctor was led into a large out-building. Obviously the stables, which were situated at the rear of the house. The building had been renovated and adapted, the old stable doors bricked up and new windows added. The windows contained frosted glass, the Doctor noticed as he was led through a small steel door in the side of the building.

He found himself in an anteroom with bright electric lights, obviously a very recent conversion. There were large coat hooks on the wall, as the Doctor might expect to find in a changing room, and these were draped with waterproof macs that were daubed in dried grey plaster or clay.

'It's probably best if you could see my work in action,' Banham told him, checking his watch. 'I'm due for a session shortly, but I'm afraid it's impossible for you to sit in. Privacy is essential if we're to get anything from these sessions. However, if you'd like to follow me, you can see from a vantage point which I had written into the plans for this place. It's very useful for keeping a check on the progress of my patients.'

The Doctor was shown through another steel door into a narrow corridor with an immensely high ceiling that seemed to be the rafters of the original hayloft. At the bottom of the short corridor was a set of metal steps leading up. The two men climbed and the Doctor emerged finally on to a raised viewing platform. The area was in darkness except for light coming up from the rooms below, and this was filtered through sheets of gauze that made up the ceilings. The platform was small with an iron railing around its perimeter, and it overlooked four rooms. Gangplanks led off from the central stage, and these were intersected halfway across each room by other planks. The gauze was suspended from the underside of the planks.

'From here you can see them, but they can't see you,' Banham said, his voice little more than a whisper even though the rooms were all empty. 'I have four patients at a time undergoing this therapy. Although it's very dirty, they usually find it extremely cleansing.'

He grasped the railing and the Doctor stood at his side, gazing down. Below, he could see a room plastered in clay, walls and floor daubed completely. In the centre of the floor was a mound of clay in the crude shape of a man, except that it was a thing of giant proportions with thick trunks for legs and vastly oversized arms. The head was simply a great misshapen ball, featureless but for the nightmarish suggestion of eyes and nose created by what looked like purely accidental damage inflicted on the face.

'Very pretty,' the Doctor mused.

Banham saw the Doctor's features up-lit, and found them disturbing and alien. Like something straight out of a Gothic fantasy. The Doctor's Victorian clothing added to the disconcerting impression.

'The whole point here is that the men are able to create things of twisted, abstract horror. They pour their pent-up emotions into these works, Doctor, and those emotions are often violent, frightening, horrific. These men are deeply scarred by their war experiences. They have seen things that would make your blood curdle. Enough to send a man insane. But here they are able to exorcise their innermost torments. Get them out in the open. Make them malleable. Give them form. Make them *external*.'

'Intriguing theory,' the Doctor breathed, gazing into the empty darkness above the rooms.

'And with extremely rewarding, *demonstrable* results.'

'Fascinating –'

There was a sudden roar that shook the viewing platform. A ricochet vibration that thundered through the whole building like an explosion. The platform shuddered and the Doctor gripped the railing, gaping down to find the room below being blasted with mist.

'Sorry,' Banham yelled. 'The automated misting system. It's a bit enthusiastic. Works on a timer. I forgot.'

The spray came to a hissing stop and the water pressure made the pipes judder and thump. The Doctor gave him a grotesque, shadowy, upside-down smile.

'What startled me was the thing down there,' he admitted, nodding at the gargantuan clay monster.

'Ugly things, aren't they? But not as ugly as the reality which spawns them, I can assure you.'

'I'm sure.'

'The patient you are about to see was a corporal in the 14th Battalion, York and Lancaster Regiment. His unit was wiped out during a German assault near Berles. He was the only one left alive. They found him struck dumb. He had severe lacerations to his hands, and we've never been able to establish what happened to him. His memory of the attack is a complete blank. He communicates through written messages. Curiously, only capital letters. I get the impression he's rather incensed about something.'

The Doctor said nothing, but continued to gaze at the clay man below.

'I must go now. It's imperative that you remain absolutely silent during the session. The patient won't even know you're here if you keep quiet. The lights in there are just bright enough to stop them seeing out, although you can see in. If he realises you're here, this whole session, and perhaps the last half-dozen, may all be wasted.'

'Don't worry,' the Doctor assured him. 'I'm expert at being invisible when I want to be.'

Banham regarded the apparition in front of him. It was made up of streaks of whitish-yellow light and its face contained extruded features. 'I'm sure you are,' he said, before turning to leave.

Corporal Duncan McHale followed Banham into the antechamber. McHale swapped his jacket for a coverall and, while Banham put on his own smock and wellingtons, McHale removed his shoes and socks. The building wasn't cold. McHale understood that some sort of underground heating system had been installed. The air was warm and slightly humid, with the all-pervading aroma of damp clay. Over the past two months, it was a smell that McHale had grown to relish. In fact, he quite looked forward to these sessions now.

'Are you all right?' Banham asked.

McHale tried to speak. Sometimes he forgot he had no voice. Sometimes he opened his mouth and was shocked to hear an unexpected silence. In frustration, McHale simply nodded and gave Banham an embarrassed smile.

They went together into the clay room, and McHale met with the waiting Gargantuan. It hadn't got any prettier since he last saw it. A creature of infinite deformity, the grey monster towered over them both. This entrance always gave McHale a shiver. He still hadn't got used to meeting his own creation.

While Banham went over and sat on a stool in the corner, McHale approached the thing like a boy before an overbearing schoolteacher. For long, silent moments he simply stood and stared into its fractured face.

'Take your time,' Banham told him, voice calm and level.

McHale gazed up at the thing and tried to block out Banham's presence. Tried to focus, to shut out the world and reach the feelings locked inside. They would all come out, Banham had promised, and the creature would soak them all up for him.

Slowly, McHale bent and picked up a handful of clay from the floor. He kneaded it in his hands, feeling the stuff, damp but body-warm, ooze between his fingers. Savouring the grit against the scars in his hands, he squeezed harder. Harder. He'd lost his memory and lost his voice, but the clay man would take all his troubles. It would release his voice, and his memories. All the frustration and hatred that hid them would be sealed in the clay. Harder. His teeth were grinding now. His mind circumnavigated the dark area inside him, the terrifying blackness of uncharted territory. Here be Dragons. Here be things of such horror that they *had* to be cleared out.

McHale lashed, thrashing the clay man's chest with the gob of clay. The clay stuck like a cancerous growth. McHale despised it. He beat it with his fists until it flattened and became part of the thing's broad chest.

Then he laid into the clay for all he was worth, doing his utmost to scream his rage. But the voice wouldn't come. Only a searing, terrible silence. McHale felt the spittle streaked across his burning hot face but didn't stop to wipe. His hatred was so dazzling now that he couldn't stop. He was a tidal wave of wrath. He lashed and thrashed and beat the clay man with every trace of loathing he possessed.

From his vantage point above, the Doctor gazed down, gripping the railing with white knuckles, intimately fascinated by McHale's frenzy. Banham simply sat as if he weren't there, his stool to all intents empty.

McHale threw himself to the floor, grasping an armful of clay that he smashed on to the man-shaped mountain in the middle of the room. The creature was becoming more grotesque by the minute, and McHale pounded it in a rising delirium. The building was permeated with an indefinable atmosphere – a palpable, electrifying presence in the air.

The only sound the squelching clay.

Desperate to express himself, McHale appeared to be in the throes of a fit.

The Hun came screaming. A mass of them squelching through no-man's-land towards McHale's position. He released the locking pin on the Vickers and squeezed the trigger. The rattle of bullets exploded in his ears. He sensed movement to his left and glanced to see Johnson blown backwards with a large bloody hole in his head. McHale snatched the Vickers off its tripod and hoisted it furiously into the air, standing in plain view and letting rip. They fell in droves. A hundred men. Squirming and thrashing in the grey slime, which had been pummelled for two days nonstop before the attack. Still a few got through. The belt ran out and McHale slung the Vickers into the trench, grasping his Lee Enfield and blasting at the nearby Germans. The air swarmed with screeching steel. The crazed clatter of a thousand insane assassins.

A German private landed with a thunk *beside him and before the boy could raise his arm McHale swiped him with his trench club, exploding the boy's face like soft red fruit. The German sank to his knees, thrashing in the mud, shrieking at the top of his voice, until McHale blasted a hole in his chest and he jammed backwards on top of Johnson's body.*

Grey motion to his back. Instinctively McHale lashed out with the club. Head height. A figure grasped its face in a paroxysm of pain, and McHale blasted him three times point-blank. The body slapped back into the sludge.

Looking for trouble, McHale found stillness and a sudden vacuum from gunfire, except for the echoing thunder of his own spent bullets. Men writhed in the mid-distance, throwing up splashes of mud and blood. Some were still. Some squirmed and sloshed. McHale's ears were ringing but he could make out the cries of desperate, terrified men. The air stank of cordite. It tore at his throat, like swallowing barbs. His lungs heaved and his blood roared like a raging river coursing through him.

He turned and saw the boy-German's body lying on Johnson, the boy's chest wide open and swelling with blood. McHale remembered the look of startled fear in the boy's eyes. He was seventeen, if that. And now he lay slaughtered at McHale's feet.

Grasping the Enfield, McHale suddenly turned the gun on himself. So easy. So easy. Get out. So easy. Get out now. He pressed the trigger. The rifle refused. Pressed again. Pressed again. Rammed the muzzle hard into his throat. Felt his stinging larynx. He slammed the empty gun into the mud and grasped the trench club. Clutched the scrap-lead head, layered with barbed wire, tight in both hands. Squeezed until he felt the blood stream.

And he screamed –

McHale screamed. His voice flooding the room and bouncing off the walls, a word emerged from the animal yowl.

'*Nooo…*'

He dropped to his knees in the wet clay, sobbing uncontrollably. Banham lifted him out of the mud and transported him to the stool. McHale shuddered and trembled, dark and appalling emotions running wild in him like ferocious things on the rampage.

'There,' Banham soothed, voice warm like a cosy fire-lit room. 'We got it all out in the end.'

But McHale could only cry.

Chapter Three

When Albert Briggs got back to the station house, he found Bessie and Millicent Fry unloading the Doctor's box off Zachary Smith's cart. Norma Grealy was helping guide the box, barking orders like a sergeant major.

'Bit to the left… *Right!* Watch that corner…'

Briggs regarded them in fresh wonder every time he saw these huge women. Even after all these months, he could still not get used to seeing village girls wearing, and filling, their husbands' work clobber. They looked as if they were in fancy dress, ready for the harvest festival dance. Norma Grealy in particular appeared very brawny, with her spiky-cropped hair, great baggy jumper and heavy working trousers that disguised her shape to make her a hulking, sexless thing. A stranger would take her for a bloke, Briggs was certain. She'd worked the land for nearly two years now, and in that time she must've put on five stone, evolving to meet the demands of these brave new days.

Between the three of them, they manhandled the blue box into Briggs's lock-up at the side of the house. It landed with a solid-sounding thud on the damp brick floor, and all three women clapped their hands to remove imagined dirt, since the box seemed perfectly clean to Briggs. He realised they'd adopted their men's habits as well as their clothes: their swaggering walks with arms dangling, like great apes after physical exertion, to illustrate the effortlessness of the task.

With a thankful nod from Briggs, the Frys jumped up on to the cart, while Norma took up the draw-shaft and carried them away like a great plodding donkey.

Briggs stepped into the gloomy lock-up and gazed at the box. It towered above him, filling the space almost completely.

'What on Earth is that?' said a voice behind him.

Turning with a look of surprise, he discovered Mary Minett in the doorway.

'It's the Doctor's box,' Briggs informed her, knowingly.

Mary moved around it, peering at the curiously textured surface. The box seemed to be constructed of a cross between Bakelite and oak. It was painted a peculiarly dull blue colour, without any of the sheen Mary might expect of a modern paint. In fact, on closer inspection it looked to Mary as if the box hadn't been painted at all, but that this blue was the material's natural hue. She walked all round it to meet Briggs again.

'No doors,' he said, confirming her own conclusion.

She touched the nearest plane of the box, and snatched her hand away abruptly.

'What's up?' Briggs demanded.

Mary touched the box again, this time with more care. And this time her hand remained.

'I thought…'

Briggs watched her enquiringly.

'It's nothing,' she dismissed. 'I thought it felt hot.' She inspected her hand closely. 'Must've been a splinter or something.'

'Looks smooth enough to me,' Briggs said, running the tips of his fingers over the box.

Mary moved to the door, eager to get back into the daylight, and Briggs closed the door behind them.

'Did the Doctor ask you to lock up his box?'

'He did,' Briggs confirmed, leading Mary back to the house. 'Mind you, can't see why he wants it locking up if it hasn't got any doors.'

He entered the darkness of his kitchen and headed straight for the kettle, placing it lovingly on the range, then proceeded to rattle the teapot with preparations for elevenses.

Mary sat at the little table and watched him swilling the cups. Briggs possessed only the bare minimum of crockery, yet whenever he wanted a drink or meal he had to retrieve dirty dishes from the scummy cold water in the sink. Since his wife died, he'd let the place slip. The table top was knobbly and slightly sticky with dried old scraps of food, and the whole place was thick with dust. The curtains at the tiny window hadn't been washed since before Effie passed away, and Mary felt quite sure that, if she asked, Albert Briggs could not for the life of him point her in the direction of the mop or scrubbing brush.

With some sadness, Mary had watched the station house descend into squalor over the last four years. Her gradually less subtle hints that she might be able to come round and clean for Briggs had met with gradually more stern rebuffs from the constable. Now the station house was in a state of filthy disrepair and Effie Briggs was very probably spinning in her grave.

'Now then,' Briggs said, delivering a teapot into the middle of the table like a music hall illusionist, 'what can I do for you, Miss Minett?'

'Actually,' Mary said, taking and turning the cup he offered, 'it's about the Doctor.'

The sun was high in the sky over Hawkswick Hall. Banham sat opposite the Doctor and poured them both another cup of Earl Grey. The Doctor rewarded him with a grateful smile and dashed a small amount of milk into his drink. Both men sipped in silence.

They were at the front of the house on an elevated terrace edged by stone balustrades. Banham wore a lopsided straw boater that made him appear quite the dandy, while the Doctor preferred to lounge in the shade of a large umbrella which Dr Banham had kindly supplied.

The grounds were dotted with people. Mostly pairs of khaki-suited men, or soldiers with nurses. They strolled together enjoying the summer's day, redolent with the scent of grass and clean English air.

'Is that a rock rose I can smell?' the Doctor asked suddenly.

Banham smiled. 'It is. We can't see it from here, but it's just over the other side of the balustrade.'

'One second,' the Doctor said, depositing his cup and scrambling out of his seat. He scurried away and returned with a cutting that he caressed lovingly for Banham to admire.

'*Cistus purpureus*,' the Doctor announced, gazing into the crimson papery petals. He turned the flower and regarded it from all angles with a faraway look in his eyes. 'It's flowering very late.'

'So,' Banham said with mild amusement, 'you're a doctor of horticulture.'

The Doctor shook his head absently, entirely beguiled by the rose.

'A botanist, then,' Banham probed.

Still shaking his head, the Doctor watched Banham with a strange look of rapt detachment. Banham found the Doctor's eyes suddenly paler than they were supposed to be.

'I'm just an avid admirer of all things beautiful,' the Doctor remarked, handing the cutting over.

Banham received it with consummate care, but the petals abruptly dropped on to the table between them. Banham found himself clutching a bare twig between his fingers, a strangely barren and contorted thing. He met with a look of genuine pain residing in the Doctor's features.

Banham huffed. 'The petals fall before nightfall,' he told the Doctor plaintively.

A pathetic smile forced its way unenthusiastically into the Doctor's lips. 'It's a good job you don't have that effect on your patients,' he remarked, reaching over to scoop up the fallen petals.

Banham dropped the twig to the ground and took another sip of tea.

'You must admit, Doctor, that this morning's little demonstration was most remarkable.'

'I was suitably impressed,' the Doctor concurred. 'Tell me, this therapy, how long have you been employing it now?'

'Longer than I care to remember, Doctor. To be perfectly honest, I find it quite a drain. It's a long haul with each man. Most of my work here is preamble. It simply gets the patient comfortable with what I'm asking him to do. All of them feel extremely awkward for a good few sessions. The trick is to make them entirely relaxed with the clay and the environment. The rooms are specially heated using an underfloor plumbing system. Although it's a constant very low level of heat, I also then had to install the spray system to keep the clay workable. Some of the patients take weeks to make the full adjustment. When that comes, though, I soon see results.'

'I was stunned,' the Doctor admitted, sweeping his cup off the table and gulping with zeal. 'It really did seem to be a kind of exorcism.'

'Yes. Exactly,' Banham enthused. 'At the start I explain to them, "You have bad stuff inside you and we're going to get it out. You're going to put it into your work. Embody it. *Encapsulate* it." I discovered it helps to encourage them to work with a human form. They can relate to him more readily. Project their own emotions on to him. Kick the proverbial hell out of him if they want to.'

The Doctor put his cup down. 'You talk as if these things were real people.'

'To the patients, they *are*. But a special kind of people. Like sponges, they can soak up all my patients' fear and wrath. They're mouldable. Like God, these men are able to fashion men in their own image from the very earth itself.'

'From the earth we rise, to the earth we shall return,' the Doctor commented gloomily.

Banham lowered his head and his face became shaded by the rim of his boater. 'The religious and metaphysical overtones are important, Doctor. Don't mock them.'

The Doctor shook his head emphatically. 'Oh, I wasn't mocking, Dr Banham. Please don't think me so shallow.' He gazed again at the rose petals in the palm of his hand. 'I can see how these men regard themselves. It's as if they're looking into one of those fairground distorting mirrors. They see ugly, weak, broken, hideous forms. They create craven images, copies of themselves, and the copy-selves take on the fear and the loathing of the original. They serve to give those emotions form and identification. And, in doing so, put them in perspective. It's a beautiful therapy, Dr Banham. And one that certainly seems to work.'

'Of course it works, Doctor. I've been using it for years, invariably with spectacular success. That it works is indisputable.'

'And I'll be perfectly honest with you, Dr Banham,' the Doctor said. 'When I arrived here this morning, I brought with me the certainty that this hospital was the source of all the troubles at the village. I'm now satisfied that your patients here are entirely blameless, and I hope that if I ever suffer from shell shock, I will be delivered directly into your personal care.'

Banham touched the rim of his hat graciously.

The Doctor took another sip of tea. His smile evaporated and he fell silent, watching the grounds, lost in thought, before speaking again.

'You told Captain Thomas this morning that by the time you'd finished with him he'd be returned to his old self, whatever state that was. Do you really believe you can do that for him?'

Banham sighed and his hands fell on the table. He was shaking his head sorrily. 'Sometimes catastrophic events can change people beyond all recognition and no amount of therapy or drugs is going to undo the damage.'

'I was afraid you were going to say that,' the Doctor said, placing the rose petals carefully into his jacket pocket.

'The important thing is that they *believe* they can get back,' Banham said. 'I think in Thomas's case his accumulated experiences have had such a traumatic effect on his outlook that he'll never see the world in the same light again. It's some small comfort if he thinks he will.'

The Doctor resumed his observation of the grounds, saying nothing. Banham watched him curiously. There were times when the Doctor seemed such a zealot for life that he could be a tirelessly infuriating man. But now he seemed consumed by some private distraction, looking out over the grounds but with eyes completely unfocused. Banham got the impression that he wasn't watching the grounds at all. Perhaps he was gazing beyond into the empty blue sky. Perhaps even beyond that. The Doctor's brooding look lasted a discomforting length of time, until Banham finally picked up the teapot again.

'More tea?' he offered in a genial tone.

The Doctor regarded him darkly.

'No, thank you,' he said. 'I'm afraid I must leave now.'

He patted his jacket as if checking he had everything, then offered his hand to Banham.

'It's been an extremely instructive visit,' he announced without a trace of smile. 'I'm grateful for the time you've given me, Dr Banham. I know you're a very busy man. I'll let you get back to your work. Goodbye.'

And with that he stood and began to march purposefully across the gravel back to the steps that led to the gently sloping lawns. Banham watched his back, the teapot wavering uncertainly in the sun-drenched air above the table.

Watching from his place beyond the river, Private Daniel Corey was surprised at the Doctor's unexpectedly abrupt farewell to Banham. They had looked so contented sitting there sipping tea in the sunshine, chatting cheerfully like familiar friends. Banham had obviously managed to appease the Doctor's qualms. He had satisfied the Doctor that there was no need to fret about the patients at the hospital. But Corey would put the man right.

Making his way towards the small bridge, Corey tried to match the Doctor's speed so that they would converge somewhere near the stile that the Doctor seemed to be heading for. But as Corey reached the bridge, he saw that the Doctor had altered course and was heading straight for him. In a quick change of tack, Corey simply stopped where he was and pretended to watch a small group of four men and two nurses who were strolling along the riverbank nearby.

The bridge was a small, ornate, stone, hump-backed affair, green with moss and strangulating ivy that made it look aged and quaint. Corey leant heavily against the side, allowing the cushion created by the ivy to take his weight.

In the corner of his vision he could sense rather than see the Doctor's approach. In no time at all the man was upon him, striding across the bridge before Corey had realised he was so close.

'Doctor!'

He stopped and turned to Corey in puzzlement. For long moments, the Doctor gazed at him without quite focussing on Corey's features, as if he were trying to look right inside Corey's head.

'I'm sorry,' he declared finally. 'Do I know you?'

'No,' Corey said. He felt suddenly embarrassed. He glanced in great discomfort at the small approaching group. They were laughing and joking, the nurses giggling demurely. They were close enough to hear if they had a mind to listen, and Corey wasn't sure how to put it now he actually had the Doctor here.

'I'm sorry,' Corey spluttered. 'There's this unused room above Dr Banham's office.' He nodded at the house as if to confirm what he was saying. 'It's just got some old furniture and stuff stored in it. They share the same chimney and the sound carries. Sometimes I go in there because it's so quiet and it has this wonderful view of the river. Even better than my own.'

The Doctor approached, the bafflement still evident in his eyes. Corey stepped back uneasily.

'I listened to you and Dr Banham talking this morning,' Corey confessed. 'You said something about strange things happening in the village. Animals being slaughtered.'

Corey choked up as he heard a screech from one of the nearby nurses. Two of the men had lifted her between them and were dashing for the river, apparently intending to lob her in. The whole group were in a hysterical state, the other three falling about laughing. The two men reached the bank but the nurse managed to yank free at the last minute, and instead of dunking *her*, one of the men lost his footing on the banking and slipped in head first himself. The shrieks of merriment intensified, and two of the men were laughing so much that they fell to the floor like a pair of squirming landed fish.

Corey found the Doctor's face close by, shattered into a huge grin.

'It's easy to believe that this is a happy place,' Corey said. 'All the blokes who've been here for any time seem so… well. But there's something wrong here, Doctor. Something terrible.'

One of the three dry soldiers offered his hand to the drenched one, but instead of allowing himself to be tugged out, the man pulled in the other and they both thrashed about sending great waves splashing. One of the nurses got a bit close and the two in the drink hurled water at her in unison. She caught the full blast of it and screeched again.

'What do you mean, "something terrible"?'

The two men left on the grass wiped tears from their cheeks and struggled to sit up. They grasped each other for support and fell back with a thud.

Corey shook his head restlessly. 'I'm not sure,' he admitted. 'I just know something terrible is happening here.'

Ignoring the festivities on the riverbank, the Doctor sat on the wall of the bridge with his back to them. He crossed his arms and observed Corey closely.

'How do you know, exactly?'

In for a penny, Corey thought. 'I *sense* things. My mum's got the gift, you see. She's a medium. She says some of it rubbed off on me.'

'And you believe that you can sense... what?'

'Evil!'

'Evil?'

Corey nodded. 'I thought I was getting better,' he said. 'The bad dreams were clearing up. I was starting to get a full night's sleep without waking up screaming. Then I started dreaming again. But not about the war. About something else.'

'What?'

'It was horrible. This thing. Eight feet tall. It had loads o' faces.'

'Faces?'

'Yeh. One face, then another, like it was hundreds of different men all at the same time. And they were all twisted and smashed. Covered in blood and gore. Bits hanging off them. One after another. Merging and changing. And it came for me. Bloody well *screaming* at me. I was *trapped*. Couldn't get *out* –'

He found the Doctor grasping his arms and the rising panic subsided. Out of the corner of his eye, Corey noticed that the small group was looking, and even the two men in the water appeared suddenly morose.

The Doctor took him by the arm. He ushered him off the bridge and down the river in the opposite direction. The sun was high in the sky and a light cool breeze wafted Corey's hot sweaty face. As they strolled, the Doctor spoke soothingly.

'Do you believe you have the gift?' he asked.

Corey nodded instantly. 'I knew when my gran died,' he informed the Doctor. 'I was only five and before Granddad came rattling at the door I *knew*. I didn't say anything, but I knew he was coming and I knew why. Don't ask me how. I just *knew*.'

'And you've sensed things since then?'

Corey found a pair of nearby ducks suddenly fascinating. He watched them floating on the mirror-still water, watching him back out of their little black beads-for-eyes. The Doctor shared his curiosity, and they regarded the ducks in a four-way shared silence.

'It scares me,' Corey admitted, but he still couldn't look the Doctor in the eye. 'I don't *want* it. I don't want anything to do with it.'

'Maybe there are things in the psyche we simply don't understand,' the Doctor conjectured. 'Things the human race forgot about but which lay dormant in the subconscious.' The ducks made a low kind of garbled honking sound and drifted nervously off in the opposite direction, obviously unsettled by the Doctor's words. 'But they're nothing to be afraid of. They're just part of being human. Everybody probably has the same capacity, only some people are more sensitive to it. I wouldn't let it scare you.'

'*You* wouldn't like it.'

'Possibly not.'

'Certainly not. It scares the hell outta me…'

As the ducks receded into the distance with hardly a ripple in their wake, the Doctor found Corey smack bang in front of him. The uncertainty in his face was usurped by a new determination and he began to babble again.

'There's evil here, Doctor. And it's growing. Every day it gets stronger. Some of it's already escaped, by the sound of what you said to Dr Banham. But there's a whole lot more at the house. Soon it's going to get out, and woe betide us when it does.'

'These dreams may be a resurgence of your nightmares from the war,' the Doctor reminded him.

The hesitancy now had completely vanished from Corey. He was entirely convinced of what he was about to tell the Doctor, and that conviction came across loud and clear in his firm and level voice.

'I felt *evil. Here.* It's *gathering.*'

In order to admit more light into his dingy kitchen, Albert Briggs had left the door wide open. While he sat at his table with yet another pot of tea and a sandwich, Albert watched the nothingness happening in the street outside.

Hawkswick was a tiny place. A simple community of farm labourers' cottages huddled around a small church and an even smaller inn, mostly built of local stone. The station house itself was the old charge hand's cottage, and had been annexed with its lifelong-redundant brick lock-up when Briggs himself was a lad. He could remember playing on the great stack of bricks that had been brought in to build it, and getting a right old telling off from his dad for trying to throw a good few of the bricks at Nanny Coggings's dog. Luckily for the dog, the bricks were so heavy he could manage to chuck them only about halfway to the yapping little gargoyle.

Briggs poured a fresh cup of rich red tea and sipped with reflective satisfaction. In this long slow dusk since Effie died, his tea had become a real comfort to him. The ritual of preparing the pot, heating it first with boiled water, heaping in exactly the right amount of fresh leaves, splashing in the boiling water to release that first explosion of exotic aroma. All their married life Briggs had made the tea. He fancied himself expert in the field of tea making. And now the habit brought back Effie. Every time he made a cup of tea, he might be making it for both of them. But of course, when he carried the teapot to the table, Effie was no longer there.

The little kitchen these days was beginning to look shabby, he knew. He felt sure that people in the village talked about his lack of cleanliness. Mary Minett had badgered him steadfastly to let her come in and clean for him. But right to the end, Effie had been a habitually tidy and fastidiously clean woman. She had a day of the week for every task. Monday washing, Tuesday drying and ironing, Wednesday floors, and so the week went, every day finding Effie busy from dawn to dusk, rain or shine, scrubbing and swilling and mopping and brushing and scouring and cooking. In these actions passed her life. And now Briggs couldn't bear the idea of having another woman in the house doing Effie's work. And neither could he bear to break the habit of their lifetime and take over her chores for himself. There had been unspoken rules between them. He made the tea.

At the far end of the village, Briggs saw Mary Minett approaching on foot with her bicycle, the oversized basket attached to the front stuffed full of something covered with a crisp white tablecloth. He watched her straw-coloured hair blowing in the breeze, and suddenly remembered how very lovely she was. About thirty years old now, Mary still looked like a mere slip of a girl. Her skin retained its youthful complexion, her eyes their girlish sparkle, her disposition its childlike optimism and curiosity. It amazed Briggs that nobody had managed to snatch her up before now. Not that she had been short of offers. She had been pursued at some time or other by every eligible young man in the village, and probably half the eligible male population from outside of it in the last ten years or so. She had rebuffed them all to remain a determined but not in the slightest embittered spinster. If Briggs had been thirty years younger, he might have found that enigma enticing himself. But these days his interest in mysteries, as well as women, was rather dulled. There was no way he could cope with both rolled up in one.

As he observed her advance on the station house, leaning into the bicycle to counteract the weight of whatever she had in the basket, he saw her stop suddenly with a huge smile springing into her face. Then he saw the Doctor come into view and the two of them stood talking. The Doctor waved his arms about, indicating back the way he had come, and then pointed busily at various parts of the village. He seemed eager to get on, but Mary pointed out the basket and thumbed back the way she had come. The Doctor shook his head, his demeanour indicating that he was in a hurry. Mary chided him with a furrowed brow. Eventually, the Doctor, like most men Briggs had seen under her charming offensive, surrendered gracefully.

Mary pointed briefly to the station house, and they continued on their way together towards Briggs as he sat in the dark sipping his tea.

'Constable Briggs,' Mary greeted him brightly.'I believe you have a spare bicycle at your disposal.'

Briggs clambered out of his chair.

'That's right,' he confirmed.

'I wondered if we might impose upon you to borrow one for an hour or so this afternoon. I'm sure your old one will be eminently adequate for our needs.'

Briggs regarded the Doctor, who regarded him back with a look of silent resignation. The old bicycle was battered and rusty. The front wheel had a mind of its own. And years of Briggs's eminently adequate posterior had left the seat a bit on the vicious side.

'You better take this one.' Briggs offered the cycle propped up against the station door.

The Doctor did so thankfully.

'We're going to take a picnic lunch,' Mary said.'It is such a fine afternoon that I felt the Doctor might benefit from it, having not taken breakfast or lunch today.'

'Sounds like a nice idea,' Briggs agreed, shielding his eyes from the sun.

'Yes,' agreed the Doctor.'It does. Doesn't it?' He flashed Briggs a smile that may or may not have been laden with irony.

'Come on, then,' Mary ordered.'And thank you, Constable, for the loan of your bicycle.'

'You're very welcome,' Briggs told her.

The two of them headed up the road together, Mary talking incessantly, telling the Doctor that the church was to celebrate its fifth centenary this coming year, and it was such a pity – wasn't it? – that they would celebrate it in war…

With a shrug and a sigh, Briggs returned to his tea and his memories.

They stopped their bikes on top of a small hill, which afforded magnificent views of a gently sloping valley. The air was warm, alive with birdsong. A gentle breeze played catch-me-if-you-can with Mary's tablecloth as she struggled to set it down flat, and the Doctor simply stood and laughed at her.

'You might help,' she said curtly.

But the Doctor shook his head. 'This is much more fun,' he told her, leaning back on his saddle and using his bike as a prop. He folded his arms and gave her a genial smile.

'You're going to stand there and let me do all the work?' she demanded, mock-outraged.

'I never implied that I was a gentleman,' he defended.

'Indeed you did not,' Mary agreed, popping the heavy basket on one corner and tugging the cloth as square as she could manage on the uneven, tufty ground. She laid out a blanket and arranged herself beside the basket before opening it and peering inside like a child with the biscuit tin.

'I don't suppose you're going to be such a cad as to stand there and watch me make an absolute pig of myself alone?'

Laying down his bike next to Mary's, the Doctor wandered over and knelt opposite in the grass.

'Wouldn't dream of it,' he said.

She placed a large plate of buttered bread in the centre of the cloth, and this she surrounded with smaller dishes of other foods while the Doctor watched them being uncovered one at a time.

Mary waved her hands over the spread, like a chef presenting her finest speciality.

'Let the festivities commence,' she announced, and grabbed a chunk of bread.

The Doctor joined her, chewing thoughtfully as he gazed out across the valley, watching the small white dots which were far-distant sheep.

'This is a beautiful place,' he announced, the breeze ruffling his curled fringe and his eyes scrunched up from the sun.

'It's my favourite picnic spot,' she said. 'I've been coming here for years now. Never changes. This is a timeless place.'

'Yes,' the Doctor agreed, his voice as distant as the far-off sheep.

He seemed detached, she thought. Completely wrapped up in his own head. As if he were pretending to look out but actually looking in. In Cromby's field this morning, when he was investigating the demise of poor old Harold the Bloody Younger, she had witnessed an entirely different man: one whose razor-sharp eyes and piercing cleverness reminded her of her father in his hungry youth. And this morning, her very first contact with him, when he pressed himself inadvertently against her on Albert Briggs's doorstep, she had sensed at that moment an elusive *something* in him. Something of such vast complexity and clandestine subtleties that she could not begin to put the sensation into words.

From that moment, the Doctor was a deep fascination for her. He was a highly unusual man, she knew, and she was determined to resolve his mystery.

'I was intrigued by your arrival this morning,' she announced.

He gave her a playful look. 'Really?'

'Really. You arrived by train last night in Grimston. Yet you didn't stay there and you were here this morning at five o'clock in the field where Bill Cromby and Constable Briggs found their trench. Did you wander about up here all night?'

'I slept at the station.'

'Strange.' Mary chomped a chunk of bread. 'There's a perfectly comfortable hotel in Grimston.'

'I'm saving my money,' the Doctor told her earnestly.

'I was given to understand that one received expenses whilst on ministerial duties.'

'True. There was a perfectly adequate hotel. But I prefer a degree of solitude.'

'And you'll get it,' she told him flatly, 'sleeping in railway stations.' The Doctor simply smiled. 'I also happen to have a perfectly comfortable spare room,' she informed him.

'You do?'

'I do.' She balanced her bread carefully on the edge of the plate in the centre of the cloth and dabbed at her lips gently with a napkin. 'The Griffin, I believe, charges three shillings a night. I could put you up for three shillings a night less.'

'Well that'll certainly save my money.'

'So that's settled, then,' she said, picking up the bread again.

'People may gossip,' he suggested.

'People can gossip as much as they like. Now you're in Hawkswick it's either my spare room or, if you prefer, you can lodge with our most venerable Constable Briggs.'

'Given that choice,' the Doctor conceded, 'I accept your kind offer, Miss Minett.'

She smiled and raised a leg of fowl at him. 'Chicken?'

'Don't mind if I do.'

He took the chicken and nibbled at it as a fieldmouse might chip away at an ear of corn, savouring every morsel.

'Which Ministry, exactly, are you from?' Mary asked him bluntly. She had always found this frontal attack a good plan of action. Catch your enemy unawares with the big guns.

'I'm a special envoy,' the Doctor said. 'Your most venerable Constable Briggs submitted numerous reports, you know. Things of that nature, during war, get noticed.'

'Things of that nature, during war, are treated with the complete lack of regard they deserve. I know what went into Albert Briggs's reports. If I were the minister responsible for handling such matters, then I'd've filed them promptly in the circular basket-weave filing cabinet by the desk. Reports of phantoms, strange noises in the dark, Charlie Skaggs's rabbiting stock gone missing, most probably let out by Minnie Stock's two little tearaways... The only thing that Constable Briggs's reports didn't contain was Bob Marley's ghost.'

The Doctor aimed his drumstick at her pointedly. 'There's also the small matter of slaughtered livestock.'

Mary lifted her eyes in consternation. 'We're out in the sticks. There are big dogs. Your average head of department in the government of this green and pleasant land is not going to have his appetite whetted by dead cows. I would have guessed that his nearest thought might be the beef wellington he might be enjoying for his dinner tonight.'

'Well, my head of department was interested,' the Doctor asserted, a dribble of brown chicken skin dangling from the side of his mouth.

Mary's chunk of bread swam through the air in an elaborate arc. 'And he sent you on a ghost hunt.'

'He did.'

'And this is the sort of job you think is worthwhile in time of war?'

'I'm merely doing my duty.'

Mary pointed out the chicken skin as diplomatically as she possibly could. 'If you were asked to go and stick your head in a bucket of water, would you do it?'

'I have a very great respect for my King and country,' the Doctor announced with showmanship pride, removing the chicken skin and dabbing his chin with his napkin, raising his eyebrows in silent thanks. 'If they felt that my head in water, in their considered opinion, was necessary, of course I would.'

'You strike me as a man too strong of will to be sent off on wild-goose chases.'

'I'm quite partial to wild geese,' he said, tugging the last bit of chicken off the bone with his teeth.

'But the chicken is – *satisfactory*?' Mary checked politely.

'Satisfactory. Yes.'

He threw the bone into a bag which Mary had unfolded for leftovers. She unscrewed the top from a small bottle of ginger beer and handed it to him, then opened a second for herself. They both sipped contentedly in the sunlight, and Mary watched the Doctor's fringe waving in the breeze. He wore his hair uncommonly long. It marked him out from other men. She liked that. Quite a lot.

'My father works in the Department of Information,' she announced conversationally.

'He does?'

'Yes. You must be familiar with it.'

'Of course.'

'He works directly under the minister himself,' Mary told him.

'Really?'

'Really! Do you know him?'

She found the Doctor's eyes oozing amiable entertainment. 'The minister or your father?'

'Either.'

'I'm afraid I know neither,' he said. He appeared sorry for that.

'But you know the minister, surely?'

'Not personally.'

'Lord Cecil,' she urged. 'You must know *of* him, at least.'

'Of course I know *of* him,' the Doctor remembered abruptly, thumping his forehead with his clenched fist. 'Lord *Cecil*! Yes of course. I met him at one of the Department of Information's lunches. Lloyd George was there as well. *Lord Cecil*, of *course*. Charming man. I don't know him personally, but he *seemed* very nice.'

Opening a tin of small cakes, Mary offered them to the Doctor. He peered inside and plucked one out, removed the paper with exaggerated care, and munched experimentally.

'Hmm... Did you make these yourself?'

'With my own sweet hand.'

'Wonderful.'

'I'm not just a pretty face.'

'You're certainly not. With that I can agree irrefutably.'

She took a great bite out of one of the cakes, demolishing it almost in a single stroke. She chewed heartily before speaking again.

'I was curious about your box.'

The Doctor swept crumbs off his chest and regarded her meaningfully from under that beguiling dark fringe of his. 'You are very curious about many things, Miss Minett.'

'I'm very much afraid it's in my nature.'

'I'm very much afraid it is.' He took another cake.

'I've always been extremely forward.'

He sipped ginger beer. 'I can see that.'

'I'm my father's child.'

'That follows.'

'It has no doors.'

'What? Your father's child?'

'Your box.'

'Perhaps it has secret compartments,' he proposed.

'If it's supposed to keep things secret, your box is very large.'

'I have a lot of things.'

'And you take them everywhere with you?'

'Infinitely too valuable to leave behind,' he assured her.

'Most travelling men I know take a valise.'

'Perhaps I travel further than they do,' he ventured to suggest.

'*Do* you travel much?'

'I have travelled very far, yes.'

'Where?'

'Here and there. I don't care to remember most of the places. Much of the world is very much like much of the rest of the world, in my personal experience.'

'Where's the most exotic place you've ever visited?'

The Doctor considered. 'Probably right here.'

'You cannot be entirely serious, Doctor.'

'Why not?' He looked quite hurt. 'This is a very beautiful country. Dazzling seasons: glorious summer, tempestuous autumn, grinding winter, the darling buds of May.' Mary watched enthralled as the Doctor's face became animate with a passionate enthusiasm, his eyes gazing into midair, where there was nothing at all to see except what he put there himself. 'A rich heritage that comes of the mixed culture of an island state. Great historical characters: Sir Walter Raleigh, Sir Francis Drake, Oliver Cromwell, the Duke of Wellington. *Monarchs*: King Alfred, Harold, John, the Tudors, Elizabeth, Victoria.' He ran on, refusing to stop even for breath. 'The world's greatest scientists: Sir Isaac Newton, Rutherford, Newcomen, Trevithic, Sturgeon, Faraday, André-Marie Ampère…'

Mary giggled despite herself. 'Ampère was *not* an Englishman.'

'On his mother's side, I believe. Chaucer, Coleridge, Tennyson, Keats, Byron, *Shakespeare*!'

He rose to his knees and his face fell dark and menacing, eyes wild. He grasped his chest with one hand and thrust the other out to one side in a vastly overacted theatrical gesture.

'Tomorrow,' he growled, deadpan, 'and tomorrow, and tomorrow… creeps in this petty pace from day to day… to the last syllable of recorded time!'

Mary clapped. 'You like Shakespeare?'

'I loved the man.'

'Sorry?'

'Adore him. Marvellous.'

Suddenly the Doctor was on his feet, dark eyes seething.

'I have of late - but wherefore I know not - lost all my mirth.'
He began to stomp about in the grass, then was back, hair flying
with the energetic posturing of his head. 'Forgone all custom of
exercise; and indeed, it goes so heavily with my disposition that
this goodly frame -' he indicated the ground at his feet with
dramatic emphasis - 'the earth, seems to me a *sterile*
promontory.'

Mary found conviction in the words too compelling for
comfort. The Doctor seemed genuinely distressed, his face
growing red with agitation. But on he went, as if in the midst of a
serious altercation with her. He raised his arms.

'This most excellent canopy, the air -' he grasped her by the
arm, speaking fervently, the words tumbling out of him in an
avalanche - 'look you, this brave o'erhanging firmament, this
majestical roof fretted with golden fire -' he let go of her arm
roughly - 'why, it appeareth no other thing to me than a foul and
pestilent congregation of vapours!'

He stormed about on the little hill, tailcoat flying, the shaded
trees a fractured backdrop for his frightening impromptu
performance.

'What a piece of work is man!' he announced, suddenly
challenging. 'How noble in reason! How infinite in faculties!' He
smacked his head with some force. 'In form and moving how
express and admirable!' He stuck out his chest. 'In action how like
an angel! In apprehension how like a *god*!' His fist jabbed the air.
'The beauty of the world, the paragon of animals! And yet to me
what is this quintessence of dust?'

He knelt at her side by the basket, taking her hand in his. Finally
she was quite relieved to find the humour back in his eyes. He
was playing games with her, seeing how far he could push her,
and she had almost failed his silly little test.

'Man delights not me –' He grinned, and she allowed the tension to explode out of her own broad smile.

The Doctor let go of her hand abruptly and stood and marched away, telling her as he went, 'No, nor woman neither, though by your smiling you seem to say so.'

He plonked himself down on the other side of the cloth and snatched another cake. Mary gave him a hearty applause and he bowed graciously.

'My Lord Hamlet,' she laughed, 'methinks thou art truly mad.'

The Doctor's face was suddenly thunder.

'My dear Ophelia,' he said in a voice as distant as the stars themselves, 'sometimes I fear that I am.'

Bill Cromby followed Laura Rawkins up to Skews Bank Field, where she had been horse-hoeing turnips with Maggie Fowler. She had babbled on about finding bones in the field. Cromby had got little sense out of her other than to describe an awful stench, and bits of rotting meat sticking out of the ground. When they arrived, Cromby saw for himself what all the fuss was about.

'There, you see.' Laura showed him.

Maggie Fowler stood watching them from the opposite end of the turnip-strewn field, refusing to come anywhere near. Cromby didn't blame her.

He was looking at a few square yards of churned ground where he could see red meat glistening in the rich, dark soil. Lumps of flesh were exposed to the sun, some of them crawling with maggots. The air was thick with the stink of the abattoir.

Then he saw something else and picked his way through the area to get a closer look. It was in the middle of the site, and as he stepped through he disturbed a ground-cover cloud of flies. They buzzed angrily about his ankles but he ignored them.

Finally Cromby reached what had grabbed his attention and bent to inspect it closer. He had noticed it glinting, and now he recognised what it was. The khaki fabric merged, camouflaged, with the soil, but the brass button attached to it reflected the sun like a shining beacon.

Chapter Four

'So you've met the esteemed Dr Charles Banham,' Mary said as she shuffled about, trying to make herself more snug on the blanket. The sun now was beginning to descend, and she found herself wincing slightly at the Doctor, fearing that he might mistakenly believe that she was in some discomfort.

'I have indeed,' the Doctor said.

He hunched in the grass opposite. He was gazing off into the distance, his attention caught by two approaching figures whom Mary had noticed as well. They were far off. Indistinct black blobs, gaining on Mary and the Doctor from the direction of the village. One blob was substantially larger than the other, and had to keep stopping and waiting for the second to catch up. Mary knew their identities, even from here.

'And what did you make of him and his hospital?'

A nebulous look occupied the Doctor's face. The idea crossed Mary's mind that the Doctor may well have been uneasy about visiting Hawkswick Hall. She wondered if he might have been forced out of combat by psychological problems. He certainly seemed a man of mixed signals, sometimes shooting off along unexpected or uncharted paths. She knew that some of Dr Banham's patients were humiliated by what they perceived as their deficiency, and perhaps that was why the Doctor was so very cagey in his replies. Perhaps he, like the men at the Hall, had endured horrors far too abundant for his mind to remain intact.

'Dr Banham is a very remarkable man,' he said at last. 'I'm sure you'll agree.'

'Oh, wholeheartedly. From what I've seen of his work there, it's very impressive indeed. The men under his care seem to recover remarkably well. I've visited other hospitals of its kind where the atmosphere is oppressive. Shell-shocked soldiers often find it impossible to allay the ghosts of the trenches. Hawkswick Hall is marked by a certain… sense of relief, don't you think?'

'Yes.'

'Charles Banham is such a charismatic, enchanting man, I've found.'

'Yes.' A mischievous glint entered the Doctor's eyes. 'A magnetic, rather darkly attractive man, I thought.'

'I can't say that I noticed,' she told him, equally playfully.

'And yes, I think he does his patients the world of good. A real tonic, this therapy of his, it seems.'

'So you don't believe that they could be responsible for blowing up poor old Harold the Younger and his chums?'

'I hadn't formulated any theory on that,' he said. 'Dr Banham informs me there is a large munitions factory in Grimston.'

'That's right,' she confirmed. 'A disused mill. The owners went bankrupt and the Government installed their own machines. I know the building – it's very substantial – although I haven't visited it since it used to be a mill. If you're thinking of making a visit there, I could take you if you like.'

'That might be a very useful offer. Thank you.'

'You're very welcome. I'm always pleased to assist representatives of His Majesty's Government.'

'How very patriotic.'

'We all have a duty to do our bit in war.'

'Our two friends seem to be somewhat distraught,' he said.

Mary found Cromby and Briggs shambling down the narrow lane towards them, an oddly matched couple if ever she saw one. Two old men: one giant, the other short and a touch on the lean side. Cromby advanced like a gargantuan steam engine; his face was red but he seemed hardly out of breath. Briggs came up behind him at a half-run, his face also ruddy, but from exhaustion.

'Gentlemen,' the Doctor greeted, standing and sweeping the crumbs from his waistcoat. 'What a pleasant surprise.'

Briggs stood akimbo, face to the breeze, gasping for air.

Cromby scowled. 'Doctor,' he rumbled, 'we could do wi' you comin' down Skews Bank wi' us.'

'Oh,' the Doctor looked enthusiastic. 'What is it?'

Cromby turned to leave, and as he went he said over his shoulder, 'You can see that when we get there.'

The Doctor regarded Briggs for some clue, but the old constable simply shrugged breathlessly, before tramping off again at Cromby's heel.

The Doctor wished to work alone, and that was quite acceptable to all concerned. Before he went trudging off into the field, he instructed that Cromby bring up two carts, along with as many shovels and forks as he could lay his hands on, and that Briggs return to the village and make certain preparations in the village hall.

Mary waited with the bicycles near the gate, and, in the company of Laura Rawkins and Maggie Fowler, she watched the Doctor picking his way through the churned carnage. Skews Bank was a west-facing, slightly inclined field. This put the Doctor between them and the falling sun. He looked an ominous shape, like some grim reaper come to claim his spoils. The dark-green coat appeared almost black, his long hair a mane. He cut a fearful figure.

A field of flies rose around him and Mary was reminded of a reference she had come across in one of her father's mammoth dictionaries. It was a great tome which smelled of dust when she opened it as a little girl, when she used to read her father's reference books voraciously, trying to expand her vocabulary beyond his, and very often catching herself out with entirely misplaced words. Some of them had made their way into fondly quoted family lore, and her father, perfectly delighted to be entertained by her blunders, positively encouraged her. As the

Doctor rummaged through the human detritus at his feet, she remembered for the first time in her life coming across the word *Beelzebub*. To her young mind, it was a beautiful word. And now, suddenly, she remembered its etymology. *Hebrew: bá'al zebûb, literally: lord of the flies.*

Mary shivered at the thought.

'Turnin' cold, ain't it? ' Maggie commented.

'Might be a storm comin',' Laura suggested.

'I think you're probably right,' Mary agreed.

She watched the Doctor huddle to examine something in the field, and wondered what the lump of dark matter was. She remembered his complete nonchalance this morning when handling the ragged scraps of poor old Harold the Younger, but couldn't believe that he might bring himself to regard human remains with the same casual indifference. What kind of man could walk a field of the dead with such a complete vacuum of emotion?

'Who is 'e, anyway?' Laura asked.

'He's a man from the Ministry,' Mary told them. It was the most convenient lie. Elegantly simple and fitting. The mantle had been thrown around him by Bill Cromby this morning, and had been enthusiastically accepted by the careworn Constable Briggs. The Doctor had embraced it without qualms, since it seemed to suit his purposes extremely well, whatever those purposes were. The Doctor didn't know yet that she knew it to be false.

'Well I 'ope 'e's brought 'is gas mask,' Maggie said.

'Bit of a mess, ain't it?' Laura concurred.

'I think 'e's done,' Maggie said.

Mary found the Doctor marching down the field through the scattered turnips towards them. His face was a shadowy mask, impossible to read, even as he grew closer. As he approached, Mary heard the creak and clatter of Cromby and his carts as they came down the lane.

The Doctor opened the gate to let Cromby in, and immediately began to pass out shovels to everyone, including Mary. Mary was not unused to handling such implements – she had her own market garden like most people in the village – but she was a little perturbed that the Doctor would regard her so perfunctorily as simply another labourer.

'Could you bring the carts down the field, please?' the Doctor asked Cromby and the new girl he had brought along to tow the second cart. 'We've got a lot to do before it gets dark.'

The village hall was a spacious building. The windows were uncommonly high, as were the vast rafters, and now the room looked to the Reverend Clarence Forster even bigger than ever before. All the folding tables and chairs had been removed. The boxes that constituted the stage at one end had been stacked together in front of the entrance, making it impossible to see in from the door. This opened up the entire floor space and this in turn served to lend more impact to the sight when you did enter.

When Forster had opened the door, the stench had hit him instantly. The place reeked like a butcher's chopping room. Although the air was unnaturally still and cold, perhaps *supernaturally* so, it struck Forster, this did nothing to diminish the almost tangible stink of damp earth mingled with putrefied flesh.

As he stepped inside, he was dismayed to see what the Doctor had organised during his visit this afternoon. The entire floor was littered with the remains that had been excavated from Cromby's field. They were laid out in regimented rows, allowing just room for a person to walk between them to inspect the horrific piles of human fragments. They had been arranged like one might see fossilised specimens uncovered at a dig, as if the Doctor were hoping to piece together some prehistoric monster unearthed after millions of years in the ground.

With grim determination, the priest embarked on the long haul down the central aisle. As he went, he tried to avoid discerning the detail of what he was walking through, but it was difficult to ignore. There were clods of earth that didn't even appear at first glance to have any tissue embedded in them, but Forster did not wish to pry as to why the Doctor had brought them.

Forster was struck suddenly by the words from Psalm 23. He spoke them as he walked, his voice echoing.

'Yea, though I walk through the valley of the shadow of death, I will fear no evil: for thou art with me; thy rod and thy staff they comfort me.'

But as he reached the end and turned to face the carnage, his thoughts faltered. It was at such points in one's life that one's faith might be challenged.

Steeling himself, the Reverend Forster raised the large wooden crucifix which he had brought for this task, and proceeded to bless the remains in the hall.

Mary arrived with the Doctor at the village hall as the sun was descending behind the church. She paused to watch the raging sky, and found the Doctor sharing her wonder. His face had taken on a ruddy hue, and his eyes reflected the intense redness of the setting sun. He suddenly appeared to Mary to look like some theatrical representation of the Devil himself. All he needed was a fiery staff. Except that he didn't look as sham and comical as the Devils she had encountered on stage.

Even as they approached from the opposite end of the village, she had become aware of the smell. At the door to the hall, the stench was unbearable and she feared she might not be able to go ahead with this task after all.

The Doctor read her mind. 'You don't have to do this, you know.'

His voice was mild, caring, and her Devil image evaporated into the dusk.

'I want to help,' she said firmly.

'This will not be easy,' he told her.

'If *you* can do it, then so can I.'

'Very well.'

They were about to enter when the Reverend Forster emerged. He was ashen, quite obviously shaken. At first he was lost for words, but when he found his voice he directed his consternation at the Doctor.

'Ah,' he said, removing his little horn-rimmed glasses and stuffing them into his pocket. Mary knew he wore them for close work, and had therefore worn them to obscure rather than clarify the contents of the hall. 'You must be the redoubtable Doctor.'

The Doctor offered his hand amiably, but Forster only shook it with some considerable effort.

'The Reverend Forster,' the Doctor greeted him warmly.

Quite clearly perturbed, the priest indicated the hall behind him. 'Might I ask, sir, what it is you are hoping to achieve by this?'

Levelly, the Doctor replied, 'I hope to solve a most malicious and heinous crime.'

'I fail to see how this… this *method* might do that,' Forster said.

'By reconstructing the dead, I hope to get them to tell me who did it,' the Doctor informed him in all seriousness.

Forster simply glared at him dumbfounded, as indeed did Mary herself. At last the priest's voice spluttered into action.

'Tell me, Doctor, have you come across a book, by the young lady Mary Shelley, called *Frankenstein*, *or*, *the Modern Prometheus*?'

The Doctor grinned and nodded like a small boy. 'Mary Shelley. Of course. A marvellous book.'

'Then you are aware of the Christian message it contains.'

The Doctor's childish enthusiasm did not abate at this subtle chastisement. 'I am,' he said, taking the man by the arm and leading him gently into the street. 'I'm delighted to meet someone who enjoys the Gothic romances.' He completely ignored the priest's shocked gawp. 'Tell me, have you come across the newer works of a writer called Mr H.G. Wells?'

'I'm afraid I can't say that I have,' Forster said, disengaging his arm from the Doctor's grasp.

'I recently read a fantastical story entitled *The Time Machine*. I would highly recommend it to one who seeks original and stimulating reading matter. I found the concept quite enthralling. Mr Wells has written much of interest, and possesses a most passionate concern for Man and Society. You really must read him.'

Forster looked at the man as if he were quite mad, before assuring him, 'I will be certain to look out for his work, thank you, Doctor.'

And with that he turned on his heel and headed for the black, imposing outline of the church.

The Doctor returned to take Mary's arm, and the childishness was gone.

'Are you certain you're ready for this?' he asked.

She removed his hand from her arm, and instead took his arm in hers. With a deep breath of the foul air, she guided the Doctor into the hall. She was, however, unprepared for the impact the scene was to have on her. After a stunned silence, she found the Doctor holding her hand, having removed her own vicelike grip on his arm. His eyes were full of concern and kindness.

'I can manage on my own,' he said.

She shook her head.

'Very well,' he announced, removing his jacket and placing it on a hook by the door.

He began to stroll purposefully down the hall, bending occasionally to inspect a heap of dark matter, and as he went he rolled up his sleeves for business. Mary watched him go, slowly removing her coat to join him. She saw him hunch down low, picking with long exploratory fingers at a large chunk of earth which contained a substantial bone. He dropped the bone suddenly and gazed about the room.

'I asked Briggs to procure some medical supplies from Hawkswick Hall for me,' the Doctor told her.

She gazed about and found a small pile of folded white material at the bottom of the hall near where the stage was supposed to be.

'There,' she said, pointing, and the Doctor went to unfurl the material.

Inside, he discovered a number of surgical instruments and half a dozen pairs of rubber gloves. He wiped his soiled fingers briefly on the white cloth, and pushed his hands into a pair of the gloves, offering a second pair to Mary. Then he grasped a scalpel from the surgeon's roll and returned to the large bone he had found.

Mary knelt by him as he began to work, chipping away the soil to reveal a deteriorated limb below. There were maggots crawling in it and as the soil fell away the stink intensified.

'Probably been in the ground about six months, I would guess,' the Doctor mumbled, more to himself than to her, she thought. 'Although I'm no expert, of course.'

As he removed more soil and maggots to reveal more of the decomposed flesh, Mary could not force herself to keep looking. She allowed her eyes to wander across the room, and found herself staring fixedly at a scrap of khaki studded with two or three scuffed brass buttons. There were two dull white stripes visible in the dirt, but Mary was no longer able to focus on them. She fought to stop the tears, but it was simply no good. With a quick apology to the Doctor, she dashed for the door and left him to his work.

At midnight, the Reverend Forster was in the habit of visiting the church to check all was well. It was a personal, solitary sojourn which had formed a custom over the years. He was now positively unable to sleep without this small nightly pilgrimage.

As he entered he found the church in silence, and a peculiar kind of darkness flushed with stained-glass moonlight. At first the church felt empty, and this was how he was accustomed to finding it at midnight. But as he made his way down the aisle, he was surprised to see a solitary figure on the front pew.

The woman regarded him with haunted eyes, the moonlight making her face half pale moonglow, and half gloomy shadow. It appeared to Forster that she possessed no mouth, only eyes that stared out of the darkness at him pleadingly.

Overcoming his initial surprise, Forster approached with his usual air of tranquil assurance. He spoke in barely more than a whisper.

'I do not often find parishioners attending at this hour,' he confessed.

'I do not often feel the need for such close communion with God at this hour,' Mary replied. 'I'm sorry if I startled you, Vicar.'

He shook his head. 'No. Please. This is a most pleasant surprise, I assure you.'

He knelt briefly at the altar and crossed himself, before returning to sit beside Mary. They shared many minutes in silence before he spoke again.

'Have you been here very long?' he asked.

'All evening.'

'I thought you were helping your friend the Doctor.'

'My friend the Doctor is quite capable of doing his job without my presence.'

'I'm afraid I was quite appalled to see what he had done to the village hall,' Forster confided. 'I must admit I fail to understand what he could possibly achieve by all of this.'

'The Doctor is a man of unusual methods,' Mary told him, 'but I feel that his heart is in the right place.'

'The ends will justify the means...'

'We are in the midst of strange times, Vicar,' Mary reminded him, 'both on a global and a rather more insular scale. Perhaps these circumstances demand strange techniques to resolve them.'

'I do not wish to cast aspersions upon the activities of a government official, but I find it very difficult to reconcile his procedures with any aims he might have.'

'That is partly why I am here tonight,' Mary admitted suddenly.

'I'm sorry?'

'The dead in the village hall includes the body of a soldier. When I saw it lying there, I was not able to continue to assist the Doctor with his investigations.'

Forster watched her compassionately out of his shadow.

She said nothing.

'God calls those who are ready to go,' he ventured.

'Does he?' she responded instantly. There was a hard edge to her voice which made Forster look up in surprise.

'I don't understand,' he said.

'I do not wish to cast aspersions upon the activities of one so mighty,' she told him with equanimity, 'but I find it very difficult to reconcile his procedures with any aims he might have.'

Forster gazed at her for a good few seconds in silence, before looking to the altar for inspiration. He found the cast figure of Christ looking down on him out of blank, staring eyes.

'It is not for us to understand his ways,' he said. 'But as Christians, what we must keep sight of is the fact of redemption. Christ died and was resurrected. You can be sure that God would not allow a good soul to die in vain. David is freed from all earthly pain now. He is released from this world to a far, far better one.'

'Amen,' Mary said, but the word was a hollow custom.

'Your brother died in the cause of a great Good.'

'God is British, is he? I take it he's not a Hun, then?'

'I can see why you are so full of resentment. It will take time for the wound to heal. But you will come to terms with his good work eventually.'

'The good Lord works in mysterious ways,' she said sarcastically.

'He does indeed,' Forster echoed. 'Indeed he does.'

'But you don't blame me for wondering, Clarence?'

He found her eyes glimmering wet in the dark and touched her hand lightly.

'Of course not. We all wonder sometimes. These are terrible, terrible days. But salvation will come, I'm sure.'

'I sometimes think he's not looking,' she confided. 'I think he's turned his back on us because he's busy with some other job on some other planet far off in this infinite universe. And then I think, sometimes, what if... what if he's not there at all?'

'Oh, he's there! He's listening and watching and he's very aware of all our suffering. And I'm sure he'll make his presence felt before this war is over.'

'I wish I could be so certain.'

Forster took her hand and led her to the altar. They knelt together, side by side, under the figure of Christ. Mary said a silent prayer to her uncertain God, and after a moment Forster began to speak, his voice now strident, filling the church to the rafters with his faith.

'Lift up your heads, O ye gates; and be ye lift up, ye everlasting doors; and the King of glory shall come in.'

Mary sensed movement behind her and glanced back to see the Doctor at the back of the church. He was lost in the shadow, standing there, hesitant. The moonlight entering through the stained-glass windows was imbued with curious qualities of light, and out of the corner of Mary's eye she saw the Doctor shrouded in this strange mist. Forster had not heard him enter, and continued to recite Psalm 24.

'Who is this King of glory? The Lord strong and mighty, the Lord mighty in battle.'

And the moonlight held them all in a still, cold grip.

* * *

Emma Braithwaite marched in silence down the vast first-floor corridor and stopped outside Private Corey's room. She put her ear to the door and listened. Nothing. She tapped lightly and tried the door, only to find it already partially open. She pushed her way quietly inside to find the room empty. The bed had not been slept in. She checked her watch. Twelve thirty. Corey wasn't one of those patients you would expect to be up and about at this hour, and she felt a rush of concern for him.

Closing the door lightly, she set off to search.

Corey stood at the window to the storage room and listened to the soft footsteps that he presumed belonged to Emma Braithwaite. They faded with distance and he resumed his silent, lonely vigil amid the gargantuan, angular shadows cast by the stowed furniture of the house. Outside, the silver moonlit trees swayed in the building winds. Portentous dark clouds gathered above, black against the navy sky, dim moonlight presenting their billowing boundaries.

Autumn was coming. And so was something else.

The world was a boiling cauldron as the Doctor walked Mary home. Seething clouds cut and released the moonlight, and the trees around the village swayed about them like strangely anchored wailing apparitions.

'Did your dead men talk?' Mary asked him as they went, raising her voice above the bedlam.

'It was an extremely useful exercise, yes,' the Doctor told her.

They huddled together, walking side by side, rubbing shoulders against the coming squall.

'And are you able to divulge what they told you? Or is that official government information?'

The Doctor tugged his jacket tight around his shoulders in a gesture that suggested to Mary more shutting *her* out than the storm. His face was screwed up against a wind that seemed to have suddenly sprouted invisible teeth.

'There were two men,' he announced. 'One was a corporal. The other I'm not sure about. There is still a good amount of material missing. Both heads, for example. I couldn't determine the actual cause of death from what we found, but what I *can* say is that they were torn apart in exactly the same way that Cromby's bull was torn apart.'

'You found no unequivocal identification, then?'

'Not as such, no,' the Doctor said as they reached Mary's house on the outskirts of the village. 'But our friend Constable Briggs called by. When I told him there were two bodies, he remembered that two men went missing from Hawkswick Hall last March. That fitted in with my rough estimation of how long the bodies had been in the soil. And he recalled that one of them was a corporal.'

'I remember that,' Mary said. 'They turned up again a day later, apparently, and were returned to the fighting.'

As she reached for the door, she found the Doctor regarding her with sceptical eyes.

'I don't think they turned up anywhere,' he told her, 'until today.'

Mary's was a large house, which immediately set it apart from the rest of the village. She bustled the Doctor into the drawing room and proceeded to attack the fire with a poker. The fire began to fight back and Mary smiled in satisfaction. The room was filled with ochre ghosts, and immediately felt much warmer than it actually was.

She discovered the Doctor engulfed in orange shadows that waxed and waned as the fire uncurled in the grate. Mary found herself drawn inexplicably close to him. He watched her curiously out of amber eyes, but for long moments they shared a silence disturbed only by the crackling of the coals.

'Do you feel a little better now?' he asked, his voice thick with concern.

Mary nodded.

'It was grossly inconsiderate of me to allow you to help me tonight,' he said. 'I'm sorry you were so upset. I really should have known better. I seem to have a talent for distressing people. It was unforgivable.'

'It's fine,' she said. 'I'm normally much more resilient.'

He shot her a whimsical look, then gazed into the fire lost in secret thought.

She shivered, and fleetingly expected him to put his arms around her.

'Cold?'

'Yes.'

'Would you like me to bring in more coal?'

'No.'

She gazed into his eyes again, remembering their first contact this morning on Briggs's step in the sunlight. She found the Doctor a powerfully attractive man. And she found herself wondering what he might think of her.

He rubbed his hands and gazed about the room.

'This is a lovely little place,' he told her.

'My grandfather built it in 1863. This was his summer retreat. My father was born here in this house. In my bedroom, as a matter of fact. Although, of course, it wasn't my bedroom then.'

'Of course.'

'It's a very special place to me. I spent most of my childhood in the city, but I gravitate back here. I have fond memories of playing in the surrounding countryside as a child.'

The mantelpiece contained a number of photographs and the Doctor peered into them while Mary gazed over his shoulder. One was a picture of her grandfather in sombre Victorian suit. Another a family shot which contained the entire Minett clan stretching back over four generations. It reminded Mary of those battalion photos so often published and bandied about these days. In pride of place in the centre was a sepia image of a young man. The Doctor picked up the photograph and inspected it closely.

'Boyfriend?'

She shook her head and removed the picture from him without taking her eyes from the man's. 'Brother,' she said, her voice a patchwork. She tried to pull herself together but found herself choking back tears. 'He was killed.'

'In the fighting?'

Single, painful nod. 'The Somme.'

He took the photograph and replaced it on the mantel.

'It must be difficult,' he said.

She nodded again, avoiding his eyes. She touched the end of her nose and sniffed.

'It is.'

'You were close.'

'Yes.'

'There's nothing I can say to heal the pain,' the Doctor told her simply.

She wanted so much for him to hold her. She expected a hug, at least. He was close enough and this was the most opportune moment she could possibly present to him. But the contact never came, and she was abruptly aware that he was distancing himself, moving over to the piano and allowing his fingers to brush the walnut lid. He picked up the sheet music and read it briefly without referring to the cover.

'Chopin,' he announced, checking the front to see if he was right. 'Do you play?'

'That was David's favourite piece.'

He replaced the music on the stand.

'I'm so very sorry for you.'

He was given a hard stare before she asked, 'Would you like some hot milk and honey?'

He beamed.

'There's a bathroom at the top of the stairs to your left,' she told him. 'You can freshen up there if you wish.'

The Doctor agreed that might be a good idea after his activities this afternoon.

'Let me take your jacket,' she offered. 'I'll hang it by the door.'

Slipping the jacket off, the Doctor headed for the door.

'The left…?' he checked.

'Top of the stairs,' she confirmed, and he vanished.

Mary listened to him ascending and heard the floorboards creaking in the bathroom before she slipped her fingers into the jacket pockets. The outer pockets were empty, but in the inside breast pocket she discovered a small wad of documents. She pulled them out and inspected them.

There were two sheets of folded paper, one a sheet of yellowing writing paper, which appeared ancient and worn around the edges, the other, a folded sheet of newsprint.

The newsprint was a cutting, which was headed:

THINGS GO BUMP IN THE NIGHT
IN YORKSHIRE VILLAGE

and Mary was not surprised to find a brief article about 'strange occurrences' in the 'remote, picturesque village of Hawkswick, north Yorkshire'. It was little more than a paragraph, but alluded to apparitions, and even explicitly described an eyewitness report of 'dead men walking in the night'.

Mary had frequently read such lurid, fantastical stories when her father brought cuttings to amuse her. Even during these sombre days of war, the gutter press still found profit in titillating and sensationalist hyperbole. Mary understood the compulsion for thrills in these austere times, but when such tommyrot was published at the expense of veracity, she failed to see the point. She was slightly surprised that this story had leaked out. The only place it could have come from was Constable Briggs's letters to the Ministry. And *that* she found even more disturbing than the distortions of the story. Something she found yet more surprising still was the fact that a man like the Doctor would read and believe this piffle.

She carefully refolded the cutting, slipped it back into the inside pocket and regarded the second piece of paper. It was softened with age and wear, the edges now almost worn through. With great care Mary opened it up to find a scruffily scribbled note inside. There were slices of it missing where the paper became gossamer-thin. She also noted that the message seemed to have been scribbled by means of some curious implement. There was nothing of the flow of the nib she saw in most written material. The words had been seemingly pressed into the paper under some great pressure, the ink a strange, synthetic consistency. The edges of the words failed to taper off with any kind of elaborate swirl, but came to an abrupt, deep stop. The thing that Mary found most curious of all, however, was the message itself. It said

Meet me in St Louis', February 8th 2001. Fitz.

She heard the Doctor stepping back across the bathroom upstairs and quickly folded the note and returned it to his pocket. She stepped silently into the hall and slipped the jacket on to the coat stand before rushing to the kitchen to put the milk on to boil.

In the bathroom the Doctor splashed his face with tepid water. He fumbled with the soap and rubbed his cheeks briskly before swilling and reaching for the towel. Once dry he hesitated in front of the mirror. If Mary could have observed him, she might have been very curious to witness him standing there for an impossibly long time simply gazing at his own features. In the silence of the house, he might have appeared to be entirely lost in thought, perhaps even mystified by the face he found before him.

He recovered himself only when he heard the sound of the piano from the drawing room downstairs.

Mary played the full piece, wholly consumed from the delicate opening, through the sweeping larghetto, to the sensitive conclusion, before she remembered that the Doctor was present at all. Then she sensed him behind her and turned to find him standing in the gloom by the still open door. He was swallowed up in shadow so she found it impossible to see his reaction, but he said softly, 'That was beautiful.'

'Thank you,' she said, closing the lid with consummate care.

'You wouldn't believe a man of twenty could contain such mature perfection,' he commented, coming in and taking a seat on the sofa.

'Sorry?'

'Chopin.'

Mary regarded him with sudden understanding.

'He was only twenty years old when he wrote that,' the Doctor explained. 'And the first piano concerto was actually the one he wrote second. He lost the orchestral notation for the first, so the second was published first, and so became the first.'

Mary by now was laughing at him. 'You amaze me with your familiarity with the obscure and minutiae. Where on Earth did you get all this knowledge from?'

Puzzled himself, the Doctor remarked, 'I suppose I must read a lot.'

'Music, Shakespeare, anatomy, criminal detection. That is indeed a wide scope of interest, Doctor.'

'It is indeed,' the Doctor agreed.

'It is quite unfortunate that your knowledge of the government department in which you purport to work is not so detailed and well informed,' she announced suddenly.

Silence stretched between them, but it was not a thing of malice. The Doctor regarded her with what she took to be a satisfied respect that she had found him out. She might even suspect that he was actually *pleased* that she had discovered his subterfuge.

'It isn't Lord Cecil, is it?' he said in a quietly cordial manner.

'Lord Beaverbrook.'

'Of course.'

'Lord Cecil is Minister of Blockade.'

'I think I *prefer* my intimate knowledge of Chopin,' the Doctor told her with muted amusement.

'I think so do I,' she concurred.

They said nothing for a moment, but floundered in still waters.

'Would you like your milk now?' she asked.

And in return, she secured a very contented nod.

Out of the black night, a rousing wind buffeted the large picture window until Charles Banham was forced to get out of his chair and attend to the noise. He grasped the curtains but, as he was about to close them, paused to watch the large buddleia shrubs outside his office swaying in the gale like shambling, drunken giants. The leaves gleamed dull silver in the dancing moonlight, lending the shrubs an ethereal quality, as if they were and weren't really there. Banham regarded them with detached fascination, before sweeping the curtains closed to shut out the image.

He slumped back in his chair and continued to listen to the storm brewing, before reaching into the pool of warm illumination from the electric lamp on the edge of his desk. Arranging two folders on his workspace, he opened the first to find a photograph of a young man badly scarred with facial lesions. He gazed into the picture lost in thought, then laid it carefully on one side before perusing the foolscap sheets which the folder contained. He found the form he was looking for and began to scan his own notes from six months ago.

Collins, Joseph Anthony, Lance Corporal.
13 March 1918.
I conducted an interview with Lance Corporal Collins today. He informs me that his nightmares have now stopped completely, and that he feels perfectly ready to return to action. Collins displayed agitation when I suggested that he remain at the hospital for another two weeks to ensure full recovery. He stated that he would be no more ready in two weeks' time than he was today. Nurse Gladys Wilson has eagerly endorsed this assessment, and I see no reason why I should not recommend to the Board that Lance Corporal Collins be given a clear bill of health and returned to active duty. This recommendation will be put to the Board in two weeks.

Below that entry, the sheet was blank. Banham slowly unscrewed the top from his pen while he organised his thoughts. He took himself back in time to the cold late winter, and began to write.

18 March 1918.
Lance Corporal Collins requested an informal interview with me this evening. I agreed to see him along with his colleague and friend, Corporal John Sykes. The meeting started amicably enough, with Corporal Sykes doing most of the talking. He told me that neither of them wished to remain here until next Monday when the next Board was scheduled. I told him that I could not bring the Board forward, and that his patience would be appreciated. It was less than a week away now. At this point Lance Corporal Collins became intensely agitated, informing me that he had close friends in the front line trenches. He did not wish to be incarcerated here. I told him he was not imprisoned, and that he was free to leave if he so wished. Both Corporal Sykes and Lance Corporal Collins were surprised at this. I told them that I had no powers to detain them, and

indeed no means of doing so. This initially seemed to take the wind out of their sails, but Collins again became irate, and eventually stormed out of my office. Sykes made apologies for both of them, but I received the clear impression that the subordinate officer had the upper hand in their relationship.

There were forms in the file that detailed his report to Constable Briggs in the village of the two men going missing the next day. Banham pulled a fresh form out of his drawer and headed this with Collins's name and rank.

20 March, 1918.
Lance Corporal Collins and Corporal Sykes arrived in my office at seven o'clock this morning, even before my staff was about. I was most surprised by this, but they explained that they had marched to Grimston, intending to board a train there and travel south. They had rather embarrassingly miscalculated the cost of such a journey, and had returned to request funds to make the trip. I informed them that I could not sanction such petty-cash withdrawals, and they should really await the Board, which was now only four days away. Both men offered such a compassionate, reasoned argument for their immediate return to the fighting that I offered to subsidise the trip to London myself. Once there, they would be able to rejoin their regiment and would be shipped out under army purse. This they accepted with much gratitude, and left again immediately.

Necessary arrangements were made to inform Hawkswick's constable to call off his search. The mystery was solved.

Banham blotted the sheet, as if this might seal the words with truth. Then he closed Collins's file and opened the folder for Corporal Sykes. He found the necessary forms and began the same task of falsification. As he wrote, the ink flowing with smooth fluidity through his lies, he realised suddenly that the form had become soiled with some inexplicable contamination. Checking the nib of his pen under the lamp, he found it perfectly clear. He brushed the dirt from the sheet, only to find more of it smeared right across the page. Irritated, Banham held the document under the lamp and peered at it closely. Then he caught his breath.

The mark was a pale-grey wash. The colour of clay. Turning his hands, he was dismayed to find them smeared with the dirt. Rubbing his hands together frantically, he was appalled to see the substance coming from nowhere until they were completely daubed. His eyes began to sting as if he had sand in them. He felt the stuff between his teeth. Tasted it in his mouth. Cold and gritty. Like clay or earth.

With a sudden startled gasp, Banham clutched his face.

Rubbing his eyes, he stumbled from his desk to the mirror in the corner. When he saw the thing gaping back from inside the mirror, a low groan emerged from him. He slumped forward, grasping the drinks cabinet under the mirror, almost collapsing as his knees gave way beneath him. Several bottles clattered to the floor and a decanter of brandy exploded into the carpet. Struggling to recover himself, Banham observed the horrific reflection, and it regarded him back with hysteria etched into its ancient lines. The face was that of a man long dead. A cadaver with sunken cheeks and shadowy pockmarks. But worst of all were the eyes. There was no colour at all, just a dull grey sheen that gazed blindly but seeing.

The colour of clay.

Daniel Corey came out of his reverie with a startled gasp when he heard the shattering glass. He listened intently to the sounds of muffled fury coming from Banham's office below. There was the distinct clatter of bottles toppling, then a groan of anguish. A guttural sound, like a growling dog. The bottles rattled again and Corey heard the door to Banham's office slam shut.

He marched from the room and gazed down into the hall below, keeping well back from the banister. He could see the administration area, but the hall was in darkness. The door to Banham's offices opened and a lumbering shape spilled out. Indistinct in the shadows, it stumbled across the hall and vanished into the corner, where Corey knew there was the door to the basement. The door slammed, and Corey heard the wooden stairs creaking under a substantial weight. Then silence.

Corey set off in pursuit, down the stairs and up to the basement door. He listened for signs of life on the other side, but there was nothing. Taking the handle with caution, he pulled open the door and plunged into the pitch black beyond.

For a second he didn't move a muscle. Simply listened to the howling wind outside. Then he was certain he heard another howling as well. A sound mingled with the weather, but distinct from it. A sound of equal squall, but a sound Corey could swear was made up of human cries.

He forced himself to move into the darkness, and the stairs groaned under his weight. He stopped. Listened. There were murmurs in the dark that he wasn't at all sure about. After an uncertain pause, he descended to tread warily down the corridor. He was able to make out only obscure shapes, shadows within shadows. The rest was an unfathomable blackness full of something he could almost sense, but not quite.

A *presence*.

He stopped again and listened for any hint of movement, but all he could hear was the distant wind. The basement smelled thick with damp. Corey could taste it in the back of his throat. It reminded him of Banham's therapy rooms, except it was so cold. Much colder than it had any right to be, even for a cellar.

Corey stepped towards the door to the yard at the far end of the corridor, but about halfway down he came to another door that caught his attention. It was closed. No different from the other doors in the dark. Except he could hear something inside. When he put his ear against the door, he could definitely hear the faint sound of somebody weeping. A man's shattered voice.

Corey tested the handle and found the door unlocked. He pushed at it silently, but stopped when he heard the click behind him.

He turned to see a dead man, gun raised. The man had a corpse for a body. Through the khaki uniform Corey could see gaping wounds seeping blood and gore. Shreds of fresh torn skin peeled from his face. One eye hung from its socket, lying on his cheek like a lump of sloppy jelly. The other eye burned with hatred, staring straight at Corey. The smashed teeth ground together, and for an instant Corey got the crystal-clear impression the man was in excruciating pain.

He sensed it for a split second.

And then the gun went off.

Chapter Five

There was a peculiar kind of cosiness to the house at night, Emma Braithwaite thought as she marched down the ground-level corridor that connected the rooms of the east wing. The jaded white paintwork reflected the low electric lighting with a warm glow that felt calming. The corridor served rooms to one side only, and so had views of the back of the house: the more functional gardens, the greenhouses and the old stable block. The windows in the corridor didn't have curtains, and it could look quite stark and clinical in the bright light of day. But at night the place changed completely, becoming much more subdued.

Examining the door to the dispensary, Emma was satisfied to find it secure. As she turned, she was shaken to see a dark-eyed woman gazing at her from outside the window. A haunted-looking woman in white. The woman looked drawn and pale, and was also *transparent*. For a good few seconds Emma stared back in startled amazement at the apparition, before realisation dawned that it was her own reflection. She gasped with relief and approached her other self, checking her appearance in the black night.

Her eyes were shadowy and she looked exhausted. She'd considered requesting a change back to day work, but she knew the hospital was desperate for night-time volunteers, and she felt she'd be letting them and the men down badly if she changed her mind now. At first she'd thought she'd get used to it, but the tiredness hadn't abated over the weeks.

Wouldn't be so bad if she wasn't so het up about Daniel Corey. She found increasingly lately that she couldn't get him off her mind. Worried about him constantly. She'd followed his progress with a singular interest since she first laid eyes on him. She'd observed his gradual recovery and then this recent sudden slide back into torment.

And she felt, oddly, as if she were joining him. By the look of her reflection in the window, she was well on her way.

Abruptly another body joined hers outside, commandeering her features with its own. In shock and confusion, she adjusted her focus to see a man in uniform glaring at her out of wide, wild eyes. Emma relaxed when she recognised the figure as Corporal Davies. He was pleading, pointing into the dark behind him. Emma touched her ears to let him know she couldn't hear a word he was saying, and headed for the door at the end of the corridor.

She opened the door to a chill, rising wind that had been a pleasant breeze when she started her shift. Davies scurried around the corner to meet her.

'It's walking,' he ranted, trying to grasp her sleeve and pull her outside.

Emma brushed him off.

'What's walking?' she demanded, half agitated and half concerned.

'The *Golem*,' he urged.

'Golem?'

'It's walking. I've seen it.'

Emma gazed at the seething dark and listened to the howling wind.

'It's getting very cold,' she told him, her voice as soothing as she could make it. 'Why don't you come in and let me get you a nice hot cup of tea?'

Staring wildly at the shrubs that waved in the wind, Davies shook his head.

'Gotta keep guard,' he raved. 'They'll take us in our sleep… Get us in our beds… Eyes peeled, soldier…'

'Well I'm afraid it's a bit cold for me to go gallivanting off,' Emma told him. 'You just keep an eye on them for us, would you? Report back when your watch is finished.'

For a moment she found his eyes imploring, then he came to a snap decision.

'I'll keep an eye on them,' he assured her.

He patted his hip, as if checking he had his pistol holstered there, which of course he didn't. Then he went stumbling and tripping into the night and Emma closed the door thankfully. She breathed a sigh of relief and turned back down the corridor, deciding that a cup of tea might not be such a bad idea after all.

Something rattled in the distance. Bill Cromby emerged from sleep and listened. It had been a long, strange day, and now he was shrouded in a drowsy fuzz that refused to clear. The rattle was a door, and it sounded to Cromby like the door to the stables. A growling wind prowled through the farmyard outside, slinking between the buildings, keeping low, not yet expanding to its full fervour.

Cromby's bones told him worse was to come. He'd sensed an approaching storm tonight, and it wasn't too distant now. But it certainly wasn't strong enough yet to blow open the stables door.

'What's up?' Iris Cromby's voice, syrupy with sleep, spilled into the dark.

'Nowt,' Cromby told her. 'You get back to sleep. Just a door blowin'.'

He pulled on his trousers and left Iris in the warm bed to trek downstairs and through the kitchen. There, he discovered his two sheepdogs crouched uneasily by the range. Kneeling to check on them, he found deeply troubled eyes, and was disconcerted to realise that the dogs were actually shivering with fear.

'Ey,' he soothed. 'What's up wi' you two, ey?'

Both dogs gazed at him nervously and he ruffled the long black and white hair under their muzzles.

Dragging himself reluctantly from them, Cromby hoisted the twelve-bore from its hooks above the range. He opened the sideboard drawer and felt inside for two shells, and these he slotted into the two breeches. The shotgun snapped shut with a satisfyingly grim sound. He shoved his feet into the vast boots by the door, and, not bothering to tie the laces, let himself out into the coming storm.

The stables door was a flimsy affair, designed that way for easy access in case of fire. It rattled in the wind as if trying to escape from its hinges. Cromby checked the sneck, and saw that it had been ripped open by some considerable force, the metal bent almost to a right angle. He gazed around the yard at the gathering wind and wondered if it could really do so much damage.

Crooking the twelve-bore under his arm, he stepped inside the stables and immediately sensed the tension in the air. The horses fidgeted in their bays, tugging their tethers and stamping uneasily. Cromby peered into the shadow and, finally satisfied that there was nobody about, he propped his gun in the corner and set about the task of calming the horses.

They were difficult to control tonight, as they had been last night and this morning. Like the dogs, they glared at him out of wide brown eyes full of fear. He stroked them and spoke with soothing tones, but all to little avail. In the background, the door continued to rattle and clatter. He decided the best thing he could do was to secure the door and come back early in the morning.

As he left the stables, though, he sensed a presence behind him. He was about to shut the door, but changed his mind at the last minute. Instead, he stepped back inside and proceeded deeper into the darkness with his gun at the ready. As he thought before, the stables were empty. Still not satisfied, however, Cromby approached the ladder in the far corner that led up to the hayloft. Jamming the gun into the crook of his arm, Cromby began to climb.

The loft was pitch black. As he lifted himself up, the dark was filled with the sounds of creaking boards. Cromby stopped. So did the sound. The loft ran the entire length of the stables, one big open space, and every inch was imbued with an oily blackness. The slate roof let in no light. The only source of illumination was the dull glow from the opening Cromby had just come through.

As he stepped into the dark, Cromby held his breath, and the loft was saturated with the echoing sounds of his own movement. He heard the horses below shuffling and stamping uneasily.

He stopped again, suddenly alert. The wind rattled some loose slates. His own heart thudded like a wild caged thing in his chest. Otherwise the stables were silent.

Cromby turned and made his way carefully back to the opening. With one last look, he lowered himself down to ground level. This time he secured the flapping door with a large stone and returned to the house, where he found the dogs still cowering in the corner. Removing his boots, Cromby considered the twelve-bore in his hands. Then he headed for bed and took it with him.

In the hayloft, the dark stirred. Hay rustled. Boards creaked. Things moved.

One at a time, shadowy figures clambered down the ladder to the stables below. The horses snorted hotly, but the figures ignored them and headed straight for the door. The first figure tried the handle, only to find the door jammed shut. There was a scraping of stone from outside and the door was released. Moonlight sliced the dark, and a skeletal form peered in to greet the others. The thing wore an army uniform, tattered and torn, smeared with mud and dried clay. Three stripes were visible on its shoulder, brown with stains of blood. It waved the others out into the oncoming storm, and they vanished into the dark behind the stables.

Constable Albert Briggs woke with a start. He reached out for

Effie, and found the bed empty. Momentarily confused, he sat up and tried to materialise himself in the cold reality of here and now. Time and space swirled around him, past and future and dreams all mingled together in a confusing maelstrom as furious as the storm outside.

Briggs sat in the dark, listening. There was the rustling of the trees, the splashing of rain against the window, the sound of the wind howling down through the valley, like an unearthly ululation.

He slapped back on to the bed and tried to close his eyes, to escape into the softness of his dreams, where Effie waited with open arms. But he couldn't rest. Couldn't even close his eyes. He was sure he'd heard something beyond the storm. Some movement outside. A gathering of footsteps around the station house.

His eyes were flashing beacons in the dark as he told himself not to be so stupid. To get back to sleep and stop acting like a big baby. But he couldn't shake the feeling. Somebody was there.

In the dark.

In the storm.

Out in the tempest, dark shapes moved.

They came through the village under cover of storm. Shadows shifting among the shifting shadows. Slipping unseen from place to place. Visible in the fractured moonlight only for fractured moments. Then gone. They waved to each other silently, their movements lost in the black. Steadily they progressed.

Gradually they closed in on the station house.

One of the shapes tried the door to the lock-up and found it secure. Dropping to its knees, it fumbled in its kit bag and pulled out a jemmy. There was a sharp crack carried on the wind and the shape sprang to its feet and listened. No response. It slid inside while another shape kept watch at the door, and more hunched low in the bushes nearby.

A dead hand reached out and touched the blue box. Ragged skin and bone feeling the texture. Empty sockets full of wonder and darkness.

The shape slipped back out into the night and led the others off. They found a secure base in a lilac hedge and began their preparations with military precision. The clink of steel. The small roar of leather straps being run through bones-for-hands. The assured clunk of a magazine being driven home. The hollow dropping of a mortar into its tube.

The armies of the night on manoeuvres.

The wind rattled the windows and now it sounded like it was raining as well. Mary Minett pulled the blanket around her head and tried to shut out the frightening clamour of the night. But her blanket was pathetic insulation against such a wild storm. She imagined the damage the wind was causing in her gardens, uprooting shrubs and tearing limbs from trees. Loose tiles on the roof battered against her sleep. She heard the empty water butt rolling down the path. It came to a hollow-crashing halt. She heard the high-pitched screech of the gale as it clawed its way around the house, trying to get in.

Then she heard the explosion.

Mary jumped up in bed, startled. Was she dreaming? Had she fallen back to sleep and only imagined she was still awake? Was it the water butt again?

But then she heard the second explosion, and as she thrust herself into her clothes, the third and fourth came blasting through the night. They sounded very close. Much too close for comfort. Mary dragged on an old jumper and dashed for the door.

Downstairs she heard the back door slam and peered through the front window to see the Doctor vanishing into the night. Struggling with her boots, Mary finally grabbed her coat and set off in pursuit.

* * *

To the sickening sound of crumbling rubble, Albert Briggs scrambled out of bed and threw himself into trousers and boots. Feeling decidedly wobbly, he rushed for the door and scrambled down the stairs. In the kitchen, he listened to the sounds of movement outside. It was coming from the lock-up end of the house. The sounds of somebody forcing their way through piles of shattered bricks following the explosions that had blasted Briggs out of his lovely warm bed.

Dragging his jacket around his shoulders, Briggs opened the door to the squall. The cold storm air whipped his jacket around his face and he heard fluttering papers in the kitchen. Briggs forced himself outside and slammed the door behind him.

As he rounded the side of the house, he found the lock-up in ruins. The Doctor's box shimmered an eerie pale blue in the restless moonlight. Clambering over the surrounding pile of bricks, all that remained of Briggs's demolished lock-up, were several dark shapes in ragged uniform.

They stopped their inspection of the Doctor's box when they sensed Briggs approach. In unison, they turned on him, watching him out of shattered shadows for features. Briggs took in the detail in a single, photographic instant. Four of them. Corpses all. British army uniforms – gleaming wet in the ruptured dark, blotched with uncertain stains that could have been blood or worse. Faces tattered – hanging skin, small sheets flapping from their jowls, leaving gaping holes where their cheeks should have been.

Then searing white light and Briggs was sucked into an all-consuming blackness –

Following the road to the village, Mary Minett felt the first spots of rain spattering her face in the cold wind. She tugged her coat tight around her shoulders, but she'd dressed in such a hurry that she'd left breaches in her clothing that allowed the weather in.

She felt beset by invisible demons trying to rip the clothes from her, freezing hands groping, nipping, clawing.

Ahead, she saw the dark shape of Doctor veer off into the shrubs that lined the road. What on Earth was he up to? Where was he going now? She followed into the thicket, fighting lacerating branches. The bushes were a bewildering domain, dense dark and pale light warring for dominance, their interminable battle tearing the world to shreds. She thought she saw the Doctor just ahead, but now she couldn't be sure of anything. Her senses were ambushed. Thick scent of earth. Howl and rustle of wind. The taste of rain on her lips. Thrashing fingers whipped her face, tearing at her eyes as the bushes surged and groaned around her. The storm threw up indistinct phantasms and they crowded in from all sides. She turned back for the road, and realised with a sudden stab of panic that she was completely disorientated.

Forcing on, she became certain that she could see the Doctor ahead. She yelled his name repeatedly, her voice mingling with the wailing wind. The movement stopped. She saw him waiting, and forced her way through to meet him in the maelstrom.

Shielding her eyes from the lashing undergrowth, she reached out and at last her hands touched the material of his coat. It was wet with rain and as Mary peered at him through her fingers, she gasped.

The dead man gazed back out of eyeless sockets. The exposed sinews where his lips should have been distended, and he gave her a death-mask grin. The roaring light splashed over his features with a fluidity that made him even more grotesque. She saw glistening strands of pus around the edges of the eye sockets, the pulped flesh that remained slopped over the bare bone of the thing's skull. She had no idea what expression it was trying to convey. All she knew was the terrifying hysteria that suddenly gripped her. She let out a scream and pulled away, not daring to turn her back on the thing. She felt the intransigent shape of a large shrub pressing against her, and the corpse advanced slowly.

Outstretched fingers of bone and gristle groped for her face, until suddenly the thing was gone under a squall of confusion. It was flung aside as the bushes crashed with new movement. A vacuum of darkness appeared, abruptly refilled with shimmering shrubs. There was a chaotic moment of rustling and commotion, and the shadows curled and diminished. Mary glared into the dark, and found the Doctor clambering to his feet in front of her.

His hair was plastered to his face with rain, strands of it sticking out wildly from his dive through the undergrowth. He stood grinning, face pale in the moonlight.

'You called?' he said.

Mary collapsed into his arms, doing all she could to stifle the urge to sob on his shoulder. She pulled herself together and detached herself from him, patting down her coat and arranging her dress ashamedly.

'Forgive me,' she said, avoiding his eyes. 'I had such a fright.'

'So I saw,' the Doctor agreed, taking her by the arm and guiding her quickly the way he had come.

Covering her face, she allowed him to lead her blind, until they emerged back on to the road and she felt relief gushing up inside her. Raising her face, she took a deep breath and allowed the rain to cool her burning cheeks. When she opened her eyes again, the Doctor was already some distance down the road, dashing for the village. She set off in pursuit, amazed at his seeming ability to detach himself from the strangeness of this night and deal so determinedly with one astonishing thing after another.

In the village, a nightgowned crowd had gathered around Briggs's station house. Most of the village was present, and Mary found Briggs prostrate on the ground amid them. Pushing her way through, she knelt by him and saw a dark smudge of blood spreading around the side of his face. He was entirely lifeless, white as a sheet.

'Move back,' Mary demanded. 'Let him breathe.'

As the crowd parted reluctantly, Mary felt for a carotid pulse. It was present, but weak.

'Get me blankets,' she shouted to no one in particular, as she began a careful examination of Briggs's scalp.

Someone knelt beside her, and she turned to find the Doctor gazing with concern at the constable.

'How is he?'

'He'll live,' she said. 'He's had a very nasty blow to the back of the ear. He's going to have an unpleasant headache for a day or two, but I'm sure he'll be all right.'

Briggs stirred, automatically reaching for his head. He groaned as he tried to get up.

'Steady on, Albert,' Mary soothed. From behind her someone lowered blankets, and she took them and folded one under Briggs's head. The other she used to cover him.

'What happened?' he asked, eyes unfocused.

'I was just going to ask you the same thing,' Mary confessed.

He tried again to sit up, but Mary pushed him back with gentle admonishment.

'Don't you dare try to move, Albert Briggs.'

The Doctor stood and gazed around at the nearby faces, all full of shock and wonder at the night's events.

'Did anyone see what happened here?' he asked.

The crowd could only mumble and look at one another. Then Charlie Skaggs, a pointy-faced man as skinny as his own whippets, separated himself from the onlookers. He took the Doctor to one side and spoke confidentially.

'Them dead soldiers,' he said.

'You saw them?' the Doctor asked.

'I *followed* 'em,' Skaggs announced. 'Down through the fields from Skews Bank. Went straight for the lock-up. Broke in. Then bloody well blew it up.'

Skaggs glanced at the devastated lock-up. It was now simply a heap of rubble around the base of the Doctor's box.

'I reckon they was after that,' Skaggs told him.

'I wonder why,' Mary said, appearing suddenly at Skaggs's shoulder. She was watching the Doctor pointedly.

'Perhaps they were attacking the station house,' the Doctor pondered. 'Making some sort of point about the law around here.'

'What you reckon they are, then?' Skaggs demanded bluntly.

'That's what I intend to find out,' the Doctor told him. 'Did you see how many there were, Mr...?'

'Charlie Skaggs, sir,' Skaggs admitted cagily. 'Six of 'em. Moved like the wind, they did. But they can't beat Charlie Skaggs.'

'And you say they came down from Skews Bank?'

'Aye.'

'Isn't that where we found the bodies today?' the Doctor asked Mary.

She nodded. The Doctor appeared thoughtful. Then he was moving back to Briggs, who was trying again to rise. The Doctor knelt and helped him sit up.

'Don't know what the bloody hell hit me,' he said.

The Doctor shook his head. 'Do you feel well enough to try to stand?'

'Yeh.'

Briggs struggled unsteadily to his feet, but rested heavily on the Doctor for support. Mary watched as the Doctor led the old man gently back towards the station house, then she turned to the crowd of hungry-looking onlookers.

'I think that's about it for tonight,' she told them. 'You must all be frozen. I suggest you get back to your beds and we can sort this mess out in the morning.'

With an unenthusiastic grumbling sound, the crowd began to

disperse. Finally, only Skaggs remained, gazing abstractedly at the Doctor's box. When he realised Mary was looking with him, he said, 'Not a mark on it. What yer make o' that then, eh, Miss Minett?'

'It's a mystery, Mr Skaggs,' she agreed. 'Like everything else around here of late.'

'Makes yer wonder what the government's developed in secret for this war effort, dun't it?'

Mary smiled. 'It does indeed, Mr Skaggs.'

Touching his cap with an uncomfortable look, Skaggs began to make his way into the night.

'Ah well,' he said, 'can't be standin' round 'ere yatterin' all night. Things to do. See yer later, Miss.'

'Goodnight, Mr Skaggs.'

She watched him go, then regarded the remains of the lock-up. The smashed bricks and mortar were piled high, ragged shapes jutting out of the dark. But amidst it all, the box stood unscathed. It glowed eerily in the waning moonlight: blue, solid, immaculate. Smug.

The questions tumbling over one another in her head, Mary turned and headed for the station house.

Head thumping fit to burst, Briggs allowed the Doctor to help him into the kitchen. He slumped at the table while the Doctor rinsed a cloth and returned to dab Briggs's wound with it.

'Looks worse than it is,' the Doctor told him, inspecting the lesion through Briggs's thin grey hair. 'Stopped bleeding already.' Briggs felt a slight pressure, and realised that the Doctor was checking inside his ears.

'Can't see any other damage,' he muttered in satisfaction. 'Any nausea?'

'Not bad, no.'

Briggs suddenly discovered the Doctor's hand in front of his face.

'How many fingers?'

'Three.'

'No fuzziness?'

'No more than usual.'

The Doctor grinned. 'I think Mary was right,' he said. 'You'll be right as rain once the headache's gone. Now! Tea?'

Briggs smiled and started to climb out of his chair.

'Oh no you don't,' Mary warned, as she entered. She put on the kettle before coming over and sitting opposite Briggs at the table, regarding him with a critical gaze.

'How do you feel?' she asked, her tone brisk.

Briggs shrugged it off. 'Fine.'

'Bit sore, eh?'

Briggs fingered the area around the back of his ear gingerly. 'You could say that.'

Mary's look softened. 'Can you remember anything?'

'I can remember feeling the explosions,' Briggs said. 'Thought the bedroom floor was going through. I came down and went outside to see what was going on, and that's the last thing I remember.'

'It's common in concussion,' the Doctor said as he poured boiling water into the teapot, 'for a loss of memory of events immediately preceding the injury.' He brought the teapot over and deposited it in the middle of the table.

Mary found him watching her. 'How do *you* feel now?' he asked.

'Oh, I'm fine,' she said dismissively. 'Just a bit of a shock, that's all, facing a thing like that. I thought the stories about dead men were hysteria. Never thought they might be true.'

The Doctor fished three cups out of the sink and proceeded to dry them with a scabby-looking tea towel. 'There are more things in heaven and earth, Horatio, than are dreamt of in your philosophy.' He placed the cups on the table and balanced the strainer on Mary's cup before pouring. 'Milk?'

'No, thank you.'

After pouring tea for himself and Briggs, the Doctor plunged into a seat and sighed heavily across the table at them.

'Well, now. This is very jolly, isn't it?'

The rain grew heavier as Charlie Skaggs made his way back to Skews Bank. The wind battered his face raw, and his clothes were so wet now that he was finding it hard work even walking. A constant stream of water poured from the rim of his cap, but he pressed on. He'd never been stopped by bad weather yet, and he wasn't about to let a bit of rain make him go hungry tomorrow.

Returning to his traps along Long Sceil, Skaggs discovered two rabbits in the snares he'd set the night before. Binding the legs with twine, he shouldered the two small carcasses and began to reset the snares before picking up his rifle and continuing on his way.

Before he'd finished he heard the movement. He stopped and listened. They were moving up by Scarrs Wood, crashing through the undergrowth along the perimeter of the trees. Although he couldn't see them, Skaggs made out perhaps a handful of men. The sounds of men were utterly different from the sounds of deer or other large beasts. The voice of the boot has a distinct and characteristic tone.

Crouching in silence until the furore died down, Skaggs made his way swiftly to the edge of the wood where he discovered fresh prints in the mud of the path. Maybe six sets in all, leading straight into the wood. Skaggs gazed into the deep shadow for a good while, then glanced back down the fields towards home with a brief, uncertain look, before committing himself to investigate. There was a good chance, he realised, that it was the dead men who'd returned this way. But Charlie Skaggs prided himself on his intimate relationship with nature, and even if the wood was crawling with them, he felt certain he could elude them with ease.

As a boy, Skaggs had been cursed with an unnatural dread of ghosts. His father told him stories that he was far too young to hear. Like the story of Old George Mullings who refused to stay dead. Every night Old George would clamber back out of his grave and go looking for children who wouldn't sleep. If he found one, he'd chop off its head and boil it in a big iron pot. To the terrified little Charlie Skaggs, every sound in the dark became Old George, and he'd spent many a childhood night with his eyes fixed open watching the shadows.

Later, he'd attributed his heightened awareness to those torturous nights. Charlie Skaggs – the man who could hear a pin drop at a thousand paces in a storm!

Now he was older and wiser he didn't believe in ghosts. Not until he'd seen the walking dead men. When he saw them shifting like shadows through Skews Bank, when he saw how dreadful they looked, just like his childhood image of Old George Mullings, as if they'd been rotting in the grave for months, Charlie Skaggs was amazed at how calm he felt, how he'd conquered his childhood dread.

Now, he sensed someone watching him from the deep black shadows of the wood. He had a sudden image of Old George Mullings observing him though the trees. Skaggs shivered. The idea crossed his mind that he must be bloody mad. He could turn back now while he was still on the edge of the wood. He had tomorrow's dinner over his shoulder. He could be climbing into a nice warm bed now.

But Skaggs wasn't a child any more. He wasn't afraid of the dark any more. This was *his* wood. And he wasn't about to be scared out of it by a bunch of dead men.

He prowled through the undergrowth near to the path, keeping an eye on the prints until they left the path and entered the shrubs themselves. Skaggs knelt to investigate, and found more prints in the leafy detritus at his feet, although now they were much harder to follow. There were snapped branches here, and Skaggs realised that, whoever they were, they'd headed for the middle of the forest. He set off in pursuit.

The torrential rain stopped in the shelter of the wood. The air was moist and smelled fresh. The canopy overhead heaved and waved in the wind, opening sporadically to let the occasional gleam of moonlight gush in and vanish just as quickly. With the light came the rain, brothers in arms, spattering noisily on the dense buckler fern. Skaggs stopped and listened to the forest. It was harder in the wind, but he could hear nothing unusual.

Deeper he plunged, stopping intermittently to check the trail, sometimes anxious he'd lost it, then picking it up again in the clearings and cross hatches of natural paths. Skaggs moved like an animal, his senses tuned to the nature he cherished. The fragrance of the wood filled his lungs, and he breathed it lovingly.

At the core of the wood he found the ancient pollarded oak, encrusted with lichens, moss and ferns, which had constituted the heart of Scarrs Wood for five hundred years. It rose like a groping, deformed hand amid the slender birch, beech and elms that towered around it. But now, in the tangled dark and light, Skaggs was perplexed to find the tree strung with adornments. At first he found it difficult to make out the shapes that turned in the breeze. He waded steadily closer through the fern, ears still keen on the surrounding wood, his entire body on a hair trigger ready to bolt.

He stopped abruptly when he recognised the shapes suspended in the tree. They hung on dirty twine, turning slightly in the shifting air. Little dark forms like lumps of rag hung there to dry. From the shadow they suddenly took form, and Skaggs realised with horror and fascination that the tree was full of dead things.

Having kept a close eye on Briggs for nearly an hour, Mary and the

Doctor had decided to call it a night and return to Mary's house. As they sat in the cool drawing room with the dying embers of the fire glowing feebly in the grate, Mary removed her boots unashamedly and rubbed her wet, aching feet.

Slumped in the chair by the piano, the Doctor regarded her from inside his shadow. He looked brooding, she thought, as though something weighed heavy on his mind. Mary decided to revert to form, and hit him with the heavy artillery while he was frail.

'Although you reached the village ahead of me, I was the first to attend to poor Constable Briggs,' she pointed out.

'Indeed you were,' the Doctor agreed, his voice as dark as the shadow.

'I just wondered where you had disappeared to,' she said.

'I was checking on my box,' he told her.

'That's what I thought,' she said.

He remained silent.

'I thought it unusual that you would attend to your box *before* attending to the constable. You are not a man of callous disregard for human life.'

'I am certainly not.'

Short silence.

'It also seems very strange that your box sustained no damage whatsoever, despite the fact that the station lock-up was completely razed to the ground around it, don't you agree?'

'Perhaps it's made from a very resilient material,' he suggested.

Mary considered this. 'I can't imagine a material that might withstand such damage unscathed.'

'There are landships in France that can sail straight through the heaviest bombardment,' he informed her. 'They are made of substantial armour plating, and will withstand even direct hits from all but the largest shells. They will make a great difference to the war effort, I am sure.'

'I am sure they will. But I am also quite certain that, were they to have a ton of bricks quite literally fall upon them, they would not come out of the encounter entirely unmarked. Please do not insult my intelligence, Doctor.'

'I would never consider attempting to insult your intelligence, Miss Minett, please believe me.'

She watched him watching her out of his private darkness.

'You are a very secretive man, Doctor,' she told him flatly.

'I suppose I am.'

'Your responses do nothing to answer any of my enquiries about you.'

'I am sorry you find me so intriguing, Miss Minett. I wish I were able to enlighten you. But I'm afraid I am an intensely private person. It seems I was just made that way.'

'It seems we have a conflict here, my dear Doctor. Something of the irresistible force meeting the immovable object.'

She saw him smile transiently and he leaned out of the shadow at her.

'Who's the irresistible one?' he asked in all seriousness.

She grinned back but refused to reply. Two could play at that game. After an appropriate pause of silence, she spoke again, keeping her voice light and chatty.

'You seem quite comfortable with all this strangeness, I must say. It's not every day one comes face to face with the animate dead. Most people would have some considerable difficulty in coming to terms with such encounters, and yet you seem to take all this entirely in your stride. Am I to assume you are accustomed to facing such horrors in your daily life?'

'As I said, there are more things in this life than one might sometimes imagine. I simply accept the evidence of my own eyes.' He gazed momentarily into the fading fire. Pale flames emerged intermittently from the ashes, rippling around the black edges of the coal's remains, but they were transparent blue things without substance or heat. The Doctor watched them, and Mary watched the flickering light reflected in his pensive eyes. Suddenly he looked askance at her.

'I must admit, I do seem to find it surprisingly easy to come to terms with that evidence. Perhaps more easy than most people. I really can't say why that is.'

'What do you think provoked the attack on your box?'

'I don't know.'

'Why would supernatural forces, if indeed that is what they are, show any interest at all in your box if it is simply some form of container for your wardrobe and valuables?'

'Perhaps they have an interest in high fashion.'

'Perhaps they have an interest in magic.'

'Magic?'

'A box that can withstand such destructive forces must have certain qualities which they might find very interesting. I feel I really must tell you something about your box, Doctor.'

'Oh, yes?'

'Yes. I have a certain... *empathy* with living things.'

'Empathy?'

'Please do not scoff, Doctor. As you said yourself twice tonight already, there are more things... *et cetera*. This is an extremely delicate faculty of which I have been aware all my life. I do not affect to be some theatrical sort who can read minds and tell you what playing card you have in your hand. I simply feel in some vague way what others feel when I am in close contact with them.'

Raising his hands in surrender, the Doctor was waving the white flag of a genial smile at her. 'Please, Miss Minett, I was not about to scoff. As I said, I am very much open to ideas to which others might be more closed.'

Straightening her dress, as if to compose her mind as well as her appearance, Mary went on. 'This talent has proven singularly useful in my dealings with the local animals in my role as sometime village vet. I seem to be extremely sensitive to emotions, whether they be human or not.'

'Oh, yes?'

'Yes.'

'And this talent has some relevance to my box, I take it.'

'When your box was delivered this morning, I was puzzled by its texture and its hue, as was Constable Briggs. I had occasion to... *touch* your box...'

'*And?*'

'I sensed a very great deal of what I could only describe as... pain.'

'Pain?' The Doctor looked abruptly curious.

She had thought he might laugh out loud, but he seemed genuinely intrigued. It was not the reaction she'd expected at all.

'Pain,' she confirmed.

The Doctor gazed off into space. He remained silent for a long time, and she got the impression there were many things he wanted to say but couldn't.

'To what might you attribute that sensation?' he asked at last.

Mary had considered this. In fact, it had occupied her mind for much of the day, and indeed, driven her almost to distraction. 'I thought at first it may have been an impression endowed by those responsible for transporting your box. Perhaps the box attracted and retained traces of their emotive energies.'

'But you don't think that now?'

'The sensation was very intense. In fact, it was as powerful to me as an electric shock. Traces from other people on an inanimate object could not have been so very potent, I am sure.'

Settling back into his seat, the Doctor became a shapeless, featureless being. Only his voice remained. And that was as soft as a voice in a dream.

'Perhaps you imagined it.'

Mary peered into the darkness. She could see nothing of the Doctor now, as the fire withered and even the dim orange of the grate extinguished at long last. There was much to discuss with this man. Many questions she must ask. But it was very late. And it had been an exceptionally long and arduous day. And she was now suddenly so very weary. She decided to postpone her interrogations until later.

'Perhaps I did,' she agreed.

She rose and headed for the door. There she paused.

'I'm afraid I must really get some sleep now. I do hope we can continue our most interesting conversation tomorrow.'

'I do hope so,' he said.

'Goodnight, Doctor.'

'Goodnight, Mary.'

Finishing off the last dregs of her tea, Emma Braithwaite gazed abstractedly into the dark-brown sludge which remained in the bottom of her cup. Dorothy Winstanley observed her silence from the other side of the room for a good minute until she couldn't stand it any longer.

'What's up?' she demanded, and found Emma giving her a surprised, questioning look.

'What d'you mean?'

'You were miles away,' Dorothy informed her plaintively.

'I was not.'

A mischievous smile schemed its way into Dorothy's lips. She was a thin woman with a long, bony nose that reminded Emma of a parrot's beak. At least ten years older than Emma, she was a woman Emma nevertheless harboured only a guarded respect for. Age, Emma had realised, did not always bring with it a deepening of wisdom.

'Not thinking about that Danny Corey, I don't suppose?'

Emma grinned back. 'No!'

'I can read you like a book, Emma Braithwaite.'

'You cannot!'

'Go on, then, tell me that you wasn't thinking about him, and swear it on yer mother's deathbed.'

'I will not!'

'See!'

'See what? I'm just tired, that's all. Haven't been sleeping well for a while.'

'No,' Dorothy said. 'Probably 'cause you're sleeping in the wrong bed…'

Emma managed to stifle the indiscreet giggle that was dying to escape. 'Dot Winstanley, you're rude as they come.'

'But I'm right, aren't I? You can't sleep for thinking about him!'

'I can't get to sleep 'cause it's bloody well daylight. That's the truth. How do you manage to sleep in the day?'

'After a night on duty here, I have a job on keeping me eyes open, I can tell yer.'

'I'm probably just not cut out for regular nights,' Emma reflected. 'I never was much good at getting out of my sleep routine.'

'You wanna get him *asked*!'

'What are you on about?'

'Private Corey! Ask him out down the pub or something. If he's not going to make the first move, you're gunna 'ave to do it yourself. We live in liberated times, now, you know. Nothing wrong with a lady suggesting a civilised *parlé* with a gentleman. They do it all the time in London.'

'Do they?'

'Course they do.' Dorothy nodded enthusiasm, then put on her poshy-oshy voice. ''Scuse me sir. Would you care to take me out for a sophisticated glass of alcoholic beverage tonight? I really do fancy getting quite tipsy and having a right good old knees-up. What?'

Shaking her head, Emma fell quiet and introspective again. Dorothy allowed her to brood for a full minute before she jumped up and grasped Emma's cup and saucer from her.

'Tell you what, let's read yer tea leaves, eh?'

'You can't read tea leaves!'

'Course I can. Been doing it for years.'

'You haven't…'

'Call me a liar, Emma Braithwaite –'

'I will, too.'

Dorothy checked the level of liquid in the cup before swirling it around, turning it over suddenly on to the saucer and allowing the dregs to drain.

'I thought I was supposed to turn me *own* cup over…'

'No.' Dorothy put her right. 'It works just as well if I do it for you. Now…'

She carefully turned the cup three times, before lifting it back off the saucer and peering inside. After a moment's serious turning and cogitation, she shook her head ruefully at Emma.

'My, you're a dark horse, Emma Braithwaite!'

Emma grinned. 'Go on then… What can you see?'

Dorothy's eyes grew wide and bulging in her skinny face. Her voice dropped a note or two for full effect.

'I see wedding bells,' she announced.

'When?'

'Soo-oon… Very soo-oon…' She glanced back into the cup, this time at a slightly new angle. 'And I see the patter of tiny feet, Emma Braithwaite.'

'When?'

'Soo-oon… Very soo-oon… Before the wedding bells –'

Emma burst out laughing and grabbed the cup back. 'Get out with you, Dot Winstanley.' She glanced at the random patterns of tea leaves left inside the cup, an arbitrary residue that meant absolutely nothing except that the cup needed a swill.

'You mock the gift, child?' Dorothy crooned, laying on the evil eye.

Emma laughed despite herself.

'You shall be struck down by lightning!' Dorothy warned.

'I shall wash my cup up this minute,' Emma replied.

'Nothing shall alter that which has been ordained.'

Shaking her head, Emma turned to the sink and attended to her washing up. When she turned back, Dorothy was sitting again in the little armchair in the corner. The possession had finally left her. Now she looked simply tired and in need of a good early night.

'I better get on,' Emma told her.

'I'm serious, you know,' Dorothy said as Emma swung open the door.

This time Emma could tell she *was*. She paused.

'What about?'

'Asking him out.'

Emma considered this. Then she threw Dorothy an uncertain smile.

'I'll think about it,' she said, and left.

From the kitchenette, Emma made her way back upstairs to the first-floor landing of the central hall. Dorothy might well be right. Maybe she did ought to ask Daniel Corey out. Nothing wrong with suggesting it, was there? If he got back on his feet again, he'd be back in France before she knew it, and then she might never see him again. And maybe it might be just the thing he needed, to get out a bit rather than moping around this dreary place day in and day out.

As she passed Corey's door, she gave a light knock again. The door was still ajar, as it had been earlier, so she was surprised to see the bedclothes ruffled and someone inside.

'Daniel?' she said softly.

He didn't respond. She told herself not to be so ridiculous. Leave him to sleep. It wasn't fair to impose on him like this. But then she reminded herself that he'd been out all night and it was now nearly four o'clock in the morning, and it really was her duty to check if he was all right.

She stepped into the room uncertainly.

'Daniel?'

Silence. The curtains were open to let in the stormy moonlight. Otherwise, the room was in darkness apart from a wedge of dissipated yellow light from the landing. She stepped across to tidy his blankets, and found him sleeping soundly, oblivious to her presence.

The blankets were hoisted around him in an untidy heap, and she was positive he couldn't be comfortable like that. She started to straighten them, and was puzzled at first at the complete lack of response from him when she disturbed the sheets. Then she saw the dark shadows around his pillow, and when she bent to investigate, she realised the pillow was soaked with dark liquid.

She froze. The storm buffeted the window, doing its utmost to get into the room, but the world to Emma Braithwaite was suddenly a static, motionless place. As if time had stopped still. All she could do was stare at Corey's white face against the dark pillow.

With trembling fingers, she reached out to touch him, and saw herself as if she were in a dream. He was cold. The pillow was wet. She pulled him to face her. In the deep shadow she saw the dark hole in his head, and the scream burst out of her like a wild thing let loose in the night.

The old oak tree was covered completely in dangling things. A gathering of death. Small corpses, dead birds, rabbits, mice, squirrels, stoats, even severed dogs' heads. A menagerie of tortured creatures. Suspended head down. Turning slowly in the breeze. As Skaggs gazed on horrified, he recognised one of the heads in the tree. The head of one of his own dogs.

Legs trembling, Charlie Skaggs made his way through the ferns and took the cranium in his hands. He untied the cord and released the head, manoeuvring it to face him. The eyes, grey with patina, gazed at him blindly out of the cold, bloody skull.

With a numb kind of detachment, he stepped back through the ferns into a small clearing and laid the dog's head on the ground. Kneeling and opening his bag, he carefully placed the head inside before rising to leave.

And only then did he see them. The dead men all around him, watching him silently as he stood in the small clearing. He couldn't imagine how they'd got there without his hearing. He gazed at them one after another, and they watched him out of their ragged faces. For long, terrible moments, not one of them moved. They stood like a ring of scarecrows, scraps of torn clothing and flesh fluttering slightly in the breeze.

Slowly, Skaggs reached for his gun and levelled it at the nearest of the dead men. The thing's face retained much of its flesh, particularly around the mouth, and when it grinned Skaggs could not mistake the grim humour in the remaining features. The thing shook its head with deliberate slowness. It raised its hand, signalled the others, and Skaggs watched in horror as they began to close in.

He turned the gun on them, one then another, but there wasn't even a glimmer of hesitation. In a flash he was a child again, all the terrors of the night clawing at him. These were the walking dead, an Old George Mullings every last one. They moved with a shambling motion, some of them with badly injured limbs. Dull yellowing bones visible through decaying flesh. Vacant chasms for eyes. He remembered the old oak tree. Full of slaughter. Full of torture. Full of evil. The corpse-soldiers closed in steadily. Six of them. He had one shot only. His heart raced and he was dripping with sweat. His legs were shivering and the rifle shook uselessly in his slack grasp.

One shot.

The soldiers were dead already.

One shot.

The tree full of slaughter. Full of torture. Full of *evil*.

One shot.

He was a child again, and the horrors of the world were about to tear him apart.

One shot.

Skaggs brought up the barrel and lodged it under his own chin.

One shot.

Chapter Six

Waking to the sound of voices downstairs, Mary sat up in bed to find the room suffused with the kind of fresh sunlight that comes only on a clear summer morning after a night of violent storms. The voices were distant, coming up through the floor from the kitchen. She recognised them as the Doctor and Briggs. They were talking with some urgency, but it was impossible to make out the words. She decided that now might be an opportune moment to rise.

When she arrived downstairs, the Doctor was following Briggs out into the morning sunshine. He paused at the door when he saw her enter the kitchen behind him.

'Good morning,' he said, throwing her a very delighted smile, hanging on to the door perhaps a little longer than he should have done considering his urgency of only a moment ago.

'Good morning,' she said, still tugging her clothes straight around her shoulders. She caught sight of herself inadvertently in the kitchen mirror and proceeded to calm her wild hair with combing gestures of her fingers.

'I trust you slept well?' he asked.

Mary nodded, feeling actually that she had not slept in the least well at all. The Doctor appeared so very radiant and brimming with energy that she felt suddenly inadequate.

'I did,' she lied. She stepped over the kitchen and brought herself to within a very short distance of the Doctor's face. There wasn't even a trace of fatigue in those childlike eyes. 'And you?'

'Like a log.' He seemed to remember Briggs standing there in the background and said with apology, 'I'm afraid I really must dash. There's been a rather gruesome development.'

'Gruesome development?'

'A murder,' he told her. 'At Hawkswick Hall. One of the patients.

131

And Mr Skaggs went missing last night.'

'In that case you will need some assistance,' Mary informed him, taking the door from him and ushering him out into the garden.

'Good morning, Albert,' she announced with considerably more cheer than she felt.

Briggs doffed his cap. 'Good morning, Miss Minett.'

'I see you're feeling much better this morning,' she observed.

'Just a bit of a thick head,' he told her. 'I'll be right as rain.'

'I'm sure.' Mary smiled as they made their way together down the path and out into the road.

The sun lay low in the east, not quite risen yet over the surrounding trees. The air smelled damp, but the road was already perfectly dry after the night's rain. The sky was a fierce, magnificently clear blue, and the morning was saturated with birdsong. Despite a lingering muzziness, and the terrible news that Briggs had brought, Mary sensed a sudden lifting of her spirits.

The Doctor marched ahead, apparently having taken charge of proceedings, and glanced back to the other two as he went.

'I'll go to Hawkswick Hall,' he announced. 'It might be useful if you could perhaps accompany Constable Briggs in a search for our missing Mr Skaggs.'

Having a natural antipathy to being ordered around, Mary was about to dispute these arrangements, but she immediately thought better of it. Constable Briggs was not the sprightliest or the most sharp-eyed or dynamic upholder of law that Mary had ever encountered. Constable Briggs was a plodder, quite at home helping to organise summer fêtes, or writing reports on the various outbreaks of fowl disease that occasionally erupted. He was even quite skilful at dealing with the very infrequent drunken brawls which also broke out on occasion, but that was because all the young men of the village regarded him with a fatherly respect. Poor Constable Briggs would not be quite so at home, Mary was certain, in real-life investigative work. He was, unfortunately, no Sherlock Holmes.

And besides, she thought contritely, the Doctor was much better at dealing with dead soldiers than she was.

For all these reasons, she found herself smiling agreement at the Doctor, and when they reached the village he went marching off in the direction of the Hall.

'Now, Albert, presumably Mrs Skaggs spoke to you this morning about Charlie.'

'She did,' he said, rubbing the back of his aching neck. 'Twenty to six this morning, to be precise.'

Mary gave him a sympathetic look. 'A policeman's lot is not always an easy one,' she remarked.

He smiled in grim accord. 'Not these days, it isn't.'

Mary felt sorry for Constable Albert Briggs, truth be known. Briggs's entire career had been one of essentially secretarial skills. Filling in forms. Keeping records in the highly individual filing system built into his kitchen. He had enjoyed an uneventful life, in terms of actual policing. But events over the last few months had evolved out of all proportion.

'These are strange days indeed,' Mary said.

They were walking by the station house, with its pile of rubble where the lock-up should have been. The Doctor's box stood resplendent, as if it had been added to the pile after the damage had been done.

'Strange indeed,' Briggs echoed.

Mary realised that he too was gazing at the box. Then she found his pale-blue eyes searching her own.

'What do you make of it, then?' he asked directly.

'The Doctor's box?'

'Yes.'

Mary shrugged. 'Like everything else around here at the moment, I find it quite mysterious.'

'Not even a scratch,' Briggs noted.

'No.'

'When I woke up this morning, I remembered what happened last night,' Briggs told her. 'I didn't exactly see who attacked me, but I saw who was attacking the lock-up.'

Mary watched him expectantly.

'There were four of them,' he said. 'All in army uniform. Nobody walks about with the injuries they had. One of them must have come up behind me.'

'I saw one in the thicket,' Mary confided.

'The really puzzling thing,' Briggs said, 'is that I could swear they were here after the Doctor's box.'

In the kitchenette, Emma Braithwaite still sobbed inconsolably, while Dorothy Winstanley fussed at the sink making tea. Dorothy looked up when the door opened and Dr Banham poked his head around the door.

'Ah,' Banham said, uncertain when he saw the state Nurse Braithwaite was in. He stepped inside and plonked himself in the seat next to her.

'Hmm...'

Dorothy had met Dr Banham only once before, during the interview process to get her job here. At that brief meeting he came across as extremely efficient and a powerfully dominating man. Now he looked entirely unsure of himself in the face of a weeping girl.

'Miss Braithwaite...' he began.

Emma watched him out of red eyes, her cheeks wet with tears.

'I'm afraid I must ask you to accompany me,' he finally managed to get the words out, 'to meet a gentleman from the Ministry. There are some formal procedures connected with the events of this morning.'

Emma simply continued to gaze at him, incomprehension written all over her white, exhausted face.

Taking her gently by the arm, Banham rose to his feet and Emma stood with him. As they were about to leave, he turned back to Dorothy.

'Might I prevail upon you to wait a little longer, please, Mrs Winstanley?'

Dorothy didn't understand.

'I'm very much afraid this will prove extremely distressing for Miss Braithwaite.'

'Right,' Dorothy nodded. 'Course. I'll wait here.'

'Thank you,' Banham said. 'We'll be back as quickly as possible.'

The door sliced shut, and Dorothy Winstanley gazed at it for a good minute before carrying on with her task of making tea. She very rarely had so much excitement in one night. There was the usual fare of shrieking loons, but she'd never worked a shift when one of them had been found dead in his bed. Now she really had some juicy scandal to take home. Despite the long night behind her, she felt a curling anticipation of recounting events to Patricia Dobbins over a cup of tea and the woman's dry, lard-tasting biscuits.

A man shot dead! Right through the middle of his head! Blood spattered everywhere! Nurse Braithwaite screaming blue murder! Dorothy'd never worked such an exciting shift!

The details of the house swam about Emma as if she were being led through thick liquid instead of the air. The familiar trip from the kitchenette to the first-floor landing was suddenly a frightening and unreal ordeal. The walls and the stairs seemed such insubstantial things.

She finally arrived at the top of the stairs where she found a man waiting outside Daniel's room. The man regarded her with a melancholic look. She heard Dr Banham's voice, as if it were something in the far distance, speaking to her in reassuring tones.

'This is the Doctor,' he said. 'The Man from the Ministry. He needs to ask you a few questions.'

135

The Man from the Ministry took her by the arm and watched her closely. She avoided his eyes, preferring to stare at the empty space in front of her feet. She didn't want to talk to anybody at the moment. She didn't want to talk. She didn't want to be here. Outside his room. On this landing. This place was a nightmare. A big bad dream. She didn't want to be here at all –

'I'm sorry I have to put you through this,' said the Man from the Ministry. His voice was surprisingly soothing. It contained undercurrents of sorrow and caring which Emma would have warmed to at any other time. 'I need to ask you about last night.'

She felt the man's arm around her shoulder and realised he was guiding her with gentle pressure away from Daniel's room. He manoeuvred her to the banister that overlooked the entrance hall and let go. She stood hugging herself, doing her level best to shut out the world and the truth of what happened.

'You found Private Corey,' the Ministry Man said.

Her head jerked of its own volition, as if her mind were no longer in control.

'And you found him in there?'

Emma glanced at the door to Corey's room, and nodded again.

'Can you tell me what happened?'

For a long time she said nothing. Then she was as surprised as anyone to hear her own voice, a disconnected sound as if someone else were telling him the story.

'I came from the kitchen,' the voice told the Ministry Man. 'I'd been looking for Daniel all night. He wasn't in his room. Then I found him –'

The sound of her voice cut abruptly.

'What time was that?'

Shrug. 'Four? Quarter past?'

'And there was no one else about?'

Her head shook.

'You didn't hear anyone about just before you came up here?'

136

Shake.

'And you hadn't heard a shot?'

Shake.

'Thank you, Miss Braithwaite. I'm sorry I had to ask you all that.'

She felt Dr Banham's hand again on her arm, and the stairs arrived below her feet. She moved down with a slow, mesmerising rhythm, until the stairs began to lift themselves from under her and float about with a disconcerting fluidity. They swept up past her and the world was sucked briskly down a black plughole in the depths of her head.

The Man from the Ministry's face materialised in front of Emma out of the swirling mass of space and time. His eyes were full of concern and he reached out and touched her shoulder.

'How do you feel?' he asked.

Taking a deep breath, Emma responded with uncertainty.

'All right.'

'I'm sorry,' he told her. 'I hadn't realised you were so close to Daniel Corey.'

Dragging herself upright on the sofa, Emma recognised Banham's reception. The room was empty and she was alone with the Ministry Man. Her brain struggled to come to terms with the facts that seemed to jig around excitedly inside it.

'How did you know –'

'You *were* close?' the man said, appearing suddenly a little unsure of himself.

'I cared a great deal for Daniel Corey,' she admitted. 'I don't know if he ever realised how much.'

'I see.'

The man gazed into the midair where there was nothing at all to see.

'He would have died instantly,' he told her. 'There would have been no pain.'

Silence. He was trying to help, she knew, but she could say nothing in response. Now he looked uncomfortable, on edge, as if he were itching to be somewhere else. This was quite obviously a part of his job that he did not enjoy.

'I must go now,' he said simply. 'I'll get Dr Banham to come straight in.'

He headed for the door. As he was about to leave, he paused and looked back at her with an odd, unreadable expression. The look lasted an uncommonly long time, before the door swept him from her view.

After clearing the reception area of milling onlookers, Banham had waited edgily outside the reception room until the Doctor reappeared.

'I'd pay poor Nurse Braithwaite some careful attention,' the Doctor advised him with quiet urgency. 'I suspect she's exhausted. But there was also some romantic connection between her and Private Corey. I think they were closer than you may have realised. Or at least *she* was.'

'We don't encourage such close association,' Banham began, 'but I suppose it's inevitable when you consider the situation here.'

The Doctor regarded him in brooding silence. Then came to a snap decision.

'I want to carry out an extensive search of this hospital. I'd like assistance, if you could please arrange that.'

Banham appeared nonplussed.

'I don't know if I can –'

'Dr Banham, in a clear-cut case of murder certain formalities must be put aside. If we don't act very quickly, we could lose the evidence for ever.'

'Evidence of what?'

'Of the place where Daniel Corey was killed.'

'But the bedroom,' Banham blustered, 'surely –'

The Doctor grasped Banham by the arm and led him away from the door to the reception. As they went he spoke quietly but firmly.

'Private Corey was not killed in his bedroom.'

'But the blood –'

'There was a lot of blood, yes. Considering the wound there would be, obviously. But I could find no spray marks anywhere in Private Corey's room.'

'Spray?'

'You shoot someone through the head and there is something of a mess in the immediate vicinity, Dr Banham.'

'But surely his head was against the pillow.'

'His head was nowhere near his pillow when he was shot.' The Doctor glanced nervously at the reception door, obviously concerned that they might be overheard by Nurse Braithwaite. 'The bullet went straight through. The pillow was covered in blood, but no other damage at all.'

Banham fell silent.

'Now if you could please arrange for a member of your staff to assist, I'd like to take a very close look around this establishment.'

'I could show you round myself,' Banham suggested helpfully.

The Doctor shook his head. 'I'm quite sure, Dr Banham, that you have far more pressing matters in the light of what happened here last night. I'm quite certain that your time could be put to much better use than showing me around. A member of your staff will suffice.'

Banham gave him a forbidding look.

'Very well,' he said. 'I'll arrange for one of the orderlies to assist you.'

'Thank you.'

'You're very welcome,' Banham said tightly. 'If I can be of any further service, please don't hesitate to get back to me.'

'Don't worry,' the Doctor told him. 'I'll be sure to do that.'

* * *

'*Bloody queer as buggery!*' Bill Cromby stomped across the yard in the direction of the stables. The large rock he'd dragged in front of the door had been moved in the night. When he got up first thing to feed the horses, he'd thought the door must've pushed the stone as it blew open in the wind. He'd replaced the stone after feeding the horses, but now there wasn't a hint of breeze, and the stone was moved again.

Cromby heaved a mightily puzzled sigh and scratched the back of his neck. He lumbered into the stables and discovered the horses yet again agitated and edgy. The hay hadn't even been touched. Two days now, and they hadn't eaten a thing. Cromby had checked the hay, and it was completely fresh and clean. Nothing at all wrong with the stuff.

So what was wrong with them?

Cromby stood and considered. The stable was a perfectly comfortable environment. He had no problem with rats or any other infestation. There were no draughts. No leaks. The place was as comfortable as his own kitchen. The feed was good. The horses seemed not to ail for anything physical at all.

Again, he gazed lost in thought up at the hatch to the hayloft. Maybe there was something up there. Maybe something he hadn't seen.

Making his way to the ladder, Cromby began to climb. Hoisting himself into the loft, he stood and gazed into the stillness. There was a small opening in each end of the roof. Light came through, but it was a precious commodity. The large stacks of straw were lost in deep shadow that his eyes could not penetrate. There were areas of vague nothingness where it was impossible to see anything.

A pitchfork lay by the hatch, and Cromby snatched it up before plodding into the dark. The boards creaked and moaned under his weight, and he stopped abruptly, positive he'd heard movement other than his own. There was only silence. A musty, straw-scented silence thick with his own anticipation.

He made his way to the bottom end of the loft and began to poke the fork into the straw, turning it and gazing into the shadow, trying to see the telltale signs of infestation.

(He didn't see the large shadowy shapes stirring near the hatch while he worked. They were half consumed in shadow, their damp, glistening features picked out in fragile light. They watched him work with the straw, then began to emerge from their hiding places.)

Cromby heard voices outside, and recognised them as Albert Briggs and Mary Minett. They were approaching across the yard. He heard them open the door below and Briggs shouted his name.

'Up here,' Cromby yelled back.

He stomped back down the loft to the hatch, and as he prepared to descend into the daylight below, he thrust the fork into a large pile of straw nearby.

'Mr Cromby,' Mary greeted him with a breezy formality. 'We are in need of your assistance.'

'Oh yeh?'

'Yes indeed,' she affirmed. 'We are looking for Charlie Skaggs.'

'Well you won't find 'im if 'e dun't want yer to,' Cromby warned her.

'Mrs Skaggs expected him home last night, and he never arrived back from his travels.'

Cromby got to the bottom of the ladder and brushed himself off.

''E'll not be lost,' he told them flatly. ''E'll be swannin' off somewhere for a bit o' peace an' quiet from 'is missus. Probably down Far Glenn doin' a spot o' fishin'.'

'Well Mrs Skaggs seemed quite anxious this morning when she reported Charlie missing. After the troubles we've experienced lately, I think it might be prudent of us to organise a search, don't you agree?'

'An' you want me to 'elp look for 'im?'

Mary regarded the red-faced giant. 'I thought the one person who would know almost as much about his traps as Charlie Skaggs is the person upon whose land Skaggs sets those traps.'

Cromby threw Briggs a slightly baffled look.

'I can show yer where 'e sets 'em,' he said, 'but they're a bit spread out. I 'ope yer've got yer walkin' boots on.'

Mary beamed a highly satisfied smile at him, and led them immediately back out into the yard. As they went she asked him about his horses, and he told her about the trouble he'd had with the door.

There was movement in the darkness of the hayloft. The large bank of hay by the hatch began to stir, and there emerged a bedraggled corpse with the pitchfork jutting out of its already badly injured leg. The thing reached down and yanked the fork out of the swollen, blotchy flesh. It regarded the blood-smeared tines before wiping the points with its fingers and licking them with grisly curiosity.

Henry McGuff was a mountain, not a man. He moved with a gigantically slow gait, advancing his stupendous frame down the corridor with very little in the way of grace. The Doctor was a slender thing at his side, and McGuff was deliberately making it extremely difficult for him to strike up anything like a conversation.

'So you weren't on duty last night?' the Doctor asked as they made their way down the east wing to the door at the end of the corridor.

McGuff shook his head. 'Came on at seven this morning.'

'It's a terrible thing,' the Doctor said, obviously trying to coax some response.

But all he got was a nod.

Sweeping open the door, the Doctor stepped out into the daylight, his face scrunched up against the ferocity of the sun.

'Such a waste,' he continued as McGuff lumbered out after him.

McGuff said nothing.

They made their way over the yard towards Banham's therapy block. The Doctor gazed into the clear blue sky as they went, and stood enraptured for a moment in the middle of the expanse of gravel. McGuff stopped and watched him in puzzlement. The Doctor's eyes were sparkling with childlike intensity.

'Have you ever seen such a beautiful day?' he asked.

McGuff gawked about then shrugged noncommittally.

All at once, the Doctor was gone, and McGuff had to hurry along in an elephantine kind of plod to catch up. They let themselves into the cool and quiet of the therapy building and when the Doctor closed the door, they were plunged into a grey semidarkness. Without any help from McGuff, the Doctor found the light switch and the electric lamps flamed into burning yellow life.

'Now,' the Doctor announced, 'I'm going to take a look around in here first, and then I'm going to ask you to show me the nooks and crannies which polite visitors don't normally get to see. Would you like to come with me, or would you prefer to wait here?'

'I'll wait,' McGuff grunted.

'Yes,' the Doctor agreed. 'Probably just as well.'

He vanished through the metal door that led to the therapy cubicles and McGuff was left standing alone in the anteroom. He gazed round and began to tap his foot to a silent tune. In the distance, he could hear doors opening one after another. As the Doctor continued on his search, McGuff remembered Dr Banham's instructions: 'Go with him. Do what he says. But don't offer any help unless he specifically asks for it.'

This Ministry bigwig was obviously poking into places where

Dr Banham didn't really think he belonged. If it were up to McGuff, he'd tell the little weasel exactly where to go. But there were, he supposed, subtle diplomatic games to be played out. He understood that it was prudent sometimes to *appear* to be helpful. Especially to men from the Ministry. McGuff was just glad that he didn't have Dr Banham's job, having to sniff round these official types like they were somebody important. McGuff was no respecter of authority. And he liked to call a spade a spade when it came to dealing with people, wherever they were from.

He'd show the Ministry Man the nooks and crannies all right. But only the ones the Ministry Man could find for himself.

The day was wearing on and Mary was beginning to regret rushing out without breakfast. She was starting to feel rather tired, particularly after such a traumatic sleepless night. Briggs, she noted, was also flagging. His face was crimson, covered with glinting droplets of perspiration that he wiped habitually with his handkerchief. He'd lost a lot of sleep and not a little blood last night, and just now he obviously wasn't in the mood for a long hard foot-march through the baked fields. Only Cromby kept going at the same metronome pace, as if he were out on a leisurely stroll. His great legs seemed to have only one speed, whether they were taking him over the flat or up hills of any gradient. In the strong sun, it was not a pleasant task trying to keep up with the great farmer.

'Mr Cromby,' Mary gasped finally, as they made their way around the edge of Long Sceil, 'I really think I should remind you that our friend Constable Briggs had a rather nasty knock on the head last night. It might be wise to stop for a little rest at this juncture.'

Grinding to a halt, Cromby wiped the sweat from his forehead on the back of his arm. At the sight of Briggs, he nodded agreement.

''Ow yer feelin', Bert?'

'I could do with a minute,' he admitted.

'There's a bit of shelter up 'ere,' Cromby said. 'On the edge o' the wood. Come on. Not far.'

And he was off again like some amazing perpetual-motion machine, trudging up the field towards the gate in the top corner. After a few yards he stopped unexpectedly and dropped to the ground.

'Queer,' he mumbled.

'What is it?' asked Mary.

Cromby regarded her with a meaningful look. 'This snare. It's been left unset.'

Mary looked down at the delicate noose hanging in Cromby's sausage fingers.

'What does that mean?' she asked.

Shrugging uncertainly, Cromby clambered back to his feet and gazed about the field. He arrived at a conclusion and regarded Mary uneasily.

'Most likely means Charlie Skaggs was disturbed by summat while 'e was checkin' these snares.'

'My dear Mr Cromby,' Mary said with some delight, 'you are a treasure.'

Briggs took the cord from Cromby and inspected it closely.

'The question is,' he wheezed, 'what disturbed him?'

'That is what we are here to find out,' Mary announced. 'I propose a short respite on the perimeter of the wood. Allow us all to catch our breath and collect our thoughts. Hmm?'

Briggs nodded agreement, and Cromby shrugged a half-hearted gesture of compliance. They emerged from the field and found a fallen tree on the edge of Scarrs Wood, where Mary sat thankfully with Briggs while Cromby marched about testily.

Removing his cap, Constable Briggs patted the top of his bare head with his already damp hanky. He took a good deep breath and leaned forward on his knees, allowing his poor throbbing legs to support the weight of his sagging old body.

He wasn't up to this chasing about like he used to be. Gone were the days when he could gallivant about the countryside like a lad. He'd reached the point four years ago when he'd considered retiring from his duties as village constable, but the war had put paid to that idea. Now it was all hands on deck, all shoulders to the wheel. Old and young alike doing their bit. He didn't mind that, of course, having a good idea what England's finest were up against in the Fields of France. The trouble was that his *bit* had suddenly transformed into quite a huge amount. With the arrival of this energetic young Ministry Man, Briggs had entertained the fanciful notion that he might take a back seat, return to his kitchen and his form-filling. But that obviously was not to be.

Mary studied the sun-drenched Long Sceil Field. A lone rook swooped down to rummage in the dry stubble. She watched it peck and poke, then set sail again into the clear blue sky. The sun was now high, and it was probably nearly midday, although Mary had neglected to bring a watch. Her stomach felt like a void, and she really wished now that she'd had the good sense to grant herself a hearty breakfast. But the Doctor had swept her along, as usual, with his boundless energy and enthusiasm. The Man from the Ministry – who ran on some mysterious invisible fuel which never required topping up. The man who did not apparently have any call for sleep. The man of so many singular conundrums that she was beginning to wonder if he was really a man at all, or rather some supernatural entity himself.

'Come and look at this.' Cromby broke into her thoughts.

Both Mary and Briggs stumbled over to see what Cromby had found.

'Prints,' said Briggs.

'First rain we've 'ad to call owt was last night,' Cromby

reminded them. 'These're fresh prints. About six sets, I reckon. They *must* a' been made last night.'

He regarded Mary with an implacable look.

'I reckon we could do worse than follow these,' he suggested.

Glancing fretfully into the deep green and black shadows of Scarrs Wood, Mary could not disagree with him even if she wanted to.

When the Doctor had finished his search of the therapy block, McGuff led him to the large garage where the gardening implements and mowers were stored. They then made their way back to the house, but the Doctor was intent on taking a detour around the side of the building instead of returning to the door on the east wing. They clambered briskly down the steps to the front of the house, but en route came across the small side entrance to the basement.

The Doctor gazed up at the house, then up at McGuff.

'I take it this is an entrance to the cellars.'

McGuff nodded. 'Yeh.'

'Shall we see?'

The door was unlocked and they plunged together into the gloom. Despite his size and churlish manner, McGuff found this an unnerving part of the house. It was always deserted, yet he felt every time he came down here that there was somebody watching him. The Ministry Man seemed unbothered by any such notion. He pulled the door shut behind them and immediately marched off down the corridor as if he had no need to let his eyes adjust to the dark. Overcoming an initial hesitation, McGuff set off shambling after him. He felt a vague sense of relief when he finally caught up with the man.

The Ministry Man had stopped and knelt with his ear to the gun store.

'Did you hear that?' he asked.

McGuff listened, but he could hear nothing at all. He shook his head.

'I could swear I heard someone scream.'

'It'll be somebody up in the house,' McGuff told him. 'The sounds carry down here.'

He'd heard the screams himself once on a night shift. It was easy to let your imagination get carried away down here. But the rooms in the cellar were empty except for the locked gun store and a few rusty old garden tools.

The Ministry Man tried the door and was disappointed to discover it was locked.

'Do you know what's in here?' he asked.

'Gun store,' McGuff informed him.

'I see.'

Looking around in the dark, the Ministry Man paced about a bit before asking, 'Are any of the other rooms used down here?'

McGuff shook his head. 'Too damp.'

'Of course,' the Ministry Man said, returning his attention to the locked door.

He grasped the handle and held it for a few moments before letting go and gazing at the nearby walls. McGuff felt edgy and more than ready to leave, but the Ministry Man seemed to have discovered something that intrigued him. He stepped across and peered closely at the opposite wall, carefully exploring the texture of the crumbling damp plaster with his fingertips.

Captain Thomas had enjoyed a pleasant walk in the sunshine with Nurse Wright. They had strolled by the river for an hour, and he'd relished the company of a woman who shared his delight in simply walking in silence. The sun was high above them as they climbed the steps to the main entrance. Nurse Wright stopped abruptly and Thomas realised she was staring fixedly into Banham's office.

Through the open curtains, they could see Banham at his desk. He sat with his hands outstretched, head thrust back, and he seemed to be contorted in agony. His torso arched, as if he were suffering a sustained electric shock.

The Ministry Man shook his head, and McGuff was relieved when he resumed his march down the basement corridor. He tried another couple of the doors and found the rooms beyond empty. They reached the wooden steps at the end of the corridor and as he prepared to climb them, the Ministry Man took a last, long look into the dark. Then he ascended to find himself in the main reception area of the house.

Thomas watched as Banham slumped forward abruptly over his desk. He remained still and lifeless. Leaving Nurse Wright with a startled look, Thomas scrambled up the steps and into the house.

When Cromby lost track of the footprints, they all stopped and helped him search, but the undergrowth was dense and it was impossible to see where the trail had gone. There were obscure natural paths between the trees, perhaps created by the habitual migration of deer, but they were haphazard and vague in places, disappearing and reappearing without apparent rhyme or reason. Cromby and the little search party spent a short time scouting around, but to no avail. Finally, Cromby had a suggestion.

'We should split up,' he announced.

Mary managed to cover the shock she felt at this notion, but Briggs was not so proficient at disguising his feelings.

'Are you joking?' he said. 'I vote we bloody well stick together – pardon my French, my dear.'

Cromby was dumbfounded. 'What's up?'

'What's up?' Briggs was astonished. 'We've got dead men walking about the village, a man murdered up at the Hall last night, Charlie Skaggs gone missing, and you want us to split up in the middle o' the woods?'

Cromby shot Mary a slightly embarrassed look.

'Perhaps we could just split up a little,' Mary suggested helpfully. 'Just fan out a bit.'

Cromby and Briggs thought this was a good idea, and they continued their progress in a loose arrowhead formation, Cromby storming ahead with his usual balletic prowess. As they moved, Mary became aware of motion at the very edge of her perception. She had a vague misgiving that they were being observed, but when she looked she saw no one. The feeling was subtle but stubborn, and as they got closer to the heart of the wood she was growing gradually more jittery.

The trees around them erupted with a raucous screech. Mary screamed, glared at the kaleidoscope of circling shadows, and saw a pair of huge jackdaws engaged in territorial dispute. They met briefly in midair with a battering of black wings. Then they were gone, soaring out through the canopy to leave a hollow silence in their wake.

Clapping her hand over her mouth, Mary tried to calm her racing heart. She was quivering with fright, and, by the look of him, so was Constable Briggs. She tried to locate Cromby to see his reaction, but realised then that he was gone.

She glared back at Briggs, hysteria hunting through her like a predator through a still dark forest.

'Where's Bill?'

Briggs gazed about, but there was no sign of the big farmer. Only trees and shrubs. He stood rooted, apparently unable to move.

'I'm 'ere,' Cromby declared, lifting himself out of the undergrowth like a vast whale rising from water.

Mary gasped with relief, until she saw the look on his face.

'I think I found Charlie Skaggs,' he announced bleakly.

* * *

Captain Thomas clattered into reception and careered past a shocked Clara Walker to fling open the door to Banham's office. He was bemused to find Banham working studiously at a file on his desk. Banham appeared surprised, but otherwise entirely at ease. He removed the glasses from his face and waited patiently for Thomas to speak. Feeling strangely as if he were trapped in a bubble, disconnected from reality, Thomas struggled to find his voice.

'Can I help you?' Banham asked. He positioned his pen neatly across the top of the file and pressed back in his chair.

Stepping into the room, Thomas felt as if the world had taken a sudden turn for the surreal, and he didn't like it one little bit. Was he slipping back into delirium?

'I'm sorry,' he stammered.

The room was serene and Banham sat there completely unruffled by Thomas's barging in.

'Is there something wrong?' Banham asked, his voice full of concern.

Thomas shook his head. 'I could have sworn I just saw you... having some kind of... a seizure or something...'

'A seizure?'

'We were out on the steps.' Thomas indicated the window. 'You were acting very strangely, then you collapsed over your desk.'

Banham shook his head slowly. 'I've been writing reports for the last hour. I can assure you that I'm perfectly fit and well, Captain Thomas.'

'I'm sorry. I could swear –'

'The sun is particularly bright today,' Banham reminded him. 'Might I suggest that what you *thought* you saw may perhaps have been a reflection on the glass. Perhaps the nearby shrubs. You might have seen the shrubs and me superimposed. Seeing things through windows on bright days can be deceiving. A mere trick of the light.'

It was possible. And Banham certainly made it sound more than plausible. But Thomas could swear he'd had a clear view of Banham, and that what he saw was no light show. However, Banham certainly appeared, as he said, fit and well. A man who'd just suffered a violent seizure would look shaky and pasty, wouldn't he? He'd be distressed. Perhaps perspiring. He certainly wouldn't be sitting there cool as a cucumber. Would he?

'I really must apologise,' Thomas said, feeling his cheeks blushing.

'Don't worry about it.' Banham grinned generously. 'We all make mistakes.'

But Thomas remained dumbfounded, his feet glued to the polished floorboards, until Banham spoke again and snapped him out of his reverie.

'Close the door on your way out. There's a good chap.'

'Yes, sir.'

Thomas nodded and turned on his heel.

Mary's anxiety was intensifying by the minute. As Briggs and Cromby worked invisibly in the undergrowth, their labours hidden from her view by a canopy of ferns, she watched the surrounding trees. The woods had always reminded Mary of Shakespeare's *A Midsummer-Night's Dream*, and as a girl she'd even fancied she might encounter Puck on his mischievous errands in Scarrs Wood. It was a magically motionless place, as if in here time stood still. Here you were secluded from the march and bustle of the real world outside. It was a netherworld of fairies. But now that magic was being distorted into something altogether more disturbing. Rather than a place of quiet, it was suddenly a place of disquiet. A domain of evil spirits rather than fairies. Of sorcery rather than magic.

The shadows were alive with invisible things. Watching them. Encircling them. She could feel them all around her. She remembered Cromby's horses and their unexplained agitation. Abruptly she knew exactly how they felt. She remembered their emotions, which she'd sensed so vividly as if they were fresh garish paint splashed on canvas, and she recognised those very same emotions in herself.

Briggs emerged from the ferns and took her by the arm, leading her away from where Cromby still hunched over at work.

'It *is* Charlie,' he confirmed. 'But it's probably better if you don't see.'

She simply gazed at him, horrified.

'And we still need to continue the search, I'm afraid.'

'Continue the search? I don't understand –'

Briggs heaved a deep breath and hunched his shoulders.

'We really ought to find the head.'

Scribbling furiously on a report, Banham looked up when he heard a sharp rap at the door.

'Yes?'

Clara popped her head round to inform him that the Doctor wished to see him.

Banham beamed. 'Please – show him in.'

Striding round the desk, Banham shook the Doctor amicably by the hand before offering him a seat.

'My dear Mr Holmes,' Banham said playfully, 'I trust your endeavours were fruitful?'

The Doctor accepted the seat and slumped with legs crossed and his arm hooked over the back of the little chair with jaunty familiarity.

'I'm afraid not,' the Doctor told him. 'No.'

Banham gave him a reassuring, confident smile from the other side of his cluttered desk. 'Well I can put your mind at rest, I'm sure.'

'Oh, yes?'

'I have initiated an internal enquiry into the events of last night.' Banham clasped his hands loosely on top of the open files sprawled over the surface of his desk. 'I remain completely confident that there was no breach of security in the gun store, and I am positive we will ultimately uncover the truth of what happened to the unfortunate Private Corey. Indeed, I have the beginnings of a theory already.'

'Really?' The Doctor remained slouched.

'Really. There is nothing to say that Private Corey was killed by one of our weapons. We live here in the midst of a country community where it is not unusual to find guns in common ownership. I fear also that there is considerable ill feeling about our presence here, despite the good work we do. I suspect that none of my patients was responsible for Private Corey's death after all, but perhaps one of the villagers.'

The Doctor watched Banham with a detached curiosity. 'Do you have any basis for this theory?'

'I learned from Nurse Braithwaite that Corey was absent from his room all last night. She instigated her own extensive search for him. We can only assume that he was off the premises. The patients here, particularly those who are well on their way to recovery, often visit the village for a drink. It is quite possible, don't you agree, that Private Corey made such a sojourn last night himself? He may have been killed in the village, perhaps following a drunken argument. His killing may as easily have been an accident.'

'His wound was very precise for an accident,' the Doctor argued.

'Which leads me back to a deliberate act of murder,' Banham announced, pressing himself back in his chair. 'You must admit, Doctor, that antipathy in a village like Hawkswick can run frighteningly deep. They can feel sometimes, because some of these men exhibit no obvious injuries, that they are simply here on a free meal ticket. There is a great deal of ignorance connected with mental illness. There are also a great many people in Hawkswick who have lost loved ones in the fighting. Their resentment at seeing these young men, seemingly fit and well, drinking in their local pub when they should be off in the conflict, well – need I say more?'

'Oh I do understand what you are saying, Dr Banham,' the Doctor conceded, 'but I must also tell you that I have encountered no such discrimination in the acquaintances I have made already in the village. And besides, my enquiries into Private Corey's death are just part of a considerably wider investigation.'

'Ah. The slaughtered livestock. Did you get the chance to check security at the munitions factory in Grimston?'

'I did not.'

'Then might I suggest that you do so? And might I also remind you that a number of the women who reside in Hawkswick work at that factory? *And* that we hold no such explosive materials here, even in the gun store?'

Leaning forward on his seat, the Doctor gave Banham an even look. 'It is not just the slaughtered livestock –'

Laughing out loud, Banham jumped to his feet and stepped over to the window, from where he proceeded to gaze out over the rolling countryside. He spoke without looking back at the Doctor.

'I assume you refer now to the haunting of Hawkswick, Doctor?'

'I do.'

Banham's look conveyed his scorn of the subject.

'You know my thoughts on that matter,' he said simply.

'I do,' the Doctor agreed. 'You have made yourself quite clear. But I still fail to see how an entire village could report such similar sightings over such a long period.'

Banham remained standing as if to attention at the window. For a moment he seemed a statue, like some memorial in the likeness of an important dignitary. Then he lifted his glasses and played with them between his fingers before giving the Doctor a louring look.

'Have you ever come across the notion of mass hysteria, Doctor?'

'I have.'

'Then there is your explanation. We are dealing here with simple country folk. Uneducated. They work with their hands, not their minds. My God! In these parts they still believe in witchcraft and goblins. It comes as no surprise to me that such hysteria has spread in this way. People very often see, Doctor, precisely what they *expect* to see.'

'You are acquainted with Miss Mary Minett, Dr Banham?'

'Ah, yes –' Banham smiled fondly – 'the delightful Miss Minett. I have met her on several occasions. She frequently makes use of our pharmacy.'

'You know her, then?'

'Not intimately.'

'But you would not categorise her as one of your country bumpkins? As the kind of person who might be swept along by a tide of general hysteria?'

'Miss Minett is a highly intelligent and extremely astute young woman.'

'She also has seen one of these dead soldiers.'

Banham shook his head. 'Hysteria can affect anyone, Doctor, however bright they may be. It does not respect breeding or education. It is an indiscriminate and tenacious assailant.'

'I've seen one myself,' the Doctor announced suddenly.

Banham regarded him darkly, as though this assertion represented a direct assault on his argument.

'Last night,' the Doctor informed him. 'At very close quarters.'

'Last night, you say?'

'That's right.'

'There was quite a violent storm last night.'

'Dr Banham, I know what you are going to say. Please don't bother. I know what I saw.'

'It is only a pity you did not see what you saw *before* you were caught up in the village hysteria yourself, Doctor.'

'It is indeed.' The Doctor nodded casually. 'But I believe that even had I done so, you would have attributed it to a retrospective psychosis.'

With a cheerful, expansive gesture of his arms, Banham smiled. 'Very likely.'

'Did I mention the bodies we found in the fields near the village?' the Doctor asked suddenly.

The smile was wiped from Banham's face. 'Bodies?'

The Doctor suddenly took to his feet and marched across to inspect Banham's clock, which sat on the mantel behind the desk. He peered at it with keen interest. The clock possessed an intricately ornate gilt frame in the shape of a climbing rose, and this was set with ceramic figures and a plethora of delicate ceramic flowers.

'This is a Julien le Roi, isn't it?'

'It is,' Banham confirmed edgily. 'You have an interest in horology, Doctor?'

'Passing, yes. I find time and its measurement an intriguing subject.' He peered closely at the detail of the clock. 'Beautiful. Quite remarkable workmanship. Meisson porcelain figures. The flowers are stunning. The detail is beguiling, don't you agree?'

'Bodies, Doctor, I believe you mentioned.'

The Doctor turned back to him and discovered Banham to be a large amorphous mass in front of the window, the glorious sunshine that framed him making it appear that he was nothing but a black shadow with indefinable edges.

'I believe I did,' said the Doctor, manoeuvring himself so that he might see Banham's reaction.

'Two of them. In the fields around the village. I estimated they'd been buried there about six months ago.'

If his composure had crumbled, and it was by no means certain that it had, Banham very quickly recovered it.

'About the time you lost two of your patients, if I'm not mistaken, Dr Banham.'

The smile re-established itself in Banham's features. When he spoke, it was in a cordial manner.

'My dear Doctor, I have never *lost* a patient in my life. I am not dealing here with life-or-death illnesses.'

'You know what I mean,' the Doctor said, keeping his voice even.

'It is true that two men went missing from here in March. However, they turned up again a day later. They were returned to the front very shortly afterwards. It's all in the files if you would like to see them.'

'I'm sure that won't be necessary,' the Doctor said dismissively. 'However, I found it very curious that the bodies should be in uniform.'

Banham fell pensive. He wiped his lips briefly with his fingers. It may or may not have been a nervous gesture. The man seemed to possess immaculate self-control.

'You will find, Doctor, that a large number of the village men served in the army. Some of them returned with quite severe wounds from which they died. They are buried in the local graveyard. Do you think it might be wise to exhume the bodies?'

'That thought had crossed my mind,' the Doctor told him. 'But I'm sure I would find it an extremely difficult and tedious job to get permission to do that.'

'I'm sure you would. The war dead should be left in peace,' said Banham.

'Well that's better than being left in pieces,' the Doctor said.

The joke was in terrible taste, and it didn't go down well with

158

Banham. He abruptly resumed his contemplative gaze out of the window and for a moment the room was silent except for the unusually loud ticking of the clock.

'I'm not a believer in ghosts,' Banham said quietly. 'As I told you before, I am a man of science.'

'There are sciences,' the Doctor reminded him, 'and there are sciences.'

Banham grinned. 'It seems, my dear Doctor, that we are approaching this highly unusual situation from diametrically opposite angles. I fear we will fail to agree on an interpretation of events until I can show you categorically that you are wrong and I am right.'

He stepped over the office to the door and grasped the handle.

'I am sure that this whole situation will make a fascinating paper which we will both read with some amusement in our old age. I will be certain to forward you a copy when it is complete.'

The Doctor took the hint and stood to leave.

'In the meantime, I will be happy to let you know how my internal enquiry is progressing. Once I have established all the facts here, I am quite certain that I will have to broaden my enquiries. If you are staying at the village, I am sure our paths will cross again.'

'Oh, I'm sure they will,' the Doctor agreed, offering his hand for Banham to shake again. He left with a genial smile in his happy-go-lucky face.

As he stepped across the reception room he waved to Clara, who was busy with her interminable filing. She waved back and was puzzled to hear him mumbling to himself contentedly as he went.

'I'm sure they will...'

Having marked the position of Skaggs's body by tying a handkerchief into the overhanging branches, the small party had made their way in a methodical pattern through the trees. It seemed as if they were dragged inevitably by the inescapable gravity of the huge force at the heart of Scarrs Wood.

The first to see the tree was Cromby. Briggs and Mary arrived only a moment later. They stood speechless and appalled, unable to avert their gaze. No one spoke. An eerie silence fell over them.

Cromby shook his head. He'd visited slaughterhouses, and he'd even had the haunting task of putting his own dogs to rest. Lifetime companions. Bullet through the brain. Kindest way. He'd watched animals dying in agonies that he could only guess at. Death was his stock in trade, in many ways. There was generally, though, a balance in Life's equation. Death equals Life. You butcher one life to sustain another, and nature maintains her complex, callous equilibrium.

Over recent months he'd become quite accustomed to finding his own livestock torn to shreds and splattered across his land in a mess of waste. He was a God-fearing man, and his faith had never been shaken by anything he had ever seen. There was, he assured himself, some poetic justice to all this suffering and all this pain.

But the oak tree made him think again. How could God stand by and watch this happen? What was the point of this macabre spectacle? How could you extract any poetic justice at all from a thing so dreadful and pointless?

Briggs had often thought recently that he was near the end of his life. Effie waited for him over the other side. He was ready to go, and sometimes even relished the idea of God's taking him now.

As he gazed into the sightless eyes of the gathered animals in the old oak tree, he thought that at least they had all earned their escape from this torment. They were free now from the agony of living. The daily grind. The moment-to-moment hair-trigger replies to a terrifying world that screamed down at you and never gave you a single minute's rest. At least now they had peace.

In the centre of the tree, turning slowly on yet another length of twine, was Charlie Skaggs's blind-staring face. The jaw had been ripped open by some kind of explosion. The back of the skull was a gaping hole. The pain had been brief, Briggs hoped. But now the relief would last for ever.

Mary could hardly take it in. She had never imagined anything so horrible in all her life. Even after all the things she had seen in recent days, nothing could possibly have prepared her for such a shock as this. She had felt it before, particularly on the way into the centre of the woods, but now she knew for sure without a shadow of a doubt. There was evil at work. An immense evil.

And this was just the beginning.

Chapter Seven

'It has been a singularly harrowing day,' Mary said as she dished the boiled potatoes on to the Doctor's plate beside the portion of roasted chicken.

'I would agree with you there,' the Doctor agreed with her.

'I'm not entirely certain my nerves could stand much more of this sort of assault,' she admitted candidly.

'Oh, Miss Minett, you are an extraordinarily resilient woman,' the Doctor reminded her. 'And in my experience, people generally have a remarkable capacity for coping with adversity, even of this grotesque nature.'

Distributing cabbage and carrots to both plates, Mary returned the pan to the range and sat opposite the Doctor at the little kitchen table.

'You have much experience of adversity of this grotesque nature?' she asked.

'Some,' he told her. 'Do you mind if I get a glass of water?'

'Oh, I am sorry. Let me –'

She left the table and returned a moment later with two glasses and a large jug of water. She placed these strategically on the already cramped table, and lifted the gravy boat above the Doctor's steaming plate.

'Would you like gravy?'

'Just a dash, please.'

'You don't mind if I play mother?'

'Of course not. It's a very long time since I was mothered.'

Mary poured, stopped, and the jug hovered while she watched him questioningly.

'Fine, thank you,' he assured her with a generous smile.

'Do you mind me asking what other experience you have had of such strange adventuring?' she asked conversationally while she poured gravy over her own meal.

'I was once engaged in a rather curious exploit,' the Doctor said, dissecting his largest potato and popping a small piece of it into his mouth. He chewed briefly and continued to speak while he ate, which Mary thought was an endearing habit he had. 'It involved a number of seemingly ordinary people who were able to burn others to death simply by the act of touching them.'

Stopping mid-chew, Mary gazed at him with a mixture of fascination and scepticism.

'They sound like nice friends to have,' she said eventually.

'Very handy at a barbecue.' The Doctor cut a morsel of chicken and popped it in. 'But they could get a bit hot under the collar.'

Mary continued to observe him as he chewed heartily. He was apparently quite serious, and going by the way he took in his stride the situation around Hawkswick, she could well believe that he braved such bizarre encounters every day of his life.

'I don't remember reading about any such thing in the newspapers,' she said to test his reaction.

'It was some time ago now,' he said. 'And besides, things of that nature tend not to get into the newspapers. I very much doubt if you would find any serious reporting of the incidents we are experiencing here.'

Not unless I looked through your pockets, Mary thought. But she said nothing.

'Of course,' he continued while he worked busily at the food on his plate, 'the more frivolous journals might run a story that intimates something strange, but you never get the detail, and the more outrageous aspects never find their way into print. People who tell such stories are often thought quite mad. So the truth often lies buried. Eventually gets forgotten. This chicken is absolutely perfect. Thank you.'

'I'm afraid I have a surfeit of chicken,' Mary admitted. 'William Cromby has a large number of the fowl, and he thinks he owes me a favour or two. I very often find a dead, plucked bird on my doorstep on a morning. I think he believes that I believe they've dropped out of the sky overnight.'

'Stranger things have happened.'

'Oh, don't I know it. Stranger things happen daily at the moment.' She teased a carrot from her plate and paused before putting it into her mouth. 'What do you think was the significance of the tree in Scarrs Wood?'

The Doctor's jaw ground to a halt and he stared for a moment at the carrot on her fork.

'I'm not entirely certain,' he admitted. 'I suspect it's some form of Offering Tree.'

'Offering?'

'Sacrifice. I've heard that such offerings are made on the Black Sabbath or other special occasions. In return for supernatural powers or longevity.'

The carrot hung there for a moment longer. 'I am rather frightened,' Mary admitted suddenly.

The Doctor regarded her with a brooding look. There was no assuagement in his eyes. But there was resolution and a stern determination.

'Don't be afraid,' he said. 'I'll protect you. That's why I'm here.'

'Is it?'

The look in his face didn't change. He said nothing, and she found it impossible to read his thoughts. She remembered her intention to eat the carrot, and placed it carefully into her mouth. She rearranged the contents of her plate and cut another chunk of meat. As she did so she saw a flash image of Charlie Skaggs's staring, bulging eyes. She remembered the torn flesh under his chin as his head turned steadily in the tree. She stopped cutting and looked up at the Doctor. The look on his face had not changed at all, except that now he was staring off into space.

'Are you all right?' she asked.

He focused on her over the table. 'I'm sorry?'

'I said are you all right?'

The Doctor glanced down at his dinner, then back at her, as if he'd forgotten where he was.

'Just a little preoccupied, I'm afraid. I am sorry.'

'Don't apologise,' Mary chided. 'You have a lot on your plate at the moment.'

He looked down again and studied his dinner.

'I mean the murder at the Hall,' she told him.

'Ah. Yes.'

Seeming to bring himself together again, the Doctor continued to eat, though now his face contained a trace of what Mary might have taken for a frown.

'Who do you think did it?' she asked directly.

The Doctor stuffed a large piece of potato into his mouth and his jaw whirled around the bottom half of his face for a moment. 'Well, since there isn't a butler at the Hall these days, I'm rather afraid that it leaves the possibilities fairly open.'

'Do you have a theory?'

'Oh, yes,' the Doctor assured her. 'And so does our mutual friend Dr Banham.'

'He does?'

'He does.'

Infuriatingly, the Doctor continued to eat without another word. Mary watched him do so for a minute or two before she cracked.

'And what might that be?'

'He thinks Private Daniel Corey was murdered by a mad yokel.'

'I beg your pardon.'

'But I think he's just trying to muddy the waters and throw me off the scent. Anything to get me away from the Hall.'

'He seriously thinks one of *us* killed that poor man?'

'One of *them*,' the Doctor corrected. 'I don't think Dr Banham tars you with the same brush as the rest of the village. You don't have the brains of a donkey. You don't have the emotional capacity of a sheep.'

'I can't believe that is how the distinguished Dr Banham sees these people.'

'I'm afraid, when it suits his purposes, he does,' the Doctor confirmed. 'He is quite adamant that Corey was murdered by one of the villagers. He's given me weapon, motive and opportunity. Except that there are facts that don't quite square with his theory.'

'Such as?'

'Dry clothes, for a start. No mud on Corey's boots.'

'I don't follow.'

'Nurse Braithwaite found Private Corey around four to four thirty this morning. When I saw the body, I noticed that the clothing was completely dry. I checked his boots, and there wasn't a sign of mud on them. Dr Banham is keen to prove that he was killed in this village, or at least in the countryside around it. But if that had been the case, and his body didn't turn up again until around four, he would have been caught in the same storm as we were. What time did the rain start?'

Mary shrugged. 'Around two, probably.'

'And the other curious thing is that the body was returned to Corey's room. If he had been killed in the village, there is no way his murderers could know which room to return the body to. And that still leaves the question of *why* he was returned to his room at all.'

'And do you have an answer to that question?'

'Obviously, whoever killed Private Corey *wanted* him to be found,' the Doctor said. 'Otherwise they would have made attempts to hide the body.'

'So if Private Corey was not killed in his bed, it might be useful to find where he *was* killed. There must be clues there.'

'I've already looked,' the Doctor informed her. 'I spent half the day with one of Dr Banham's disorderlies. As far as I can tell, there is only one place I was not able to check.'

'And where might that be?'

'The locked gun store. Dr Banham insists that it is secure at all times and that he is the only one who holds a key.'

A terrible thought struck Mary as her fork hovered over her potatoes. 'That means Dr Banham himself could have murdered Private Corey!'

The Doctor rewarded her with a grim smile. 'I'm very much afraid it does. Except that it is unlikely Dr Banham would have returned Corey's body to his room to be discovered. If Dr Banham wants me away from the Hall and investigating the village, surely he would have dumped the body in the fields.'

'So it couldn't have been Dr Banham then.'

'Maybe. Maybe not.'

'Oh, this is all very confusing.'

'One thing is clear to me. Dr Banham is clutching at straws. He is not normally a man to flounder in this way, I am sure. He is panicking and he most certainly has something to hide. There is a skeleton of some very sinister nature in his cupboard.'

'So you need evidence,' Mary said.

'I do,' the Doctor agreed.

'But Dr Banham is a very astute man,' she said.

'He is,' he agreed.

'And obtaining that evidence will not be easy,' she told him.

'It will not,' he concurred.

They sat and ate. Mary mulled over the idea that the highly principled Dr Banham might not be as immaculate as she had thought. She had taken away with her a very strong impression of a good man after she met him. His staff had nothing but praise for him. He worked for the benefit of his patients, and toiled long hard hours in their service. Could it really be that he was also a murderer? Surely it was much more likely that Corey's death was in some way connected to all the supernatural occurrences that had plagued the village. After finding poor Skaggs's head in that tree, Mary could believe those responsible were capable of any amount of evil, torture and carnage.

She thought about the two dead soldiers uncovered in Skews Bank Field. They could only be the two men who went missing last March. Which meant that Dr Banham may well have lied about their return to France. Which would implicate him in their murder. And if he was somehow involved in *their* killing, he might also be somehow involved in the murder of Corey.

'One thing is certain,' the Doctor announced, demolishing the last piece of chicken on his plate. 'Corey's dry clothes do place the murder firmly at the Hall.' He dabbed his lips with a napkin. 'Which is why I'm going back there tonight under cover of darkness.'

Mary opened her mouth to speak, but the Doctor cut her off before a word could emerge.

'Alone.'

Motion. Dark. Shadow. Man. Hun. Golem. Who goes there?

Corporal Davies's mind was a crazy-fractured domain of instantaneous ideas. Here. There. Gone. Concepts born and dead in the blinking of an eye. Sometimes… Merciful relief from the shattered, pot-holed no-man's-land that was his understanding of the world.

Sometimes…

The night sky was clear black, cloudless and pricked with crystal starlight. After the storm of last night, which made excellent cover for any enemy manoeuvres, Corporal Davies felt confident that he could locate and destroy the enemy tonight. They were coming in on a covert assault. Davies had received the rumours. The enemy was to take the Hall. New base of ops. Tactical importance. Orders come down from top brass. Hold your positions at all cost. All cost. To the last man. Last man. Vital.

Eyes peeled. Here he comes. Hun filth. Golem filth. Here. Now. Moving in. Stealth of a fox. Flash of gunmetal in the dark. Scuffle of movement. How many? One?

Positions. All cost. Davies dug his heels in. Prepared the Enfield. Got the man in his sights. Looked for others. Saw no one. Mad bastard. Lone assault. Easy pickings. Davies had him in his sights as the man moved through the shadow towards the Hall. Clear shot. Bang. Dead. Easy.

Banham's office contained a dim illumination. It was now nearly midnight, but the Doctor wasn't surprised that the man was still working. He had a mighty reputation for dedication to duty. He worked while others slept. Or, at least, he did *something* while others slept. Managing to position himself in the buddleia that lined the terrace outside Banham's office, the Doctor got close enough to see that there was a crack in the curtains. Unfortunately, it was high up, well above eye level, and he'd have to drag something to stand on to see in. Too dangerous, he decided. And besides, it wasn't essential to know where Banham was, just to know where he wasn't.

The Doctor detached himself from the shrubs and made his way silently down the steps. In the shadow at the bottom, on the edge of the lawn, he stopped and checked his wake. There were lights all over the house. Windows with life behind them. This was a place that didn't subscribe to the normal sleep patterns of the rest of the world. However, the Doctor was quickly satisfied that nobody had noticed his progress.

Engulfed in black shadow, he continued round to the east wing. He would have preferred more cover, more movement in the background, more noise. A repeat performance of last night's storm would have been perfect. But he was lumbered with a clear summer sky and a bright moon overhead. And if he positioned himself wrongly, he would cast shadows that might be noticed.

A window opened nearby with a croak of infrequently used hinges. The small cry insinuated itself on the air and the Doctor dropped instantly. The ground was dry and smelled of moss and grass. Sharp twigs pressed into the palms of his hands as he waited in silence until he was certain that he hadn't been discovered. A new silence descended, and he gazed around at the black cover he had found. It was a shrub with large, broad leaves but he couldn't put a name to it in the dark. It made excellent cover, the branches falling around him to very nearly ground level at their tips. He could just see out from this position, and he was certain nobody had seen him.

When he made his move to emerge, he felt the cold steel muzzle against the back of his neck. A voice warned quietly, menacingly, in his ear.

'One move and you're dead.'

Cromby slept on a tightrope these days, ever aware of the restlessness of his animals. The horses refused to settle. The chickens had stopped laying. Even the dogs were nervous and disturbingly quiet. There was a tension on the farm. Something he couldn't put his finger on. But it was there on the edge of his consciousness. As he'd sensed the oncoming storm last night, he felt an oncoming *something* tonight. Not storm. But like storm.

'What's up, love?' Iris asked.

Cromby was surprised that she was still awake. They'd been in bed an hour and she normally slept like a log.

'Nothin',' Cromby told her.

'Why aren't you asleep, then?'

'Not tired.'

'Why?'

'I think I'll just go an' check on the 'orses.'

'Aye,' she said.

He clambered out of bed and pushed his legs into his trousers before padding to the door.

'Don't worry,' he said to the dark bed. 'Get some sleep.'

Iris didn't answer.

Stoking up the fire despite the warmth of the night, Mary Minett watched the glowing flames lick the coals in the grate. She loved the smell of the fire. It whispered of childhood, and innocent long-gone days. She would make up the fire with her brother – a shared task that left them both contentedly misted with coal dust. David would do the heavy share, lugging in the coal scuttle while she twisted the old newspapers into tight knots and arranged them in the grate layered with kindling wood. David tipped on the bricks of coal and with great ceremony he would strike up the lucifer and touch the exposed edges of the paper. Together they would hunch in front of the fire while they watched the flames take hold, and it was a fascination that had remained with Mary all her life.

The fire was full of magic. The swelling flames suggested phantoms and fairies, blues and yellows and strange smoky colours that appeared and vanished like exotic dancers. It was a daily theatre visit to their young imaginations, and now when she watched the same show she felt that David was there at her side.

Mary looked. Nobody there. But she felt his presence nevertheless, and she felt quite certain that he was never far away.

Heaving a sigh, Mary rose to her feet and opened the dresser to find the bottle of port she'd been saving for her father's next visit. It was his favourite drink at home, although she knew he feigned a taste for brandy when he socialised in the city. She took the bottle to the little occasional table by the rocking chair. Then she returned to the dresser for a glass and David's watch.

The room was dark except for the glow from the fire. There

were deep shadows in the corners that could have been full of anything. Mary sat in the rocking chair while she wound the watch. Then she poured a small amount of port into the glass and took a sip. The warmth of the drink spread through her like a burning. She had been six when her father gave her her first taste of port. It was only a touch of the tongue, but it was enough to send frantic flames cavorting through her. The sensation had been beguiling. She remembered his face breaking into a broad smile when she looked at him in wonder. But he hadn't let her have any more. One sip was enough, he'd said, at such a tender age. Any more and her liver would rot clean away in the night.

The image of her putrefying liver curbed her taste for the firewater, but it had never managed to quash completely the enticing seduction of her father's bottle of port.

The fire cracked and spooked. The room felt cosy and warm. Mary rocked gently and opened the cover of the watch. The small tinkling tune, which reminded her of an unnameable Mozart melody, played its course of twenty-nine notes before she closed the lid again. The watch felt comfortable in the palm of her hand, such a beautiful piece of workmanship. Her father had come across it on his travels in Switzerland. It dated back about a hundred years and nothing like it was made any more. It was a rare thing to own. Being mesmerised by it when her father came back, Mary had purchased the watch from him. And for David's twenty-first birthday, she'd presented it to her brother. He'd kept it on him every minute of every day until the day he left for France. Then he'd given it to her for safekeeping until his return.

And then he had never returned.

Mary sipped the port and opened the watch. The tune played again, and this time she found it impossible to hold back the tears.

The Doctor lay prostrate, hands clamped to the back of his neck under orders from his captor, face scratched by the fallen twigs and dried leaves that covered the ground, the gun's muzzle pressed to his head. His captor pressed his knee into the small of the Doctor's back, while he rummaged systematically through the Doctor's pockets.

'I'm on your side, you know,' the Doctor said calmly.

'Shut up,' his captor snapped. The muzzle jerked hard against the Doctor's skull.

The rifling through coat pockets continued until his captor seemed resigned to finding nothing.

'Where are your papers?'

'I'm afraid I don't have any. I'm a special agent. I'm not allowed to carry ID.'

'Liar!'

The muzzle moved, only to return to the middle of Doctor's back.

'Now. I'm going to tell you to get up in a minute. Then I want this jacket off. One funny move and you're dead! Understand?'

'Loud and clear,' the Doctor muttered in resignation.

There was the scuffling of his captor rising, and the Doctor clambered to his feet, very careful to leave his hands in clear view as far as he could. When he turned, he found a young British corporal standing in the moonlight with a suspicious sneer fixed on his face. The man was watching him with wild eyes, and he kept the Doctor covered with a brass-tipped cane that he brandished as if it were a rifle.

The Hun spy stood and raised his hands. Davies jerked the Enfield menacingly and there was fear in the Hun's eyes.

'Now,' Davies snarled, 'jacket off. Drop it there, on the ground. And no funny moves.'

The spy did as he was told and Davies pulled the jacket towards him with the toe of his boot. The Hun was apparently unarmed, but Davies was not so stupid as to trust appearances. They were sneaky bastards, the lot of them.

'Turn around,' Davies ordered. 'And keep your hands well up so I can see them.'

The Hun did as he was told and Davies was satisfied to see no visible bulge of any secreted weapons. The spy wore no holster. Keeping the Enfield cocked, Davies lifted the jacket and checked the inside pockets. Now the spy was speaking.

'If you look in my inside pocket, you'll find a letter signed by Lloyd George himself.'

Davies checked, at first unable to feel anything. Then he felt the papers and lifted them out. The spy made a move to turn but Davies was ready for him.

'I said *don't move*!'

The spy stopped abruptly mid-turn, jerking his hands higher into the air, but now he was able to observe Davies as he checked the letter of authority. It was a small document, folded many times, but sure enough it was legit. As Davies read the letter, outlining the spy's instructions and authority, he lowered his Enfield and the spy lowered his arms.

'I'm sorry, sir,' Davies apologised. 'You can't be too careful.'

He handed the man his jacket back and the papers.

'Don't worry about it,' the man said. 'You did a damn good job, soldier.'

'Thank you, sir.'

'What's your name, Corporal?'

'Davies, sir. L.P. Davies, Manchester Regiment, Twenty-Fourth Division, sir.'

'I'll put in a good word with your captain. It's a relief to think we've got such enthusiastic men watching our backs.' He offered his hand and Davies shook it uncertainly. 'I'm working under codename "the Doctor". Pleased to meet you, Corporal Davies.'

* * *

Sometimes…

Davies tore open his cigarette packet and offered one to the German NCO. The German took it and placed the cig between his lips, automatically feeling for matches before remembering where he was. Davies struck up and gave the man a light, and together they took a good long drag.

The two men stood face to face, each with an arm thrust into a pocket while the other arm managed the cigarette. Between them was a chain-link fence, seven feet tall, topped with barbed wire, and it was the German who was on the wrong side of it. Davies studied the other man's muddy face with its four days of stubble. If it wasn't for the uniform he might be taken for a Brit, or a Frog. When it came down to it, from any kind of distance you couldn't bloody well tell who were your friends and who was the enemy. Even when you got up close it was hard to tell. Veidt was the same height as Davies, same weight, give or take a pound or two, same colour hair, same bloody hair cut! Take off their uniforms and you probably couldn't tell them apart, until they opened their mouths to speak, that is.

They had first struck up a conversation four days ago, when the German prisoners were marched in and it turned out that Veidt was the only one with a smattering of English. Having a smattering of German, Davies was volunteered to question him about the German plans. He'd done so with a gun in his hand, and the gun was waved menacingly in front of Veidt's face throughout the 'interview'. They'd got nothing new or useful out of him and finally the order came through to pack him in with the others until the top brass could decide what to do with them.

The next night Davies was posted on guard duty. There were supposed to be three of them, but the other two were called off on special fatigues because some poncy lieutenant was making a surprise visit. Veidt and Davies got talking again, only this time there was no gun in evidence, and they learned that they were very alike in many ways. Veidt was an obergerfrieter, *the German equivalent of a corporal. Besides their physical similarity, they were both the same age, both from the same background, both doing the same job before they were called up, both married and both with kids the same age. Davies's son was three days older than Veidt's.*

Davies and Veidt marvelled at the divine accident that had made these mirror images face one another through this chain-link fence in this insane hell.

Veidt told him about his life back home, about the oppressive home front, about the constant drive at the expense of everything else to feed this war effort, about the severe shortages of food, about the talk of surrender, about the despondency of the German nation. Of course, it wasn't always like that. This had been a popular war in the early days. There was rejoicing in the streets. The Kaiser's image plastered everywhere. Nationalist songs sung into the night.

On the third night after the prisoners were captured, Davies was posted on lookout and he didn't see Veidt at all. On the fourth night, they continued their exploration of their not-so-different cultures and their not-so-different views.

'I remember going home on leave at Easter 1915,' Veidt mused through their cloud of intermingled cigarette smoke. 'Then there was still much good feeling about the war. Me and Elsa went to the, hmm, cinema, you say. We saw this film called Der Golem. *So frightening. I shit my pants. Really. This giant clay man. At first he is just a… statue. Then he is bring alive. He is a giant thing made out of clay yet he walks. Terrifying. I ask myself, Why do we make such stories when we have so much real horror in the world? Why do we need clay men when we have real men covered in mud and they too are the walking dead?'*

Davies shook his head. 'I took Phyllis to see Charlie Chaplin,' he said. 'Shoulder Arms. This is an American film about the* trenches. And it is a comedy. I think that's about as scary as your clay-monster film, don't you?'

'They do not understand the reality of this war,' Veidt said in reflective mood. 'I think it will be a long time after it ends before people realise the real cost and the real horror of this war. I think we are living through a nightmare. I think the world does not realise.'

'I think you're bloody right,' Davies agreed.

There was the sound of men approaching though the mud, and Davies turned to see three uniforms only a few yards away. He shot Veidt a harsh look, and the German dropped his cigarette and trod it into the mud.

'What's this?' asked one of the approaching men. 'Consorting with the filth?'

Davies's heart sank when he realised it was Frank Watson and his pair of gun-happy stooges.

'Hiya, Frank,' he said, trying to keep his voice light.

But Frank Watson wasn't in the mood for light tonight. He approached Davies with a dark scowl on his muddy face.

'Some little bird tells me you been fraternisin' with the murderin' Hun bastards.'

Davies shook his head. 'Well some little bird got his wires crossed, then, didn't he?'

Watson was a wide man, with shoulders as broad as barn doors and a mean-as-they-come sneer installed permanently in his features. He was one of the very few men that Davies knew who seemed to actually enjoy being here in the front line.

'Wouldn't say that,' Watson said with a trace of humour. 'Looks like we caught you red-handed. What you two up to, then, eh?'

'Just talking,' Davies said.

'Just talkin'? No such thing as just bloody talkin' to these filthy swine.' Watson drew up close and grasped Davies's lapel. 'What you doin'? Plannin' a break-out with your mate here? Eh? Slip

177

us a few Deutschmarks and I'll see what I can do? Is that it?'

'Don't be such a blockhead, Watson,' said Davies.

Watson took offence at this. He swung Davies round by the collar and threw him in the mud. The stooges laughed.

Davies scrambled to his feet and pointed furiously at Watson. 'You're an ass, Watson. You know? A complete and utter –'

'Point that finger at me, Davies, and I'll soddin' well snap it off.'

Another grumble of merriment. Davies regarded Watson with fire in his eyes.

'What the hell's wrong with you, you fat stupid bastard? Whose side do you think I'm on?'

'I was just wonderin' that,' Watson growled, making a move for Davies while the other two blocked any chance Davies might have had of a retreat.

'Hey,' Veidt yelled suddenly, clinging to the fence, 'he was just talking. That's all.'

Watson turned abruptly. 'Who the hell asked you, Fritz?'

Suddenly there was an Enfield raised and Veidt lifted his arms and stepped back from the fence, a shocked look on his shadowy face. Watson advanced, rifle rock-steady in his arms. There had been a steady background murmur in the compound, but instantly there was silence. As Watson advanced, Veidt retreated step for step.

'For God's sake, Watson,' Davies said.

But Watson took no notice. He raised the rifle and took aim. There was a crack and Veidt dropped to the ground with a scream. He was clutching at his right knee and floundering in the mud.

'Don't walk away from me,' Watson yelled.

Davies ran to grasp his arm, but Watson sensed his approach and Davies collapsed back with the Enfield butt in his face. For a moment he was shocked and disorientated, then he heard another blast from the rifle and Veidt cried out again. When

Davies scrambled to his feet he saw Veidt slumped in a pool of blood, both legs smashed from under him by the close-range fire. The other prisoners in the compound had moved to the back of the fenced area like silent sheep. They all looked on with terror written clear in their pale faces. No language barrier.

'You evil bastard,' Veidt cried. He tried to support himself on his arms but fell over to one side in a paroxysm of agony. 'You evil English animal.'

Watson took careful aim and pumped another single bullet between Veidt's eyes. The angry yelling cut abruptly and there was complete silence.

Until Davies launched himself like a wild thing at Watson's back. He tore at the big man's face with his nails, pressing his fingers into Watson's eyes, feeling them give like soft jelly under the pressure. Watson screamed out loud and Davies was flung to the mud. The other two swept forward to grab his arms but he was like a thing possessed, a desperate cornered beast, and they could do nothing to hold him. He scooped up Watson's rifle and levelled it at the stooges. They raised their hands, waving slowly and watching him with wide eyes. He took aim at the first one and as he was about to pull the trigger, managed to stop himself. Grasping the gun by the barrel, he proceeded to pummel Watson with it about the head. Watson cried out in confusion and pain and stumbled about in the mud. The other two watched in frozen panic.

Davies battered the big man for all he was worth. Every ounce of hatred he possessed he poured into his assault on the man's head, until Watson lay in a pool of his own blood, still grasping at his face with jittery motions of his arms. His legs thrust about in the mud and his whole body jerked in wild spasms.

Falling to his knees, Davies watched him writhing, and in his head the only thing he could see was his son. Same age as Veidt's. His son's angelic, round face gazing at him out of the *blazing storm. He saw his boy running towards him, arms outstretched, joy in his eyes, as Davies stepped off the train. Their bodies slapped together and he swept him up and hugged him so fiercely that he feared he would burst his soft little body. And he imagined what he would feel like at the moment of his death, knowing he would never see his little boy again. Knowing that somebody had taken that reunion from him. He could imagine the last spark of life in his body pulsing with hatred at the world. He could imagine lying in the mud of France, three hundred miles from home, and his body rotting but his hatred as strong as ever beyond the grave.*

Hatred. Beyond the grave. The last spark of life. The mud of France.

They came through the fields at the back of the house, closing in across open country, finally reaching the hedge of hawthorn and holly that separated the tended garden from the open lands beyond. Five dark shapes, crouching low, scurrying along the edge of nature's own barbed-wire defence. They found a breach and slipped through, one keeping watch while the others advanced in fan formation.

The garden had been turned over to self-sufficiency, flower beds stocked with cabbage and carrots. A narrow winding path of end-on-end bricks meandered through the miniature forest of witch hazel, weeping birch and spindly acer, and the shapes progressed along it, snaking down the garden towards the house in fluid, silent motion.

There were outer buildings near the back corner of the main house, and the shapes used them as cover. One of the dark things wore three stripes. It raised its hand and the others waited for the signal.

The house was in gloom except for one room whose window contained the suggestion of a light inside. The three-striped corpse crept across to listen under the window. The sounds inside were almost nonexistent. Crackle of fire. No movement. No voices. Then the tinkling tune of a tiny music box. The thing listened, turning its ragged ear to the window, and the sound might have stirred memories if the soggy grey stuff in its skull had contained any.

'I'm on a mission,' the Doctor confided as he and Davies crouched together in the shadow. 'One of our men was murdered here last night.'

'Private Corey,' Davies said.

'You know about it?'

'I heard. Yes. Murdered in his bed. Hun bastards.'

The Doctor regarded the man's shining mad eyes. Davies was on edge, fingering the short cane as if it were a rifle. His eyes were everywhere, as, no doubt, was his poor shattered mind.

'But he wasn't murdered in his bed,' Davies said suddenly.

'I'm sorry?'

Davies stared at him. 'Cover-up. I heard the shot. Saw the mess. The body was taken away.'

'You know where he was killed?'

'Yes.'

'Can you show me?'

Davies shook his head, and continued to shake it enthusiastically while he spoke. 'Can't. Can't. Too dangerous. They're walking tonight. Walking. They always walk at night.'

'Walking?' the Doctor said. 'Who's walking?'

'The Golem.'

'Golem,' the Doctor echoed. 'That's very interesting.'

'Walk at night. Round the house. Statues walking. Alive. At night.'

'You've seen these Golem?'

The shaking of the head was replaced by a frantic nodding. 'Seen them. Walking. Night. Statues. Big things. Alive.'

He grasped the Doctor's sleeve and spoke calmly and earnestly.

'They're made of clay. Giant deformed things. But they walk at night.'

Cromby found the door to the stables open again. This time the rock had been positioned neatly to one side, obviously not moved there by the door blowing in any wind. He entered the stable and peered into the thick black shadow. The horses beat their hooves and tugged their tethers, and Cromby sensed something not right in the air. He stood and listened, but the place was silent. Propping his shotgun by the door, he stepped into the dark and tended the horses, doing his best to soothe their fraught nerves, but they watched him fearfully out of manic brown eyes.

No amount of soothing and cajoling was going to work. They were terrified. And Cromby was going to get to the bottom of this once and for all. He marched down the barn and clambered up the steps into the loft above. Grasping the pitchfork in both hands, he stepped into the dark and listened. Silence. But now he felt that he was being watched. He thrust the fork into the nearest bail of straw, deep as he could. Then again. And again. Working his way down the entire length of the hayloft, he found nothing.

It *had* to be here! *Had* to be!

At the hatch he stood and listened, but again found only silence. Dropping the fork in disgust, Cromby lowered himself back down to the stables and, as his feet foraged for the ground, he felt the cold steel muzzle of a rifle against his ear.

The rifle was cocked and Cromby froze.

After much inveigling, the Doctor was able to coax Davies into leading the way to where Corey was murdered. Davies took him round the side of the house, by the east wing, and they crept in silence to the basement door. Davies glared back nervously over the expanse of gravel towards the therapy block.

'The Golem,' he muttered, more to himself than the Doctor.

The Doctor laid a hand on his shoulder. 'Nobody there.'

'The Golem. In there.'

The Doctor grabbed both shoulders and turned Davies to face him squarely.

'You mean the clay men? The figures Dr Banham uses in his therapy?'

'They walk. At night.'

'And where do they go?'

Davies glanced at the door to the basement, over the Doctor's shoulder. 'In there.'

'What do they do in there?'

'Go in. And don't come out.'

Davies was afire, eyes all over the place.

'Alive. They're alive.'

He made a move to run but the Doctor held him tight and grasped his jaw with one hand. He forced Davies to look into his eyes, and spoke reassuringly.

'All right, Corporal Davies. They're not here now. You're going to show me where Private Corey was shot. All right? There's nobody here. No Golem. Just you and me.'

Finally Davies settled down and they moved together into the jet-black of the basement. From the pockets that Davies could have sworn were empty when he searched them, the Doctor produced a bicycle lamp, which he used to light the way. They had got about halfway down the corridor when Davies stopped him outside the gun store.

'What is it?' the Doctor asked.

'This is the place.'

'Here?'

'Yes.'

'I checked here earlier.' The Doctor shook his head, panning the torchlight round to the door.

Davies grasped the torch and cast the pool of white illumination over the opposite wall, then seemed aghast at what he saw. The wall was stained with damp patches, and pitted with damage from years of being accidentally bumped. The plaster was crumbling and chunks of it had fallen away to leave craters.

'The blood,' he said. 'It was there. Everywhere. Splattered.'

The Doctor found crazed eyes peering at him in bewilderment.

'There was a bullet hole,' Davies assured him.

The Doctor took the torch and inspected the wall.

'Are you sure it was here?'

'Here. Yes.' Davies shook his head. 'It's gone.'

Running his fingers over the cold, rough surface to see if had been repaired, the Doctor gave Davies a shrug. If there had been blood and a bullet hole, they were certainly not there now. And you might clean blood and fill a hole, but you certainly wouldn't be able to age the plaster in this way without waiting about forty years or so, at a rough guess.

Davies was insistent. He felt the wall himself.

'There,' he said. '*There!*'

When he turned to the Doctor again, there was pain and confusion in his face.

Cromby lowered himself slowly off the bottom rung of the ladder, careful to leave his hands high. He turned to look at his captor, and was horrified at what he saw. A single eye gazed at him out of a face pitted with holes and shrapnel damage. There were still small chunks of metal sticking out of the side of the thing's head. The second eye, on the side that was the more ravaged, was an empty socket. Remnants of facial tissue remained around the mouth, but when the thing smiled Cromby watched in horror as some bits actually fell off on to the floor. He was stunned by the apparition in front of him, but not so stunned as to stand there and let the thing shoot him in the head.

Lashing out, Cromby sent the gun hurtling through the air and it rattled to the floor in the last bay. The creature seemed momentarily dazed, and this was just the chance Cromby needed to send a fist into the thing's face that contained all the punch Cromby's giant frame could muster. The corpse hit the back wall and recoiled to the ladder. It sprawled to the floor in a slow sinking motion that left bits of skin hanging off the rungs.

Towering over the disgusting thing, Cromby became aware of the stench that came off it. Like the compost bin on a hot summer's day. The tang of stuff long decayed. The thing looked like a wind-battered scarecrow, as if someone with a sick sense of humour had made one in the shape of a Tommy. It lay slumped and lifeless at his feet. The head lolled and the single eye gazed sightlessly into space.

Cromby bent to inspect the wrecked remains, but there were hands at his throat. As he was launched through the air to land in a crumpled heap in the corner, the thought passed through Cromby's startled brain that it was easy for a thing already dead to play dead.

The wind gushed out of Cromby's chest in a sickening blast and he felt the bone of his shoulder dislodge before he recognised the crack and felt the intense pain that followed. Gritting his teeth, he tried to clamber to his feet, but the corpse had already retrieved its gun and now it stood in front of him and took careful aim.

Through the mist of red-hot pain, Cromby saw the single gleaming eye, then the dark hole in the end of the thing's poised rifle. The firing pin cocked with a distinctive click, and the explosion filled the stables and made the horses slam and puff like steam engines.

The sergeant corpse outside Mary Minett's window raised its hand to give the order for attack. But the hand remained suspended in the air as the thing lifted its head, as if listening to some silent signal. With a startled swing of its head that sent small droplets of liquid glinting though the air, it motioned suddenly to the others to retreat. Without a word they skulked back up the path and vanished into the dark.

Cromby gazed in amazement at the empty space where the dead man had stood only a second before. There was the repeated thud of body parts hitting the ground and Cromby was spattered with cold visceral liquid. Still squirming in agony from his dislocated shoulder, he gaped about, trying to make sense of what was happening.

Then he saw Iris in the doorway, shotgun at her shoulder, a grim look in her tired, flabby, oh-so-pretty face. With a giant sigh of relief, Cromby collapsed back against the wall.

Under the light from his torch, the Doctor knelt and tried to peer through the keyhole into the locked gun store. But all he could see was darkness. Davies watched as the Doctor patted his jacket in a methodical search, and finally reached into the same pocket as he'd retrieved the torch from earlier. He brought out a large key and tried it in the lock. It rewarded him with a very satisfyingly loud click.

Then there was the clatter of movement down the corridor. Davies turned to sprint for the door, but there was a massive lumbering shape advancing at him though the dark. The corridor was filled with ferocious motion, the sounds of boots clattering, the slamming of doors, the creaking of distant steps.

In blind panic, Davies pelted down the corridor but after a moment of confused pandemonium, he was brought to his knees in the black shadow.

The Doctor remained on one knee, swinging the torchlight to bear on their discoverers. He grinned up at the shadowy shapes that loomed over him.

'Good evening, Dr Banham,' he said, rising to his feet. 'And the voluble Mr McGuff. What a pleasant surprise.'

Chapter Eight

The Doctor was shown into Banham's office without ceremony. Banham swept over to his desk, his face full of ire. He seemed on the brink of losing his composure, but he gritted his teeth and just about managed to keep himself under control. The desk became a no-man's-land between them, and they faced one another like armies across the battlefield, their uneasy truce a fragile, brittle agreement.

'Do you mind telling me the purpose of this intrusion?' Banham asked tightly.

The Doctor returned his hot stare with a cool fury. 'As you are fully aware, I am in the middle of a murder investigation. I was acting on evidence that Private Corey was killed here at the Hall. Despite your insistence that that would not be possible, I have an eyewitness statement that Corey was murdered in your basement. Immediately outside your gun store, to be precise.'

Banham clenched his fists and leaned to dominate the airspace over the desk. 'And who might this eyewitness be?'

'Corporal L.P. Davies.'

'Corporal Davies!' Banham said in obvious delight. 'Our esteemed Corporal Lionel Davies is not the most trustworthy of sources, I might tell you.'

'He was quite certain about what he had heard and seen.'

'The man's as mad as a hatter,' Banham said dismissively. 'And so, I fear, are you, Doctor.'

'Mad as a hatter. That's your professional diagnosis, is it?'

'Corporal Davies suffers from a complete neuropathological breakdown. He has a functional psychosis that can manifest itself in delusions, hallucinations, serious defects in judgement and, at times, a complete inability to objectively evaluate reality. Now, this is becoming exceedingly tiresome, Doctor. Wherever I turn, you are there under my feet. I have important and, might I remind you, well-respected work to do here. I really think these poor men deserve some peace and quiet. I would request formally that you leave these premises and not return.'

Shaking his head resolutely, the Doctor said, 'I have a murder enquiry to conclude.'

'Not here!'

'Yes, here.'

'As you are aware, I am in the process of carrying out my own enquiry. When it is complete, I will be happy to liaise with you and your department with my findings.'

'This is *my* enquiry,' the Doctor insisted evenly. 'I will do whatever I think necessary to draw it to a satisfactory conclusion.'

Banham erupted, arms sweeping. 'You are exceeding your authority, Doctor.' His face was red and his dark eyes seethed. 'This is a psychiatric hospital for our war wounded. You are a damnable nuisance. Sneaking about in the middle of the night. Encouraging one of our more seriously disturbed patients to break into the locked gun store. I cannot believe you would be so reckless and foolhardy. Now, if you do not leave this instant, I will ring your superiors and lodge a formal complaint. Do I make myself clear?'

The Doctor fell quiet. He gazed at his shoes for a moment before looking Banham in the eye again.

'Oh, yes,' he said. 'You make yourself very clear indeed.'

He retreated to the door but hesitated before he left, watching Banham with a brooding look. The look evaporated instantly and a transient smile flashed through his face.

'Thank you, Dr Banham,' he said mildly, before the door sliced him from view.

Banham glared at the closed door, fists still clenched on the desk. For a very long time, he didn't move a muscle. Then he gathered himself together and stepped over to the mirror. He wasn't surprised to find a haggard face reflected back. A face lined as if with a hundred years of life and pain. He rubbed his eyes, and when he looked again, the face was back to normal.

While she sat in the rocking chair beside the fire, her father's port and her brother's watch clasped one in each hand, something significant struck Mary Minett. She had had only two men in her life. Father. Brother. They were both equally important to her. Other men had courted an interest over the years. More than she cared to remember. But not one of them could hold a candle to her father or brother.

Her father was a successful tycoon, who had built an empire from nothing but a driving desire for success. He was a man of very many strengths and immense complexity. A powerful man, yet a man who harboured for Mary a great tenderness. He possessed a comforting reassurance that all was right with the world, whatever adversity they might face.

As they grew up together, she recognised the same traits in her brother. He could be pig-headed at times, but he had the capacity to care in more measure than she had ever met in any other man.

In any search she might conduct for a partner, she suffered a double handicap. First, the towering examples set by her father and brother, and, second, this affliction of being able to detect shallowness and lack of sincerity in others. Given the two combined, it was no wonder to Mary that she had remained unmarried.

The back door opened and closed again quietly.

She had met in her life only one man whom she felt she might trust to treat her with honesty, humour and respect. And she'd met him only yesterday. The curse that enabled her to detect shallowness had ironically turned out to be an equal curse when it came to identifying the vast complexities that made up the Doctor, a man who seemed, despite these complexities, uniquely oblivious to the idea of romance of any variety.

Someone stepped across the kitchen without turning on the light.

People to Mary Minett were abstract art, made up of surface pigments and layers of what she might only describe as 'further colour'. Some had few layers, others many. Some had pale watercolours that reminded Mary of spring mornings; others had dark and violent oils beyond the surface. The Doctor seemed to contain all of these at one time. Far too many colours, hues and textures to grasp. Reassuring, frightening, contradictory. But also, oddly, distanced. He seemed capable of perhaps hiding some of the colour she knew was there inside him. And she had never in her life encountered that before. Above all else, he was a mystery.

Someone hesitated behind the kitchen door, removing a jacket, she suspected, and hanging it on the hook there.

Perhaps there was something of the dangerous maverick that attracted her. The books she had read were full of young women attracted to this kind of man. The Doctor was at once Heathcliff and Rochester and a dozen others rolled into one. Men with secrets. Men with dark corners. Men with a power of some inexpressible kind.

The door into the kitchen opened and a shadow entered the room in silence. It stopped dead in its tracks when it detected Mary there by the fire.

'Not tired?' the Doctor asked.

'I am exceedingly tired,' she admitted.

'I do hope that you have not waited up for me,' he said.

'I have been thinking,' Mary told him. 'It is a recreation that I have insufficient time to indulge recently, but one which I needed to exercise tonight.'

He came over and hunched in front of the fire, rubbing his hands.

'Is it turning cold again?' she asked.

'Not uncomfortably so,' he said. 'There's just something special about a real fire, don't you think?'

'What a curious thing to say.'

He smiled into the hearth. 'I must apologise for speaking curious things,' he said. 'They seem to just pop out of me sometimes. I really don't know where they come from.'

He noticed the bottle of port on the table beside Mary and lifted it in front of the fire, checking the level of the liquid inside.

'I do hope this was not full when you started.'

'I'm very much afraid that it was.'

'Oh.'

'As you say, oh, indeed.'

The Doctor unhunched and sat on the sofa. Mary observed the fireglow playing in the contours of his face and she watched his eyes full of darkness and magic. When he realised she was watching him, he gave her a pleasant, slightly abashed smile. It might be the smile of a little boy who had suddenly realised he was the object of some young girl's attentions. It might be a smile of one not equipped to deal with such adult concepts. Or it might not. With the Doctor, it was hard to tell.

'Did you have a fruitful night?' she asked dreamily.

'I had a frightful night,' the Doctor confessed. 'And ultimately managed to get myself kicked off the premises for good.'

Mary giggled.

'What?'

'You can be a most amusing man,' she told him.

'I suppose I can.' The Doctor smiled, then switched mood abruptly and became reflective. 'Penny for them?'

'Sorry?'

'You said you had spent the night thinking,' the Doctor reminded her.

'I was thinking about the haunting of Hawkswick village,' she told him. 'Amongst other things.'

'Oh, yes?'

'And I could not for the life of me work out why we would be the centre of any supernatural activity. To my knowledge, Hawkswick has no history whatsoever of any such torment.'

'I was thinking along the same lines.' the Doctor said. 'Why here? Why now?'

'War wounded lie in our churchyard,' Mary said. 'Perhaps they have unfinished business.'

'I checked how many recently returned soldiers you have in your graveyard,' the Doctor said. 'And there are three. Charlie Skaggs saw *six* corpse soldiers attack the station house last night. If this supernatural business were connected in some way to your village dead, you would have thought there would have been three, not six.'

'There were also the two poor dead men we found in Skews Bank Field,' Mary reminded him.

'Five in total,' the Doctor calculated.

'Plus poor Private Corey.'

'Six!' the Doctor said triumphantly.

'Six tortured souls returned from the grave,' Mary moaned gloomily.

'I still don't think that's the answer,' mused the Doctor. 'I spoke to Private Corey yesterday morning and he had something very interesting to tell me. His mother was a medium –'

'What's Private Corey's mother's size got to do with anything?'

'A *medium*,' the Doctor repeated, 'as in "in touch with those beyond the grave".' He raised his hands and waved his fingers spookily to emphasise the point.

'I'm sorry. Do continue.'

'He had the *gift*, he said. Passed down from his mother. He could *sense* things. And he told me in no uncertain terms that he sensed an evil presence at the Hall. He said it was building up and soon it was going to get out. That would tie in with our friend Dr Banham's mounting panic and his more delirious measures to get me off his premises. I believe that Private Corey was right. I believe that something very strange is going on at Hawkswick Hall. And I believe that Dr Banham knows all about it.'

'And you believe in supernatural entities and suchlike.'

'Don't you, after all we've experienced?'

'I didn't, until last night,' she admitted. 'And even now I'm beginning to doubt what I saw. It was very dark, and the light can play games with you in a storm.'

'You and Dr Banham think along the same lines.'

'We live in an age of scientific enlightenment, Doctor. We no longer burn our neighbours as witches.'

'There are good points to living in such an age,' the Doctor said. 'But I fear as society grows more complex and people become more cut off from nature, that, sadly, something is lost. Civilisation and the higher reaches of human intellect are gained at a price. And that price is a divorce from more basic, instinctual talents that man once possessed. These skills remain, buried deep in the subconscious, but sometimes, by accident of personality, or whatever, they can resurface in some people.'

'Like my empathy, or Private Corey's sixth sense,' Mary reflected.

'Exactly,' the Doctor agreed.

'But these abilities are not ghosts and spectres, Doctor.'

'Perhaps they are made of the very same stuff, though.'

'I don't understand.'

'If you accept your ability to know the feelings of others, and Private Corey's ability to sense evil at the Hall, you accept that human beings can sense invisible forces beyond their normal field of experience.'

'Yes.'

'And what are ghosts and spectres if not invisible forces?'

Mary gazed abstractedly into the nothingness of the middle of the room. 'This is all very disconcerting, Doctor.'

'There are forces at work here that hark from the dawn of

humanity,' the Doctor told her. 'Perhaps even further back than that.'

His eyes were dark and the fireglow sent macabre upshadows that made his face appear extended and distorted. Then he leaned forward abruptly and the effect disappeared. 'But I think we're big enough to cope with them, don't you?'

Mary was not so confident. 'I do hope so.'

In the stillness of Cromby's stable, something began to stir. The horses snorted. In front of the pile of straw that filled the third bay, the ground began to heave. A small motion at first, like the burrowing of a mole. Cracks appeared in the dry, compacted earth, then began to spread as something rose out of the ground.

New movement brought dark shapes into the barn to watch. They stood round in a tight semicircle, gazing at the thing that expanded out of the soil at their feet. From the earth, it took form. A crouched man coiled tightly in the foetal position. Covered in dirt and clay.

He remained still for a time, before he began to flex his muscles and test his movement. Arms appeared out of the ball of earth. Arms covered in mud. Then a head raised slowly, uncertainly. The face was shattered bone and flesh, eyes caked in mud that crawled with tiny grubs. The thing reached up and wiped the dirt out of its eyes, and grinned a death mask when it saw the others watching.

The sergeant nodded in satisfaction.

A child is born. From mother earth. A child of war and horror. A child of its father. A child of the dark.

The Doctor rattled the fire with the poker, then noticed the watch beside the bottle of port at Mary's side. Remaining hunched, he picked it up and opened the cover. The tune ran its course before he closed it again and gazed at her out of the orange glow he'd stoked.

'That is very beautiful,' he said.

'It belonged to my brother,' Mary informed him. The tears pricked her eyes and she took a deep breath. 'I'm afraid it holds intensely painful memories for me. I was to save it until he returned. All I can think now when I look at it is that he's never going to return. And I wish I could turn back the hands…' Her voice trailed into silence.

The Doctor touched her knee gently. 'None of us can do that.'

She shook her head, and felt the tears released by the motion. They trickled down her cheeks and she did nothing to remove them.

'He must have been a very special man,' the Doctor said, standing and returning to the sofa, putting some small distance between them, 'if he was anything like you.'

Mary smiled, but it sat awkwardly in her features and faded fast. 'He used to bring me flowers,' she remembered. 'Sweet peas and snapdragons. He loved the colours. He liked flowers with vivid colours.'

The Doctor said nothing.

'Yes,' she agreed, 'he was a very special man.'

They sat in shared silence amid the shadows and the desolate dark. The fire murmured. The house was still.

'Do you have any brothers or sisters, Doctor?'

'No.'

'That is very sad.'

The Doctor did not respond.

'Any children?'

'No.'

The fire heaved a sigh in the grate.

'Are you married?'

He shook his head, and gave her a forlorn look.

'You busy yourself with your travels, then?'

'I do.'

Mary nodded. 'Might I ask you a very personal question?'

A curious look passed through the Doctor's eyes. 'You have not asked permission to do so up to now.'

'Why are you not off fighting in the war?'

He pressed himself back on the sofa, as if he were trying to find shadow to hide in.

'This is not my war,' he said.

'This is everybody's war.'

The Doctor gazed into the flames of the fire.

'Perhaps I fought my war already.'

'And lived to fight another day,' Mary argued gently. 'You are not wounded. Not shell-shocked. You are a fit young man. If you were a conchie, you'd be imprisoned along with the rest of them. How can you refuse to fight?'

He gave her a look of cold steel but said nothing.

'You'd destroy the corpse-soldiers, wouldn't you?'

'They're dead already.'

She watched him evenly. 'I know you're not a slacker. I know you're not afraid. I'm just interested in the *truth* about you. If you're not a man from the Ministry, how did you escape conscription? To do that you must be off the record, not on the census. Are you a foreign national?'

'Do I sound like a foreign national?'

'No. You don't sound like one. You certainly *sound* English. So why are you not on the register? Did you fake your own death? Am I talking to yet another dead man? People in society simply *have* to be registered. You're intelligent. Where were you educated? Oxford? Cambridge? Which family are you from? Nobody can exist in society yet remain outside the web that society is.'

The Doctor remained obstinately silent.

'You don't make sense!' she told him in exasperation.

'I think you would have been wise to stop at one glass,' the

Doctor told her, his voice mildly chastising. He stood and offered her his hand, and she took it with a numb sense of surrender.

'I think it's time we went to bed,' he said quietly. 'Don't you?'

She said nothing, but felt a bright burst of sunshine open up inside her. An excitement she had not felt before chased helter-skelter through her body and soul. She felt light-headed from the port, and only now that she rose to her feet did she realise just how much the drink had affected her. The Doctor pushed her gently towards the door, and she led him slowly up the stairs.

Outside her room, she turned to face him, and he paused in front of her on the narrow landing. Forcing herself to look directly into his eyes, she found them full of unreadable stuff. Darkness and magic and danger. The curls were wild above his brow, and he looked exactly how she imagined Heathcliff to be. She felt she was in a dream, and that he might sweep her suddenly off her feet and carry her listless body to her bed.

He said nothing for a moment while she breathed hot port into the small gap between them. There were butterflies in her stomach. She'd heard the phrase, but never really felt it, until now. They were battering their fragile wings in the sunshine, cool currents whispering about them as they danced in the air inside her. So many feelings, so much emotion, so much –

'Well,' the Doctor whispered softly in her ear.

He seemed hesitant. Uncertain. She wanted to grab hold and kiss him.

'Goodnight, then,' he said.

And the butterflies died.

Chapter Nine

As the sun climbed over the horizon the sky looked like an artist's impression of peace and tranquillity. Broad but gentle washes of pale blue with the paper showing through; streaks of yellow, green, purple and red hinted with such sublime subtlety that they could be seen without being really visible. For Iris Cromby, this was the most beautiful part of the day. It was the moment when you could see God's hand in things. The time when you realised just how perfect nature actually was.

There was a childlike wonder at the break of day that had remained with Iris Cromby all her life. She might as well be in a different world, an improbable place, soundless except for coruscating birdsong. It was like a world detached from our own, into which the world of human activity bled slowly as the first hours passed.

To Bill Cromby, daybreak in August meant time to start work. Through the kitchen window, Iris watched him bringing out the horses and handing them over to Laura Rawkins and Maggie Fowler. Iris noticed that he led them using his left hand, the right arm still hanging at his side. He had snapped the dislocated shoulder back last night, but he must be in some ample pain with it, she thought. But Bill wasn't one to complain. He got on with his life regardless of the hurdles put in his way. If he'd lost his arm completely, she was quite sure he'd still be out there this morning. He spent some time explaining to Laura and Maggie what he wanted them to do today, and they left for the fields with the horses trotting behind. Then he stepped back into the barn and Iris wondered what he was up to. After the events of last night, she'd be in there as little as possible if she was him. The place was tainted. No wonder the horses refused to settle.

As she busied herself with the washing-up, Iris watched for him coming back out. And as she watched, the rattle of crockery ground to a silent full stop. Iris could see no movement inside the stable door. Only darkness.

Without bothering to dry her hands, she grasped the shotgun and rushed from the kitchen. The stable door was still wide open, but she sensed something terribly wrong. Lifting the gun to her shoulder, Iris peered round the edge of the door.

Bill Cromby gawked up at her from his position crouching on the floor about halfway down the stables. His face contained a curiously blank look and he was holding something that he raised to show her. It was a lump of earth, Iris realised, lowering the gun and stepping inside the cool shade.

Cromby gazed around at the scattered lumps of earth at his feet. Last night they were chunks of dead body. Now they were nothing but clods of dirt. Iris gazed in amazement, and began to wonder if they'd dreamed the dead man after all.

'Bloody queer,' Cromby said, rising to his feet and looking around.

He stopped abruptly. Iris could tell something was up from the way he didn't move a muscle. She stepped over to see what he'd found, and discovered a circle of disturbed ground on the edge of the third bay. The area was lifted slightly, as if somebody had been digging for something. Or maybe as if something had come up from under the ground.

She felt Bill's hand on her shoulder and he guided her out into the sunshine.

'Come on,' he rumbled, 'better get on.'

Mary's head pounded. Her eyes were unusually sensitive to the bright morning sunlight that suffused the kitchen. Bacon and eggs splattered and sizzled contentedly in the pan, but unusually she felt that she wasn't hungry for breakfast today. When he saw her, the Doctor grinned in that infuriatingly cheerful way he had that made her feel remarkably miserable in comparison.

'Good morning,' he greeted with far too much cheer in his voice.

'Good morning,' she said, dully.

'It's a beautiful day,' he informed her, flipping the bacon with a practised twist of the wrist.

'Is it?'

The beatific grin remained obstinately in his face. 'Glorious! Breakfast?'

'Just a cup of tea, if you don't mind.'

'Sit down,' he said. 'Everything's in hand.'

Before she'd even managed to sit at the table he'd placed a cup of tea in front of her, and she sipped at this while the Doctor continued to conjure breakfast as if he'd spent his entire life at the stove. He tipped the bacon and eggs on to a preheated plate and swept it to the table. The plate was piled high with dripping layers, and Mary had to avert her gaze when her stomach did an abrupt, unexpected somersault and didn't quite manage to land back on its feet.

Snatching up knife and fork, the Doctor regarded the mountain meal.

'There's far too much here for one,' he said. 'Are you certain you won't to join me?'

'Quite certain,' she assured him.

With a small shrug, the Doctor began to tuck in enthusiastically.

Mary watched him wrap a slice of bacon around his fork, removing the rind and placing it carefully on the rim of his plate. He popped the whole forkful into his mouth in one go and chewed heartily, sustaining the best smile he could manage with his mouth so stuffed.

'I feel I really must apologise for last night,' Mary admitted suddenly.

The Doctor shook his head. 'Don't ever apologise for a healthy curiosity,' he told her gravely. 'I'd be going round apologising to everybody.'

'I don't just mean the personal inquisition,' Mary said.

He regarded her questioningly.

'My behaviour was less civilised than it should have been,' she confessed with an unaccustomed awkwardness.'You are my guest here, and I tried to take advantage of that. I'm very sorry.'

The Doctor stopped chewing. 'My dear Mary, you have gone through a very great deal in recent days.'

'Nevertheless,' she insisted, 'I feel that an apology is due, and I would be grateful if you would accept it.'

Smile. Nod. The chewing resumed with renewed vigour.

She watched him devour his breakfast in great swathes, until the plate was empty and he sat back with an exceedingly contented expression. He poured himself a cup of tea and she found his eyes sparkling with some inner ebullience which she couldn't for the life of her imagine belonged in there.

'You seem extremely happy for a man who is unable to continue his vocation,' she told him.

'I'm sorry?'

'I thought you said Dr Banham forbade you from returning to the Hall.'

'He did,' the Doctor confirmed.

'Does that not cause you some obstruction?'

'Oh, I'll be back,' the Doctor assured her in all confidence. He sipped his tea. 'Due to the fact that, as you so perspicaciously discovered, I am not actually from the Ministry of Anything At All, I do need to tread very carefully with Dr Banham. However, I'm going to prove today that the two men found in Skews Bank Field were the two men who went missing from Hawkswick Hall last March.'

'And how do you propose to do that? You said you found no identification on the bodies.'

'I didn't. But I'm going to conduct an exhaustive search of the area in which they were discovered. If there's so much as a shred of evidence there, I can assure you I will uncover it.'

'And if you don't?'

The Doctor put his cup down decisively. 'Then I'll *invent* proof.'

'Surely that is somewhat unethical.'

The Doctor simply grinned.

Mary sipped thoughtfully at her tea. 'Of course,' she said, 'there is another way…'

The Doctor stopped mid-sip and regarded her in inert silence over the rim of his cup.

'I could go to the Hall myself.'

The cup returned to its saucer with a discreet *clink*. The Doctor's face filled with dark shadow that was entirely at odds with his mood of just a second ago.

'That could be very dangerous,' he warned.

'Nonsense!' she said. 'I go there frequently to stock up on medicines and what have you. They're very used to seeing me at Hawkswick Hall. It would be very easy for me to have a look at this gun room for you.'

The Doctor stared at her, but she found it impossible to guess what he was thinking.

'I can't let you take that risk, I'm afraid,' he said at length.

Mary was briefly speechless. 'My dear Doctor, I take it you have not heard of women's suffrage?'

The Doctor seemed affronted at the idea. 'I chained Mrs Emmeline Pankhurst to the railings outside Number Ten.'

'Then am I to assume that you do not consider me capable of making my own autonomous decisions for reasons of personal deficiency?'

The Doctor raised his hands in surrender. 'I was merely pointing out the dangers involved in such an undertaking…'

'I am quite mindful of the dangers involved,' she informed him hotly. 'This is *my* home. If my home is threatened, I will fight to protect it as ferociously as any man. I am perfectly capable of looking after myself, Doctor, and fighting my own battles.'

The Doctor gazed at her as if he'd just come out of a totally unexpected downpour.

'Now,' Mary continued in her that's-settled-then manner, 'where, exactly, *is* this gun room?'

The grounds of Hawkswick Hall were pleasant in the sunshine. As Mary Minett made her way across the open lawns towards the main entrance, she passed a number of strolling couples, VAD nurses with injured men, or small groups of soldiers who were apparently not injured at all. Some of them smiled as she approached. Some waved from a distance when they recognised her. Some watched her darkly from inside shadowy faces, their eyes far distant in France and the fields of horror.

Mary harboured an immense sorrow for these men. She often wondered if her brother would have returned a very different person if things had not turned out the way they had. Perhaps death was sometimes the best. In a world quite literally gone mad, perhaps it was a blessing to be granted that final peace. Perhaps. She had viewed her brother's death from all perspectives, but she was always left ultimately with the unpleasant feeling that there was the simple truth: the war was a waste. It was a huge tragedy of a waste that the human engines had ground out in their relentless stubbornness. Men who were born to great things were being thrown on the pyre. Burned in the hell that was this War to End All Wars. Some of the men who gazed at her without really seeing her now were merely ghosts. They might as well be dead. And she suspected that many of those who seemed perfectly well were not so at all. That they were simply strong enough to hide the truth. That their smiles were sticking plasters over festering wounds that would never heal.

As she got closer to the Hall, she realised that one of the figures at the house was in fact Dr Banham. He had noticed her approach and stopped in his tracks to watch. She composed herself for the encounter, sticking her most pleasant smile prominently into her cheeks as she ascended the steps towards him.

Banham held out his hand and beamed a great fat grin.

'Miss Minett,' he said, 'what a very pleasant surprise.'

'Good morning, Dr Banham.' She shook his hand. 'How are you?'

'Well,' he replied. 'Very well. I haven't seen you for some considerable time now.'

'I'm here to pick up a few supplies,' she told him.

His smile did not abate. The sun glinted in his eyes, and he seemed genuinely pleased to see her.

'You must join me for coffee,' he announced.

Mary considered turning the offer down, but changed her mind for four reasons. First, Banham was a very astute man and she did not want to seem in too much of a hurry and perhaps imply some ulterior agenda. Second, her head still thumped from last night's intemperance and she felt a coffee might help to soothe it. Third, she might discover in idle conversation some clue as to what exactly the reputable Dr Banham was trying to cover up here at the Hall. Fourth, the sun glinted in his eyes, and he seemed genuinely pleased to see her.

In Iris Cromby's kitchen, the kettle boiled. Very strange, she thought, that Bill Cromby should request a cup of tea at this time in the morning. He never normally would eat or drink until dinner. It was a habit of a lifetime, and Iris found this very puzzling behaviour for one who lived by routine and custom.

What was even more baffling was the fact that Cromby had dragged his old armchair out of the kitchen and placed it slap-bang in the middle of the yard, facing the barn. It was his chair from the side of the fire, and it hadn't been moved for twenty years to Iris's certain knowledge. Now it stood there like King Canute's throne deposited in front of the incoming tide.

While she poured the boiled water into the warmed teapot, she watched idly through the window to see Cromby vanish again into the stables, this time to emerge a few minutes later with the ladder that normally led up into the hayloft. He leaned this against the large stone that he'd been using to hold the stable door shut for the past day or so, and proceeded to jump up and down on it until the ladder snapped under the strain of his relentless battering. Holding up a broken length of ladder, Cromby peered at it briefly before seeming satisfied, then went and laid the short section down in front of the stables door.

He turned and marched back to the house, and when he came into the kitchen he went straight for his gun. He snapped it open and loaded both barrels. Then he gave Iris a quizzical look.

'That tea ready yet?' he asked.

'Just pourin' it now,' Iris answered.

He stood and waited while she poured the tea into his favourite mug, a mug the size of a bucket. She handed it over and he marched back into the yard with it.

Iris watched as he placed the cup by the chair along with the shotgun. He vanished back into the stables for a minute, before reappearing and jamming the length of broken ladder into the dirt and up under the broken handle of the door. Then Cromby returned to his armchair and plonked himself down. He reached for the tea and began to drink as if he were off on a picnic. Absolutely confounded by his behaviour, Iris watched enthralled.

It was a surreal scene: the man who never stopped, sitting there in the sunshine in his favourite armchair sipping tea as if there were not a job in the world to be done. There was corn to gather, stubble to scarify, turnips to sow, and a field of good mangelwurzel to be hoed. And there Cromby sat like Lord Muck himself.

Then she noticed it. Her eyes widened in shock. Her mouth dropped open in sheer disbelief as she saw thin tendrils of black smoke rising from the roof of the stables into the clear blue sky.

Banham poured coffee into the two cups on the tray and offered one to Mary, who accepted it with a polite smile. He reposed in his huge chair at the back of his immense desk, while she perched on the small seat in front of it. The aroma of rich fresh coffee filled the room, and Mary's headache felt better already.

'I trust you are well,' Banham was saying.

'Oh very much so, thank you,' Mary told him.

'Despite the very distressing occurrences which plague the village these days,' Banham said.

Mary sipped her coffee. 'Despite them, yes.'

Banham left a short pause but she did nothing to fill the silence.

'I understand there has been something of an intensification of events around the village in recent days,' he said. The words sounded very much as if he were making light conversation about the weather or some such mundane matter.

'There has indeed,' she acknowledged. 'Bodies unearthed in the fields, things going bump in the night, sightings of the most ghastly apparitions –'

'This all sounds very fascinating phenomena,' he declared. 'I only wish I had time to do a study of the happenings down there.'

'If I were you, Dr Banham, I would be grateful that I had not the time to be involved in village affairs at all. Things seem to be getting quite out of hand.'

'Imagination, surely, Miss Minett...'

Looking him square in the eye, Mary shook her head. 'I fear that it is more than imaginings,' she told him ominously. 'The two bodies were very real indeed, and Constable Briggs's lock-up was completely destroyed last night.'

'It was?' Banham shrugged. 'Perhaps the storm.'

'It was built of solid brick.'

'And had most probably been constructed some considerable

time ago,' he ventured to suggest. 'Do you not concede the not too remote possibility that the building crumbled due to age during a particularly severe storm?'

'There were explosions, Dr Banham. Most palpable explosions.'

Again, Banham gave her an exaggerated shrug. 'The storm, Miss Minett, surely?'

'The storm did not bury two bodies in Skews Bank Field, Dr Banham.'

Banham looked truly sorry. 'That was very sad,' he said. 'I understand that it was not possible to identify the remains since they were somewhat deteriorated.'

'They were more than deteriorated, Dr Banham. They had been quite deliberately dismembered.'

Banham appeared shocked. 'Really?'

'Oh, yes. It caused a terrible furore.'

'I can imagine,' Banham sympathised. 'It must have been a startling discovery. I wonder who they could have been.'

'They were in army uniform.'

'Most men are, these days, unfortunately, Miss Minett.'

'It was thought they might be the two men who went missing last March,' Mary said.

'But Mr Sykes and Mr Collins reported back here,' Banham reminded her. 'They were returned to the fighting very shortly afterwards. I cannot imagine how their bodies could have turned up again in your fields if they were shot in the fields of France, can you?'

'As I said,' Mary told him, 'that was what was originally thought. Constable Briggs's files contain clear reports that the two men were found and the case was closed at the time. It remains a mystery, however, who the dead men were.'

'A mystery that will no doubt be solved at some point.'

'No doubt,' Mary agreed. 'But I believe that you have a very disturbing mystery of your own here in this hospital, Dr Banham.'

Banham appeared melancholy. 'Ah, yes. You heard about poor Private Corey. A very distressing incident.'

'Do you know who did it?' Mary asked.

'I'm very much afraid it remains a riddle, as do your two bodies. But I think the two bodies in the field and Private Corey may be linked in some way.'

'Really?'

'I suspect that a murderer roams these parts, Miss Minett. A murderer who preys on convalescing soldiers.'

'How dreadful.'

'It's sickening, isn't it? But I fear it is true. Poor Private Corey may have fallen victim to the same killer as the two men. I have begun an internal enquiry that I am confident will absolve all the patients and staff here from suspicion. I fear that the murderer may well live out in the hills, or perhaps visits this area on occasion. He may also be the answer to the mystery of the haunting of Hawkswick.'

'That's a very disturbing prospect, Dr Banham.'

'It is, isn't it, Miss Minett? But what I find an even more disturbing prospect is the calibre of help we have been offered in investigating these matters.'

'The Man from the Ministry,' Mary said. 'You don't approve?'

'Our very own illustrious Mr Sherlock Holmes!' Banham said in gently mocking tone. 'I have met him. On several occasions, I regret to report.'

'I take it you were less than impressed by the man.'

Banham took a gulp of coffee and settled himself in his chair. 'I found him to be something of a bungling buffoon, I'm afraid. He seems particularly adept at charging in where others might tread with, shall we say, a little more prudence.'

'But he seems to be an extremely tenacious man,' Mary said. 'Perhaps, I would agree, rather energetic in his method.'

'Energetic!' Banham echoed with some amusement. 'Do you

know I caught him in an attempt to break into our gun store only last night?'

'Really?'

'Oh, yes. And to make matters even worse, he was being aided and abetted by one of our more severely disturbed patients in this task of breaking and entering.'

'Shocking!' Mary said, doing her utmost to sound suitably shocked.

'In my personal experience, our friend the Ministry Man has proven to be something of a fly in the ointment. I considered putting forward an official complaint about his activities.'

'And did you?'

'To be perfectly honest, Miss Minett, I have, as you can imagine, rather a lot on my plate at this moment. I have asked the Ministry Man not to interfere here, and I think he finally got the message. I hope not to have to deal with him again.'

'Well I have had dealings with this Ministry Man myself, Dr Banham, and I can tell you that he has the tendency to make himself rather ubiquitous. Don't think you've escaped him that easily.'

'If he comes around here again. Miss Minett, he will get more than he bargained for, I can assure you.'

'You would surely not wish to obstruct the wheels of justice, Dr Banham.'

'Of course not, Miss Minett. But this particular wheel has a proclivity to run out of line, I have found. We wouldn't want to run off the track entirely, would we?'

'We would not, Dr Banham,' Mary said. 'We most certainly would not.'

She sipped her coffee and remembered the Doctor's excitement this morning at breakfast. Remembered his insistence that he would be back to face Banham. Remembered his comment about inventing the proof he couldn't find. The wheels of justice might sometimes take a hazardously circuitous route, she thought, but the ride was a particularly exhilarating one.

As the flames began to lick around the edges of the slates, there came a slamming from inside the stable door. It buckled and shuddered under a terrific battering, but refused to give. Cromby put down his cup of tea and picked up the shotgun in readiness, but remained slumped in the chair.

The sky was now full of a thick black smoke, and the yard reeked of fire. It crackled and spat and Cromby could feel the intense heat from where he sat.

The banging at the door stopped, and Cromby heard in its place a great heave of collapsing wood as the roof joists finally gave and the slates crashed into the furnace. A great guffaw of thick black smoke erupted, and Cromby felt the heat slap him in the face and singe his eyebrows.

As he watched the last remaining slates around the edge of the roof fall into the conflagration, he suddenly saw movement on the top of the wall. A fiery arm waving against the swirling black smoke. It grasped the wall and a black shape dragged itself up, flames dancing around it, a mixture of what looked like smoke and steam rising from it. With awful slowness the thing managed to haul itself on to the top of the two-storey wall and suddenly pitched forward over the edge. It hit the ground with a sickening thud and Cromby was amazed to see it explode into an eruption of ash and cinders. Chunks of glowing material were flung across the yard in all directions.

Another creature wrenched itself out and plummeted to the same fate, another burst of flame and black smoking stuff. Cromby heard a hollow-sounding puff when the thing landed.

The heat was overpowering now. Cromby stood to take a few steps back, when he realised that two more of the things were lugging themselves together over the top of the wall. They plunged to the ground, and both landed with a dense thump. One of them blasted into soot like a giant lump of exploding coal, sparkling black dust lingering on the still air. The second remained intact, its lower half collapsed, but upper half a blackened shape like the flaming remnant of a Guy Fawkes. It turned its head on Cromby and he saw through the flames and smoke that it was trying to scream at him.

In fixated fascination, Cromby approached. The thing in the smog reached out with an imploring hand, and Cromby watched it suffer for a few seconds before he brought up the shotgun and blasted it into floating embers with both barrels.

The sun burned a hole in the fierce blue sky while the Doctor stabbed his spade repeatedly into the soil at the top of Skews Bank Field. The turnip hoeing and previous excavation had pulverised the ground already, and the spade sank with ease into the loose soil. But the bodies had been spread over a wide area, it was a windless, stifling day, and the task was still an arduous one. The Doctor had hoped for a little assistance from Briggs, but he was busy making safe what was left of the lock-up, and, the Doctor supposed, to expect Briggs to pull any kind of weight out here in the blazing heat was a bit much.

In the hedgerow along the perimeter of Skews Bank Field, two dark shapes watched the Doctor work. Had he seen them, the Doctor might have marvelled at their absolute stillness. Covered in dried mud over khaki green, they were perfectly camouflaged on the edge of the field. They might have been natural growths, stumps of old trees that happened to resemble crouching men. Their eyes were empty sockets and their features made up of accidents of shadow. Had he seen them, the Doctor might well have been impressed by the way they dedicated themselves so unconditionally to this sentinel duty. No fidgeting, no gestures, no smokes, no jokes to pass the time. No motion. No boredom. No breathing.

* * *

After coffee with Dr Banham, Mary collected a few sundry items from the hospital pharmacy. Odds and ends she could do with anyway. Enough to make it look as though this were not a contrived visit, but not so much that she might end up overstocked at home. After all, she was ever mindful of her budget, supplying services to the people of Hawkswick. Wages on the land were not the best.

Making her way back out through the main entrance hall, Mary noticed the first door that the Doctor had described. 'Two doors,' he'd said. 'One inside, one outside. Since the inside door is in the main reception hall, I think you'd be safer using the outside door at the end of the east wing. It was unlocked when I tried it, so you should be able to slip in unnoticed.'

Once outside, she made her way down the steps to the lawns, then strolled casually over to inspect the rock rose which grew with such vibrant splendour in the full sun against the wall that separated the two levels. With a series of furtive glances, Mary strolled east. To anyone noticing, she might be taking in the dazzling day and the stunning scenery. She feigned interest in a low-lying shrub here and a flowering bush there as she went.

In the pit of her stomach, she sensed a curling excitement. It was odd, this feeling apprehensive in the middle of such a peaceful day among people she knew. She guessed that the Doctor would have no qualms at all about making this approach. She supposed he would simply take it in his stride, strutting about in his usual way, perhaps not even bothering to check if he was being observed. And having been discovered, she felt quite certain that he would feel no embarrassment whatsoever, no shame, no mortification. They were not, she was sure, any part of the Doctor's stock of emotions.

But Mary was not the Doctor, and now she felt extremely self-conscious as she saw the door to the basement approaching. There were people about. Some nearby. She moved closer to the door and pretended to be interested in an energetic clematis that displayed a spectacular abundance of small purple flowers. The clematis happened to be conveniently near the door, and allowed Mary to slip inside at an opportune moment when she was sure that she was not being observed.

Inside was pitch black and reeked of damp. It took her eyes a while to adjust, and then all she could see was degrees of darkness. Shapes and shapeless things loomed out of the shadow. Great dismal spectres that were formed by her mind and projected on the malleable gloom. After the things she had seen around the village lately, there could be anything here in the dark.

Moving with great care, positive she could see peering faces in all the pitted surfaces of the walls, Mary began to wish she'd never volunteered to come on this errand. What if the Doctor was right? What if it really *was* dangerous? What if there were dead men here? What if…?

She reached a locked door about halfway down the corridor on the right, just as the Doctor had described. Fumbling through her purse, Mary found the peculiar key that the Doctor had assured her would unlock the door despite its having no teeth. He'd called it his 'skeleton key', and she immediately had not liked the connotations that suggested. He had explained that the key would 'know what to do', whatever on Earth *that* meant.

As Mary felt for the lock in the dark, she froze abruptly at a sound she could swear came from the locked room. Her heart raced and she felt suddenly rather light-headed. But the sound had come from upstairs, most probably. It would be carried down here in such an old house with its endless meandering corridors and possibly even secret passageways.

And, she told herself, the sounds of men screaming were a commonplace thing in Hawkswick Hall.

There were two of them. About the size of coins, except that one was round and the other was a lozenge shape. They were attached to a length of string. The round one was red, the lozenge was green, and they seemed to be made of some compressed fibre material.

The Doctor bent to pluck them out of the dirt, and as he did so his face beamed with a great self-satisfied grin. Around the outer edge of the red circular tag were the letters '15TH WEST YORKSHIRE J. SYKES'.

Slipping the dog tags into his pocket, the Doctor picked up Constable Briggs's bicycle from the dirt where it lay and proceeded to tie the spade to the crossbar. He grasped his jacket out of the tree and laid it over the handlebars, then wheeled the bike down the edge of the field and back on to the road.

(Behind him, on the perimeter of the field, shapes moved. One of them signalled to the other, indicating the road in the mid-distance where the Doctor clambered on to the bike and began to pedal contentedly back towards the village.)

The sun was still high in the sky but starting its lazy descent into oblivion. The day was breezeless and the birds were singing to their hearts' content. The Doctor pedalled happily and watched the countryside pass him by at an idle pace. There were rabbits cavorting in the fields. There was the rich dry scent of summer in the air. There was peace and quiet and such a deep tranquillity that it was hard to believe that such terrible things were happening around Hawkswick.

Then the explosion came. Like a blast out of Hell, it hurled him off the bike. A flurry of starlings erupted out of the hedgerow and scattered into the sky, squawking and flapping as they went. The Doctor hit the ground with a slap of air and fell limp and still.

Almost immediately in the shocked aftermath, two corpse soldiers stood over him with guns raised at the Doctor's head.

Mary pushed the key into the lock and, despite the Doctor's

reassurances, she was still slightly surprised when it turned with an effortless *clunk*. The handle fell under her grasp and she swept open the door.

The first thing that struck her was the cloying stench of cold damp air. It was dark, but there was a source of light in the room, and as the door opened, Mary saw that there was a bank of candles burning on a large frame of candlesticks.

As she entered, she was revolted to realise that the floor was becoming slimy. She slipped as if she were stepping through thick soft sludge. When she lifted her feet, her boots came out of the stuff with a faint slurp. Mary squinted to find the floor was, as far as she could tell, coated in a thick layer of fresh clay. The entire floor was covered in the grey slime, except that near the candles Mary could see an area that seemed to be clear. An open book lay on the floor inside the clean patch.

Checking warily back down the corridor, Mary stepped inside to investigate. It was not easy to keep upright on the slippery surface, and she slid rather than walked over to the book. As she went, she was certain she sensed movement in the dark nearby, but when she looked it stopped in an instant. She peered at the walls, and was astonished to see them glinting with a dull reflected light from the candles. She realised with a small gasp of shock that the entire room – floor, walls and even ceiling – were layered with dense damp clay.

As Mary approached, she could see that the clean area was marked by a chalk circle. The original floor showed through inside the line, but outside was coated with clay. She stepped in and picked up the book, tilting it up to the light from the candles.

It seemed to be an ancient book. It smelled of damp and candlewax. She scanned the pages to find it was written in Latin, and cursed the fact that she had never had the opportunity to learn the language. What she could read loud and clear, however, were the illustrations. They were black-and-white etchings and they depicted Hell and Damnation. Turning the leaves, she discovered page after page of human suffering. Creatures with impish faces assaulting men and women in paroxysms of agony. The candlelight gave the pages an ethereal, almost living quality.

Again, she thought she heard movement in the dark, but when she looked – nothing. The book was making her nervous. This room was making her nervous. She decided abruptly to take the book with her. Perhaps the Doctor may be able to make some sense of it all.

As she turned to leave, there was most definitely the sound of something moving in the dark. Something large slurping in the clay. Mary froze. Silence. Then a cold breeze. The door slammed shut. The candles blew out. Then blackness so thick she felt she couldn't breathe.

In the impenetrable dark, something stirred.

Chapter Ten

By the time Briggs had got the bricks and rubble stacked safely in the small garden, he was ready for a good strong cup of tea. It had been a hard day's slog. His shirt was wet with sweat, and his poor arms felt fit to drop off. He couldn't face the prospect of lifting another single thing today, except the teapot and a plate of sandwiches.

As he was about to enter the house, he sensed rather than heard someone approaching down the road, and turned to find the Doctor leaning heavily on the battered bike. His face was bloody and Briggs could see that he, like the poor old bike, was more than a little worse for wear. Hobbling over, he helped support the Doctor and the bike, bringing them together to the station house and leaning them both against the wall while he opened the door to let the Doctor inside.

'What happened?' Briggs demanded, sitting the Doctor at the table and rushing to bring a damp cloth.

'About twenty kilos of nitro-nine, by the feel of it,' the Doctor told him.

'Nitro-what?' Briggs asked, dabbing the Doctor's face with the cloth.

'Nitro…' the Doctor looked lost, and didn't finish his sentence.

Briggs dabbed gingerly at the Doctor's head with the cloth. There was a nasty cut above the eye, and a few grazes down the right side of the Doctor's face.

'Where did this happen?'

'Skews Bank Field.'

Briggs shook his head. 'Broad daylight!' he grumbled.

'About midday,' the Doctor confirmed. He glanced at Briggs's clock on the wall. 'I must've been out for about three hours. Quite a jolt.'

'How d'you feel now?' Briggs peered anxiously into his face.

'Fine,' the Doctor said, poking around in his pockets. 'The main thing is, I got what I went for.' But his face clouded. He stood and patted his coat. 'They've gone!'

'Who've gone?'

'Dog tags,' the Doctor muttered. 'Corporal John Sykes's dog tags. I found them where we uncovered the bodies in Skews Bank Field.'

'So what you done with them?' The Doctor shook his head slowly, looking entirely baffled. 'You must've dropped them.'

'No. I put them in my pocket. I remember distinctly…'

'Concussion…'

'No no no no no. The explosion. It was an ambush! Set for *me*. *They* took the tags.'

'They?'

'The dead men.'

Briggs didn't like the turn this conversation had just taken. Not one little bit. 'What would they want with them?'

'Who knows? Perhaps they wanted them as a keepsake, or a…'

'A what?'

'A trophy?'

Briggs frowned at the idea. 'I think I better get that kettle on,' he said, scuffling over to the sink.

'Did Mary call in to see you this afternoon?' the Doctor asked.

'No.' Briggs put on the kettle and proceeded to swill the old tealeaves out of the pot. 'Was she supposed to?'

'She went on an errand today,' the Doctor said. 'I expected her to catch up with me at Skews Bank.'

'Haven't seen anything of her,' Briggs said. He pulled two cups out of the dirty water and awarded them a cursory scrub with an obscene tea towel. He put them on the worktop, but turned to find the Doctor at the door with both their jackets.

'I think we should leave the tea,' he announced.

'Leave the tea?' Briggs echoed. 'Why?'

The Doctor grasped the handle and threw Briggs's jacket at him.

'We're going to find Mary Minett.'

Quite obviously feeling some considerable wrath at the Doctor's persistent intrusions, Dr Banham was doing his utmost to remain unruffled.

'I suppose you have,' he seethed, 'a particularly crucial reason for being here?' His comment was aimed at the Doctor along with a burning stare from those sullen eyes.

'I am here for a number of reasons, but my overriding objective at the moment is to locate Miss Minett.'

Banham sat behind his desk trying to look composed with, Briggs thought, an immense effort.

'Miss Minett graced us with a visit this morning,' Banham admitted. 'In fact, we had coffee around eleven. She then collected some items from our dispensary and I saw her leave, oh, early afternoon.'

'You saw her leave?' the Doctor asked.

'Yes,' Banham confirmed. 'It is my custom to stand at that window on occasion and take in the views. They are quite stunning. From here, you have a clear panorama that takes in the river and the lands beyond on the other side of the valley. Early this afternoon, only half an hour after Miss Minett left me to collect her supplies, I saw her depart across the lawns.'

The Doctor regarded Banham with what Briggs took to be a degree of scepticism. 'Can I ask which way she went?'

'Straight across, down to the stile which leads across country back to the village.'

'You saw her walk all the way and climb over the stile?'

'Yes.'

'It takes around five minutes to reach that stile at a strolling pace. That's a very long time to watch somebody simply walking away.'

Call him a liar to his face, why don't you? thought Briggs. Dr Banham was a man possessed by terrifying demons. They crawled beneath the surface, straining to burst out from under his skin. But somehow he managed to keep himself under control. It was amazing to see, this determined composure in the face of perpetual antagonism.

'I work in a stressful environment,' Banham said. 'I practise the Eastern custom of finding moments of calm during the course of the day. I can sometimes remain at the window for fifteen minutes.'

'Did you see, then, which direction Miss Minett followed when she entered the fields?'

'She turned right on the path that would take her back to the village.'

'But you can't be certain what time that would have been?'

'I can't be certain, no. Probably around one. Maybe a little earlier.'

The Doctor stepped over to the window and gazed out into the coming dusk. He was a motionless, red figure, held in the ruby light of the dying day. When he spoke again, his voice was distant, as if it were coming from somewhere else.

'I want to see your gun store,' he said.

Banham jumped to his feet. 'And I want *you* off these premises.'

The Doctor turned on him ferociously. 'A man was *murdered* here last night –'

'*Found* here,' Banham corrected with equal venom.

The Doctor ignored his comment. 'Then a visitor from the village doesn't return after visiting your hospital.' His red eyes seethed. 'And I found today positive proof that one of the men found in the fields was one of the men you say went back to France last March –'

'*Liar!*' Banham went off like an incendiary device.

The Doctor swept across the room, frock coat flying and fury in his face. He slammed his fists on to Banham's desk. '*I* am not the liar,' he screamed.

With a tremendous force of will, Banham remained silent for what seemed to Briggs an eternity. The Doctor remained apparently glued to the desk, leaning towards Banham in a blatantly challenging posture.

Constable Albert Briggs had had precious few dealings with Dr Banham. And those dealings had been brief and professional. To Briggs's mind, the good Dr Banham came across as an overbearing man. Not intentionally. But there was an underlying sense of power about him that made Briggs feel more than a little intimidated. It was a combination of the man's sheer physical bulk, his effervescent good health and vigour, his educated manner, and his colossal reputation. They all united to give Banham a certain undeniable stature. One that this Man from the Ministry simply did not seem to perceive.

The stalemate was broken when Banham marched over to the door and swung it open for them to leave.

The Doctor stood his ground, refusing to budge.

'Come on, then,' Banham said quietly, 'you want to see the gun store…'

As they stumbled down the basement corridor, even with the light from the Doctor's torch Briggs found the place unsettling. Perhaps after all the strange things around the village lately, he was developing a fear of the dark.

'Is there a reason why you never had electric lighting fitted down here?' the Doctor asked Banham pointedly.

'The damp,' Banham told him. 'There was apparently some hazard.'

'Yes,' the Doctor said without sounding too convinced.

They reached the door and Banham produced a key from his pocket. Unlocking the room, he waved the Doctor to open it. The

Doctor swept the door open to reveal a small room, little larger than a cupboard, which was lined with hooks and shelves. There were in fact very few weapons in there, just the odd holster and a couple of rifles leaning up against the wall. The Doctor seemed stunned, and swung the torchlight round to pick out the detail of the room. Finally, he gave Banham a stupefied look.

'Satisfied?' Banham said.

'No,' the Doctor responded, stepping inside the room and proceeding to bang on the walls.

A consternated look passed between Banham and Briggs, and Briggs gave him a resigned shrug. A furious look passed through Banham's features that made Briggs feel distinctly uneasy.

Watching the Doctor systematically work his way around the walls, testing for false compartments or whatever on earth he was looking for, Briggs shook his head. That explosion today had done more damage than they thought. The Doctor must be suffering from some post-shock daftness. Dr Banham would probably have a good explanation and all the right words for it, but for Briggs's money the Doctor had gone right round the bend. Briggs was shocked to see him surreptitiously slip one of the guns into his pocket as he made his way round the little room. Shooting a startled glance at Banham, Briggs was relieved to see that he was looking the other way, apparently tired of this ridiculous charade.

The Doctor emerged from the room and Banham regarded him as if he were an irksome thing.

'Have you quite finished?'

'Yes,' the Doctor said.

'No dead bodies?' Banham asked. 'No skeletons in the cupboard?'

The Doctor seemed uncomfortable under Banham's sarcastic scrutiny. 'No,' he said simply.

'Then might I ask,' Banham said evenly, 'that you now please leave this hospital and don't come back?'

The Doctor gazed at Briggs in resignation.

'If I see you here again,' Banham growled, 'I will physically remove you myself. I will telephone your superiors and lodge a complaint of the most critical nature. I will make sure that you never come again within a hundred miles of this institution. Do you understand?'

The Doctor gave him a meek nod.

'Now,' Banham turned to Briggs. 'You are the local constable in control of law and order. I would request that you please ensure that this man does not bother my patients or me again. Can I rely on you to do that?'

Briggs felt like a schoolboy. 'You can, sir,' he assured. 'Don't worry, Dr Banham. You won't be troubled by us again.'

He turned to the Doctor in some embarrassment. 'Well, come on, then.'

And they made their way down the corridor while Banham secured the door to the gun store behind them.

'What are you playing at?' Briggs hissed as they marched through the gardens towards the river. 'I saw you, you know. Pinching that gun. It's a flaming miracle that Dr Banham didn't notice.'

'Oh, I think our friend Dr Banham had quite a lot on his mind tonight,' the Doctor said.

'You can't go round pinching stuff,' Briggs said. 'I'm afraid I'll have to ask you to hand it over, Doctor.'

The Doctor's pace didn't miss a step. 'And I'm afraid I'll have to refuse.'

Briggs had to run to keep up with him, and as they approached the stile that took them from the manicured gardens to the untamed countryside, the sun was dipping behind the horizon and the ground seethed with gargantuan shadows. Briggs was finding it hard going, although the Doctor seemed to think it was still broad daylight. He skipped over the stile like a boy flinging himself over a low wall, and Briggs clambered over after him.

'I think that all went rather well,' he told the Doctor sarcastically when he caught up again.

'Oh, yes,' the Doctor grinned. 'It did, didn't it?'

'You do realise you can't go back there now,' Briggs informed him.

The Doctor stopped in his tracks and Briggs collided with him in the gathering gloom. The Doctor's eyes contained a sparkle of good humour.

'As someone once very famously said,' he gave Briggs a stern look, and spoke with a mock-foreign accent, '"*I'll be back!*"'

Then he was gone again, marching off through the dark with Briggs at his heels.

'Who famously said that then?' Briggs asked breathlessly, struggling to keep up.

'Oh, I don't know,' the Doctor replied dismissively. 'Can't remember. Probably somebody like Napoleon.'

'Oh,' Briggs said. A wave of exhaustion washed over him but the Doctor moved at an unstinting pace. He forced on with a single-minded determination, like a missile let loose on the enemy. And Briggs was just thankful that he wasn't the Doctor's target.

A shattered moon hung in the sky, visible through a lacework of dark branches. There was little movement in the hanging tree, not enough breeze to turn the soldiers' offerings.

In front of the tree, the two remaining dead men knelt with their heads bowed, as if praying at an altar. There they'd remained while the slow dusk gathered and the woods grew thick with dark.

Suddenly one of the figures moved, approaching the old oak tree and reaching up through the gnarled boughs to place a new offering in the twisted black twigs. A pair of small tags tied with string. They dangled in the dark, casting dim reflections of the fragile light.

The figure returned to kneel, and soon afterwards the breeze began to rise. At first, it was a subtle motion of the trees. Then the canopy opened and splattered the dead men with grotesque splashes of moonlight. The light storm grew swiftly more violent until the dead men had to huddle forward against a battering wind.

In the shrubs around them, things arrived. Out of the earth they rose, until they bowed like newborns, hands clenched, knees drawn, heads folded to their mother's breast. If they had breathed, they would have smelled her earthy scent.

The two kneeling dead men stood and headed for their comrades, sensing exactly where to find them in the all-consuming undergrowth. As the wind died and the dark settled in once more, they found them one by one and introduced them to the world.

At first, the new were shaky on their feet. They progressed with unsteady movements, loping about in the trees. The sergeant brought them all together before the oak tree and they stood to attention. There were no words spoken, no commands barked, no insults thrown. Just a tacit, silent, standing to order.

The sergeant inspected its motley squad. Men without eyes. Men without flesh. Men without lungs. Men without hearts. Men with guns. Perfect.

Satisfied, the sergeant waved command and they moved out together on their night-time campaign.

Back at Mary's house, the Doctor entered the kitchen and switched on the light. He laid the gun on the table and pulled up a chair. For a while he sat in complete silence, staring at the pistol as if it might jump up and do a jig. Then he stood and removed his jacket, hanging it on the hook by the door to the lounge. He went to the sink and splashed himself with cold water. Feeling for a towel, he stepped over to the mirror and dried his face.

Inside the mirror, he found his own features. Dark eyes, dark fringe, dark scowl.

He was about to leave the image, when something in the mirror caught his eye. A curling smoke that at first he thought was behind him in the room. But as he looked closer, it became evident that the mist was actually *inside* the glass. Gradually it condensed until all he could see was swirling grey smog, tinged with dark shadows. Then there was movement within. The suggestion of a face. Perhaps the fleeting wave of a groping hand that tapped briefly against the glass.

As the Doctor looked on, a definite form materialised in the mirror, and he was shocked to see Mary peering out at him. She pleaded soundlessly, face contorted with pain or dread or both. The Doctor reached out, a reflex reply, but there was only the cold surface of the mirror. Mary's features were dragged back into the churning smog, and he saw her hands reaching for him before she was rapidly consumed.

With a gunshot clap, the mirror cracked from edge to edge, eight lines snapping out from the centre of the glass. The Doctor jumped despite himself, and found eight distorted fragments of his own shocked reaction. The broken face gazed back at him, eyes distant with what could easily have been fear and confusion.

Outside, shadows moved through shadow. Six shapes swept towards the house. They advanced with practised fluidity, silent signals passing between them at intervals.

The kitchen light was on as they approached, and the curtains were still open. They crouched together under the window and a moment later the light went out.

The sergeant waved a gesture, and one of the troopers made its move.

Rocking gently to and fro in the chair by the fire, the Doctor listened as the piece of music from Mary's watch played its course. After six small performances, the spring was depleted and the music slowed to silence. The room was dark except for the glow from the fire, and now even that was dying to a red-rimmed black.

The noise was small but definite. The chair stopped rocking and the Doctor sat stock-still. There was the softest sound of footfalls in the kitchen. Rising slowly, he put the watch on the mantelpiece and stepped across to the kitchen door. Pressing his ear against it, he heard more soft scuffling as something made its way across the kitchen in the dark.

Holding his breath, the Doctor grasped the handle, but the door swung open suddenly, taking him by surprise and sending him stumbling. By the time he'd recovered, he found a face next to his. Black empty sockets and rotting flesh. The thing stank of earth and decay. It leered a permanent grin with gumless teeth, and the Doctor was gripped in a stunned stasis. A gun barrel rose into view, black orifice searching out his face.

The Doctor pushed. The dark broke around him and in an instant of chaos they clattered together into the kitchen. A chair cracked. The table groaned. Gunmetal flashed. The Doctor groped for the smashed seat and came up with a jagged fragment. Swinging it through the air at the curling shadow, he heard the crack of bone. The thing crumpled to the floor but came up again instantly, and this time they crashed together to the ground.

Shards of smashed wood littered the floor. The Doctor felt them at his throat. A weight pressed down on him and the smell of earth filled his lungs. He pushed back and the weight fell aside. Scrambling to his feet, the Doctor felt a sudden crashing pain across his back. He fell across the table and his cheek hit something hard and cold. Scrabbling for the pistol, he grasped it and thrust it into the dark.

The sounds of commotion stopped.

The Doctor found sightless sockets watching him. The dead man had his hands raised, and the Doctor could make out yellow bone where there should have been fingers. He became aware of a steady drip of liquid on the floor, and assumed that the thing was bleeding.

Tense stand-off. The thing did not make a move. It simply stood motionless with its arms in the air while the Doctor tried to make sense of it.

Then there was movement behind. Cold metal at his neck. Two rifles pinning him down. One each side at his back. The Doctor lowered the pistol. No contest.

The thing in front of him lowered its arms, drew back a fist of bones. There was the crunch of bursting bone. His face or the fist, he couldn't tell which. A white hot flash sent him careering back.

More movement. Dark and light. He saw the moon overhead, spinning momentarily. There was an overwhelming stench of rotting vegetation. The garden flooded past. Navy blue. Silver leaves. Moonlight. His arms were jerked painfully up and back, and he felt ropes around his wrists. Wrenched tight. Burning flesh.

Then calm. The Doctor found himself tied to the clothesline post halfway down the garden. Six men faced him, fresh from the grave. They lined up in front of him and raised their rifles in unison.

'Don't I get a last cigarette?' the Doctor managed to ask feebly, before the guns went off.

Chapter Eleven

Tormented by images in the dark, Albert Briggs was finding it impossible to sleep. The horrors of Hawkswick crowded in on him. A barrage of terrors. Blasted cattle, entrails glistening in the morning sun. Charlie Skaggs's staring head turning slowly in the tree. Dead men clambering over the heap of rubble that should have been his lock-up. Empty sockets turning on him. A single, gelatinous eye in a face of decrepit flesh. Gazing blind. *Watching* him.

After tossing and turning for half an hour, he'd dragged himself back downstairs and put on the kettle. Before it had even begun to work itself into a cosy little frenzy, he heard the blast. It echoed across the village, ripping the silence like a whiplash wound.

Taking the kettle off the range, Briggs jammed on his boots. Grabbing his coat at the door, he rushed out into the night and stood on the doorstep listening to the reborn silence. The sound had gone, and he hadn't heard where it came from. But he had a good idea what it was, and he had a good idea where to start looking.

Laces rattling about his ankles, pushing his nightshirt into his trousers, contorting his coat around his shoulders as if he were in the middle of some weird tribal dance, Briggs made his way towards Mary's house.

The house was in darkness as Briggs prowled up the path. He arrived at the side door to discover it wide open, and he was shocked to see the smashed furniture strewn across the little kitchen. He was about to step inside when he heard a subdued scuffling coming from the back.

Keeping himself wrapped in shadow, Briggs crept down the side of the house and peered into the garden. He saw the hunched shape of the Doctor tied to the clothes pole, straining at his bonds. The Doctor looked up suddenly, eyes flashing white in the black with frantic excitement.

'Help me,' he said. 'Get these ropes off.'

Briggs dashed across and set to work. 'What happened?'

'Firing squad,' the Doctor jabbered. 'Opened fire at ten paces.'

The ropes came loose and the Doctor paced up and down in the moonlight, rubbing his wrists. Briggs watched him warily. The man was obviously agitated and maybe just plain flipped.

'You're dead,' he reminded the Doctor, 'if you were shot at ten paces.'

The Doctor continued his pacing, tracing a short path and return while he rubbed his chin in intense thought.

'Psychic bullets,' he muttered dismissively.

'What the hell are you on about?'

'Psychic dynamics!' Briggs found wide eyes staring full of moonlight. 'Human nightmares incarnate. Spawned by war. Martial somatotypes. Telekinetic ammo. The ballistics of belief.' The Doctor resumed his pacing, yammering as he went. 'And these are just the side effects of what's happening at the Hall. Rogue forces. A breakaway unit. A guerrilla faction with its own distorted objectives.'

'What are you talking about?' Briggs beseeched.

The Doctor gave him an unsettling look and a brief silence fell.

'Armageddon.'

'Armageddon?'

'Hot war.'

Briggs shook his head. 'I'm sorry, Doctor. I just don't follow you at all.'

The Doctor grasped the nightshirt that hung loose at Briggs's chest, his eyes burning with fierce intensity.

'I was executed by a firing squad. Not one of them aimed to miss. But they used psychic bullets. The force of their will. My mind was strong enough to resist. I was convinced enough of the truth to repel them. My belief against theirs.'

'Your belief?'

A short laugh escaped the Doctor. 'The mind is a wonderful thing,' he enthused, taking Briggs by the arm and leading him back to the house. 'Untapped areas and strange hidden depths. What the village is experiencing is a psychic phenomenon of profound proportions. The forces are so ferocious they can tear apart the corporeal world. They must be connected some way to the cruelty, horror and sheer mindless slaughter of the war. Extreme human suffering.'

They entered the kitchen and the Doctor grabbed his jacket from the door. He regarded the mess on the floor with an abstracted gaze. Then he was moving again, leading Briggs out of the house and down the road. As they went he talked, an incessant babble of information that Briggs found impossible to follow but suspected contained a truth of some kind.

'I think the war is releasing the latent psychic powers of soldiers like those poor men up at the Hall. Perhaps an atavistic reversion. And somehow Dr Banham is letting it loose. Yes! Of course! That's it! He said his cure is to *exorcise*. But what's he doing with the raw energy he's tapped? Too much to handle. He's trying to store it. I think our friend Dr Banham has bitten off a little more than he can chew. That's what Private Corey could sense when he told me he felt a gathering evil. It's *growing*. At the Hall. If Banham was restraining it, he's about to lose control.'

The Doctor stopped dead in his tracks and slammed his head with the palm of his hand. '*That's* why Corey's body was returned to his bed! They were showing Banham what they were capable of. Playing games with him. *Exposing* him... Come on.'

He marched off and Briggs trotted after him towards the village. 'Where are we going?'

'Back to the Hall.'

'You are joking?'

'If we don't, I'm afraid there soon won't be much left to laugh about. *Come on!*'

They advanced through the fields, taking cover in the corn, arrow-formation, the tail checking the rear while the flanks kept up a moving guard to the sides. In the lucid moonlight their target was clear. The buildings crowded round, bustling in on the large house at their core. There were lights in most of the windows, but no sign of movement inside as the dead men made their final approach.

When they reached the side of the stables, they paused, perhaps sensing the demise of some of their kind, perhaps in a moment of respect for those lost in action.

Then they were moving on the house. Shadows lost in shadow. Dark in the dark. Making their move. The retaliatory strike.

Briggs couldn't believe he was doing this. He'd already been mightily embarrassed in front of Banham once today, and once was quite enough for Briggs and his threadbare nerves. The Doctor led him through the undergrowth, waving him on, then waving him down. They hunched together and Briggs could see the east-wing basement door.

'Look out for the guard,' the Doctor hissed.

'Guard?' Briggs didn't like the sound of that.

'Corporal L.P. Davies of the Twenty-Fourth Manchesters. He's keen as mustard and he's armed.'

'Bugger.'

'Don't worry. If he shoots you, just pretend you've been hit and fall down dead.'

Briggs was about to ask what the Doctor was on about, when he discovered an empty space at his side and saw the Doctor making a dash for it. Briggs set off in stooped pursuit. The Doctor tried the door but this time found it locked. He fumbled and produced a key. With a grumbling sound, the door opened in front of them and they slipped inside. The basement was dark as ever, and Briggs sensed again that feeling of foreboding that had struck him last time he was here. As if eyes were on him. Myriad eyes from inside the impenetrable shadow. His skin crawled.

The Doctor used the same key on the door to the gun store, and it swung open to reveal the tiny room lined with shelves.

'So what are we after?' Briggs asked.

'The truth,' the Doctor told him. 'Look.'

'At what?'

'See that back wall?'

'Yes?'

'Look at it. *Hard!*'

Briggs shot the Doctor a side glance, but the Doctor seemed to be concentrating on the wall.

'See that?' he said, without breaking his gaze.

Briggs looked, but all he saw was wall. The dark plaster was pitted, and lumps of the stuff had fallen out on to the floor. There were a couple of shelves about chest height, but nothing on them apart from small piles of plaster rubble.

'I can't see anything.'

'Look *harder*!' the Doctor demanded.

Briggs did, and was puzzled to see the wall move slightly under his gaze. Well, not *move* exactly, but shimmer, more like. As if it was fading. Or changing.

'See?' the Doctor said.

'What's happening?' Briggs was bemused but enthralled.

'We're breaking through. This room is a phantasm thrown up by the psychic forces. They're manipulating our perceptions. That's why I took the pistol. I wanted to see if it would remain solid so far from the source.'

'So the gun wasn't real?'

The Doctor shook his head. 'Only as real as that wall. And look.'

When Briggs looked back, the wall had faded even more, as if it were dissolving in front of his eyes.

'I don't believe it.'

'Believe it!' the Doctor told him. 'It's the power of your belief that's winning the battle.'

Now the wall was a ghost, like a shimmering heat haze on the far side of the small space. Beyond, Briggs could see a much larger room. There was a bank of glimmering candles on an elaborate array of candlesticks, and the room seemed to be coated in some kind of dull slime. There was a gap in the slime near the candles, and this seemed to have been marked out with a chalk circle that contained a book. The damp smell suddenly intensified, becoming the mingled stench of wet clay and candlewax.

The Doctor swept Briggs into the room and they slid to an unsteady halt in the middle of the floor. Briggs gazed in disbelief at the thick coating that covered every surface. While the Doctor stepped over to investigate the circle, Briggs found himself drawn towards the wall. Dull candlelight reflected out of the slightly glistening surface and, for a second, Briggs was certain that the wall was moving. As if the surface were so wet it was sinking into the floor.

Glancing over, Briggs saw the Doctor examining the book, flicking through the pages faster than he could possibly be reading them.

Seeing movement out of the corner of his eye, Briggs watched with fascination as the wall began to ooze in front of his face. Swirling at first, the malleable clay began to assume form, lifting itself from the wall like a tumour. The node of expanding clay reached out to him, and Briggs realised with horror that it was becoming a groping hand, blunt fingers forming in the shapeless mass.

'Doctor!'

'Hmm?' The Doctor was distant, still lost in the book.

'*Doctor!*'

Jolted out of his reverie, the Doctor dropped the book and slurped over to watch the wall. There were more nebulous shapes emerging. More hands, as if an army of people on the other side were trying to squeeze through an impermeable grey membrane. Then a burl which bloated to form the shape of a face. The face turned to them under the glossy surface, mouth gaping wide as if to scream.

'What are they?' Briggs demanded, feeling panic building to burst.

'Manifestations of the energies contained in this room,' the Doctor said hypnotically. 'They're trying to break free.'

'What do we do now?'

Without dragging his attention from the wall, the Doctor backed away slowly. 'I think a tactical withdrawal might be called for,' he said. 'Consolidate our forces. Come on.'

They turned for the door, and discovered it blocked by Banham. Continuing on his way, Briggs was stopped by the Doctor. While he floundered in brief bewilderment, Briggs saw Banham step into the room and close the door behind him.

'I see you've made yourselves at home,' Banham said.

As realisation dawned that this was no fanfare arrival of the cavalry, Briggs sensed the Doctor retreating behind him.

'It's a sweet little room,' the Doctor remarked casually. 'I do like the Gothic touch of the candles. Although the wallpaper is a little dramatic for my taste.'

Banham smiled. 'I wouldn't let the décor bother you unduly, Doctor. You're not going to be around much longer to be troubled by it.'

'Was that a thinly veiled attempt at a threat?' the Doctor mused.

'Don't mock me, Doctor,' Banham warned. 'I gave you repeated opportunities to leave, and you persistently ignored my warnings.

That seems to me to be an invitation of repercussions.'

'Actually, you could do with some more cushions in here. They'd take the sparseness off the place, don't you think?'

Shaking his head, features fixed and grim, Banham moved with deliberate slowness towards the Doctor.

'You do not understand what you have stumbled upon, Doctor,' he admonished.

'Oh, I think I understand perfectly well what you've been up to here, Dr Banham,' the Doctor said chattily. 'Releasing pent-up psychic forces. Channelling them and containing them. Even putting them, no doubt, to some diabolical use of your own. Hmm?'

Banham's advance continued relentlessly. 'You cannot begin to guess the powers I have mastered.'

'I think I can, actually,' the Doctor told him, his voice going nineteen to the dozen as he stepped back steadily through the sludge. 'Eternal youth? Material riches beyond imagining? Superhuman strength? Perhaps even extrasensory perceptions and a smattering of telekinetic powers... Am I close?'

Banham was now almost near enough to touch.

'Can you catch speeding bullets in your teeth? That's something I always wished I could do.'

When Banham got close enough to lash out, Briggs launched his offensive, hurling himself at the man with all the force he could pack into his legs. As he sailed through the air he had only the most fleeting impression of Banham's response, and the shock of pain that followed blasted the air from his lungs. He landed in a pile of mangled limbs at the Doctor's feet, and the Doctor scrambled to help him up.

'Rather foolish,' Banham said, entirely unruffled.

Clambering back on to his quivering legs, covered in clay and bruises, Briggs was shaking like a leaf.

'Didn't you listen to the bit about telekinetic powers?' the Doctor asked earnestly.

Briggs was dragged back with the Doctor as Banham lurched closer. Suddenly he stopped and, as the Doctor and Briggs looked on in mute anticipation, raised his hand at them in a vaguely threatening gesture. Briggs felt the Doctor's grip on his arm tighten, and watched Banham in bafflement.

Then a white-hot agony exploded inside him, and he was airborne and spinning. Again, he collapsed in a crumpled heap, this time his head pounding with the fiercest headache he'd ever had. The Doctor was over the opposite side of the room, scrambling to his feet in the slippery clay.

In a lightning-quick movement, Banham lifted Briggs by the throat as if the constable were a rag doll. As Briggs dangled, trying to gasp air that wasn't there and feeling consciousness seeping from him, he thought he saw a flash of something out of the corner of his eye. Then he was flying. He landed with a crash and darkness zoomed in.

Briggs came round to hear the Doctor screaming at the top of his voice.

'*Omne genus demoniorum, cecorum, claudorum, sive confusorum, attendite iussum meorum et vocationem verborum.*'

He was reading from the book, and both Briggs and the Doctor were now inside the circle. As Briggs clambered to his knees he saw the clay, two or three inches thick, stopped dead at the chalk boundary, and Banham stood seething outside the circle, apparently unable to cross the line.

'*Vos attestor, vos contestor,*' the Doctor continued, voice booming, palm raised at Banham, '*per mandatum Domini, ne zeletis, quem soletis vos vexare, homini, ut compareatis et post discedatis, et cum desperatis chaos incolatis!*'

A cold and brittle stillness ensued. Banham glared at the Doctor as he lowered the book and peered over it, seeming more than a little surprised and relieved that the invocation had worked.

'Now,' the Doctor said quietly, 'we understand each other.'

'You'll never get out of here,' Banham hissed. There was motion in his eyes. A grey curling that Briggs thought looked like the motion he'd seen in the walls. Subtle at first, but after a moment Banham's eyes had gone – replaced by what looked like clay. When Banham spoke again, Briggs was appalled to hear a demonic growl emerge.

'You are trapped. You will die.'

The thing that was and wasn't Banham stepped to the back of the room and closed its eyes, lifting its arms in silent invocation.

To Briggs's horror, the surfaces of the room began to stir. This time, not only the walls but floor and ceiling as well. Hands formed, groping. They stretched deeper into the room, until arms appeared, and eventually Briggs was alarmed to see whole torsos looming out of the clay. One appeared on the floor, dragging itself up as if climbing through a hatch.

Another came out of the ceiling, legs first, descending slowly until it dropped with a squelch to the ground. Gleaming clay resolved itself into a man. Candlelit contours concluded their slick metamorphosis. The man stood. Mud-gorged khaki and loose-hanging flesh. Straight from the grave. He gazed at them out of bulging eyes in a cratered face. The thing unshouldered a rifle and paced around the slime on the perimeter of the circle, scowling at them ominously.

Other shapes emerged from the surfaces of the room, until Briggs and the Doctor were surrounded. The dead men observed them, and Briggs stared back with a mixture of disbelief and rising terror. The troopers caressed their guns. Ragged, bony fingers toying with very solid-looking triggers.

'We are perfectly safe,' the Doctor assured Briggs with a calm and quiet voice, 'while we remain inside the circle.'

While he spoke he was flicking through the book, and Briggs

saw that it was packed with images of what looked suspiciously to him like Hell.

'Somewhere in here,' the Doctor told him as he turned the pages furiously, 'is our ticket out. There must be *something* that will grant us safe passage.'

'What is that stuff?' Briggs asked, his voice a whisper, his throat tight with fear.

'Ancient lore,' the Doctor said without looking up. 'This book is Banham's means of control. It contains archaic spells.'

'Spells?'

'Charms, conjurations, incantations. *Spells!*'

'Witchcraft?' Briggs asked in amazement.

'Black Magic. The Dark Arts,' the Doctor chanced a glance at Briggs, and Briggs realised that he was deadly serious. 'Call it what you like. The point is – they stem from a time when Man was more in touch with his real nature. Like a race memory, they're programmed into the psyche. Since that's where the Dark Forces come from, they're also programmed to respond to that control. Banham's been using this to control the forces. Now they've become so strong that they're consuming him. He's become part of them, and we can use his own weapon *against* him.'

'Surrender yourselves,' Banham growled, voice rumbling as if it were rising from the bowels of the earth.

'With you in one minute,' the Doctor said, still going through the book, now with the beginnings of a frown appearing in his face.

'Surrender *now*,' the Banham-thing demanded.

The wall by the door was swirling again, and Briggs looked over to see a new shape emerging. Another human form, hunched and decrepit, but as Briggs looked on he was startled to see that it was the shape of a woman. The Doctor hadn't noticed. He was searching the book, running his fingers over the pages with an intense frown.

'Doctor,' Briggs said.

'Yes?' He didn't look up.

'Doctor. Look.'

The Doctor glanced up to see the shape covered in wet clay, hair plastered and head bowed. She was held against the wall by half-formed hands, her arms outstretched as if she were bound to an invisible cross. Briggs could only shake his head in terror as heard the Doctor whisper at his side.

'Mary…'

Cromby lounged in his chair by the fire, although the night was warm and the fire was out. It had become habit to sit for an hour before going to bed, and it was part of life's ritual. If he didn't have his hour by the fire, he'd never sleep a wink. Iris was busy with her lace-making, slumped on the sofa, slender bobbins dancing about her dumpy fingers.

After such a hideous day, it was nice to get back to the routine. To get lost in their ordinary things. The lace cushion was Iris's rosary. Tiny repetitive patterns, ultimately creating a thing of delicate intricacy, symmetry and beauty. To Iris Cromby, it was a meditative, religious task. And over the years that they had shared this hour of silence at the end of the day, Bill Cromby had developed a warm affection for the small click and clack of the activity.

The bobbins came to an abrupt standstill. Cromby opened his eyes and watched her, puzzled. He found Iris watching him back anxiously.

'What was that?' she asked.

'What?'

'Thought I 'eard somethin'.'

Cromby shook his head. 'Didn't 'ear owt.'

'Sounded like somebody movin' about outside.'

Lifting himself out of the chair, Cromby forgot about his bad arm and rose awkwardly with a wince. He grasped his shoulder, gritted his teeth, and lurched from the room.

In the kitchen, he found the dogs cowering in the corner. They weren't even whimpering. Just cringing and trembling in silence. Cromby took one look at them and knew suddenly that today hadn't been the end of the story. His burning of the stables hadn't exterminated their little problem. The pest was back. And it was probably here for retribution.

Rushing over to the dresser, Cromby grasped a handful of cartridges and thrust them into his pockets. Then he took the shotgun from its hooks on the wall and swept across the room to the door. It was dark outside, but there was a big bright moon, which meant he would have no trouble spotting anybody on the prowl.

Loading both barrels, but leaving the gun broken across his arm, Cromby stepped out into the night and gazed about. The yard was empty and still. Not even a breeze to disturb the dust. He listened to the silence, then felt the cold touch of steel on the back of his neck –

Mary emerged from perceptual dark and gasped what felt like her first breath in a very long time. Forcing open her eyes against the grit and weight of clay, she found the Doctor and Briggs watching her horrified from inside the chalk circle. She made a weak attempt to move but found herself immobilised, arms numb and fixed securely to the wall.

Her head was spinning with a mosaic memory of recent events. She had a befuddled recollection of the door slamming shut, of darkness rushing in. Fighting for air, sinking fast, being submerged, a terrifying sensory ordeal which ended in blackness and a dreamscape vision of appealing to the Doctor for help. He'd seemed tantalisingly close as she'd reached out to him, but he'd been dragged into bleak oblivion and she was left alone in a cold and featureless void.

She'd thought it was death. In fiery spasms of dread she'd died. Now she was alive again, and the thick damp air in her lungs was sweet as a spring breeze. A reflex laugh broke out of her and she felt tears of relief pouring down her cheeks.

The human mind can cope with only so many impossible things, Briggs thought. After a while they become acceptable, however outrageous they are. He assumed that was how the men at the front must feel. They would face the horror of it all initially with panic and disbelief, but after a while become inured to the hell of everyday madness. In a life-or-death situation you adapt or die. Simple truth. Mary Minett came out of the wall, and after all he'd seen these past months and days, he accepted it now as something real.

Banham watched them all with his grey eyes, and a cruel smile insinuated itself in his rigid features. To the Doctor's dismay, the dead men took up positions across the room, shouldered arms and took aim. Mary realised suddenly what they were preparing to do, and began to squirm and fight, crying out in despair. But she was trapped and she was going to die.

'*Noooo!*'

The Doctor dived out of the circle, arms raised high, and Briggs saw Banham's smile transform into a positive grin. There was a moment of uncertainty as the dead men awaited orders, and then a moment of mêlée as the Doctor hurled himself at one of the soldiers in the firing squad. The next thing Briggs knew there was a rifle at Banham's head, and the Doctor's finger was tightening on the trigger.

'Call them off,' the Doctor breathed.

Without a word from Banham, the rifles were lowered.

'You wouldn't shoot me,' Banham assured him.

'Wouldn't I?'

'When you guessed that I possess a degree of extrasensory

perception, Doctor, you were absolutely right.'

Banham took hold of the barrel. He tried to push the muzzle aside, but the Doctor held his ground.

'You shouldn't believe everything you hear,' the Doctor told him.

Briggs saw the certainty flicker on Banham's face. In a lightning movement, Banham swiped hard and the gun was wrenched from the Doctor's grasp. A shot rang out. A patch of clay in the ceiling exploded like the surface of a lake and splashed viscously to the floor. The rifle swept through the air in a swift arc that left Banham in charge.

There was a moment of gloating. Although the Doctor might falter in killing Banham, Briggs felt certain that Banham wouldn't share the same qualms in return. The shot was coming. The Doctor was going to lose his head in a shower of blood and splattered gore.

Diving from the circle, Briggs grasped the rifle from the nearest trooper and in an elegant motion that amazed even himself, he squelched into the mud at Banham's feet. Briggs was no hero. He was an old man caught up in a nightmare he needed to end. He was tired and sore and he wanted to go home. Banham was evil incarnate. All the death and destruction Hawkswick had suffered over the months were distilled in this towering monster.

The Enfield was moving. Swinging down. Doctor to Briggs. No remorse. Just casual carnage. It *had* to end. *Now*. Briggs pulled the trigger and blasted Banham square in the chest.

The effect was not what he expected at all. Banham collapsed against the wall, clasping the gaping wound. As Briggs scrambled back through the mud, he glimpsed a swirling grey mass inside the crumpled shape of a man. Ragged edges of a chest cavity that should have been spraying blood. Instead, there was an area of darkness that Banham clutched with frenzied hands. Inside the dark were little grey shapes. Swiping hands. Flashing eyes. A commotion of frantic activity. An impossible dance of miniature demons trying to get out.

Mary pitched from the wall. The Doctor threw himself into the middle of the room. The dead men milled about in a daze.

Banham's grey eyes were wide with fear. The smooth texture of his face grew suddenly fissured with lines of age, his hands grew knobbly and ancient in the space of seconds. The darkness inside him seemed to be made of spindly arms. Trying to tear free. Black eyes gleamed out of the turmoil. Banham thrashed, panted and gasped. The clay splashed as he was flung around in paroxysms of panic.

The Doctor's voice boomed: '*Down!*'

But Briggs could only watch in wonder as Banham's ancient body was ripped open and a flaming screaming darkness rushed out –

Chapter Twelve

A split second passed. Cromby felt the weight of the open gun across his bad arm, and the pressure of the muzzle on the back of his neck. He sensed a presence at his shoulder. Looming. Shadowy. Vengeance intent. The things he'd destroyed were back. And now they were mad as buggery.

Flinging the shotgun up on to his shoulder, Cromby heard it shut with a clack, and allowed it to tug on his finger in a continuous fluid motion. There was an explosion and the cold metal pressure on his neck vanished as suddenly as it had appeared. He spun to see a headless body collapse on the step, chunks of gristle and bone still showering the ground and landing with dull thuds in the echoing silence.

More movement behind him. He turned to see shadows flitting about the other side of the yard. Chunks of dark that could have been men. They were shuffling between the buildings. Then a shot rang out and Cromby ducked. The door frame by his head exploded with a deafening crack and splintering of wood. Cromby plunged into the kitchen and kicked the door shut. After scrambling for the key, he managed to get the door locked and bolted.

When he turned, he found Iris watching him from the door, face pale, eyes goggling. He jumped up and dashed into the hall, heading for the stairs, holding the door open and ushering Iris through. They moved together without a word, reading one another's intentions even in the dark.

As they scrambled together up the stairs, they heard the crash of the back door as it shattered under assault from a grenade. Then the sound of footsteps rushing through the house.

The dead men were inside.

* * *

The throbbing pain in his left arm was the first thing that struck Briggs as he regained consciousness. He opened his eyes to see a lowering sky overhead. He struggled to sit up and saw that they had arrived in a landscape like the photographs he'd seen of France. Gnarled black trees rose like grisly hands out of the barren mud. Sludge greyed by spent artillery stretched off to greet a brooding horizon. The air was redolent of cordite, a sulphur stink that reminded Briggs of the pictures he'd seen in Banham's book.

The Doctor stooped, attending to Mary, who lay unconscious in the mud nearby. As Briggs clambered to his feet, the effort reminding him ferociously of the nagging agony in his arm, he realised that the Doctor had dressed a wound with a tourniquet made from strips of torn nightshirt and a stub of broken branch. The sleeve below the elbow was soaked with blood, and Briggs was hit by a wave of dizziness when he saw it. Pulling himself together, he made his way over to the others.

Affording him only the most cursory glance, the Doctor continued to assess Mary. 'You were bleeding badly,' he informed Briggs in a matter-of-fact tone as he worked, 'but you'll be fine now. Try not to move about too much.'

'Where the bloody hell are we?'

'I suspect we're in a netherworld created by Banham's Dark Forces,' the Doctor said, carefully turning the mud-gorged Mary on to her side.

Dark was light. Silence sound. A bloated face loomed. She pushed. Screamed. Hands attacking. Grasping. Holding. Straitjacket grip and soothing voice. *'Hey hey calm down you're all right calm down it's only me...'*

Emerging from the clutter of terrifying sensations, Mary found the Doctor restraining her by the arms. He gazed into her face, pale eyes packed with concern, and the spiky talons of hysteria faded like ghosts.

'Are you all right now?'

She nodded, trying to convince herself more than the Doctor.

'Do you think you could walk?' he asked, scrutinising the surroundings in a state of some agitation.

'Walk where?'

'Anywhere. We're sitting ducks here in the open. I've seen movement out in the field.'

Mary tried to stand, but could manage to do so only with the Doctor's support. He helped her up and she took in the battle-churned wilderness.

'Where are we?'

'Netherworld,' Briggs answered knowingly, 'created by the Dark Forces.'

'It's like an artist's impression of no-man's-land,' Mary said.

'An apt description,' the Doctor concurred, leading her through mud that came up to her ankles. 'This place is wrought from nightmares of the war.'

'This isn't a real place, then?' Mary asked, struggling to drag her feet out of the hungry slime.

'Oh, it's real, all right,' the Doctor told them. 'The forces Banham captured are of such magnitude now that I suspect they can create quite substantial realities.'

Mary shook her head. 'You're saying this place is created from the psychic energy that Dr Banham found inside those poor men's heads?'

'That's right.'

'Do you make up this twaddle as you go along?' Mary asked him earnestly. 'Or do you have specially prepared balderdash ready for just such occasions?'

At that moment the first shell dropped. And the second and several more. They whistled in and pummelled the ground, sending up a hail of mud. Luckily, the earth was already so pulverised that it dampened the worst effects, and the shells were buried deep before detonation.

The Doctor yelled but Briggs didn't need telling to run.

Her whole body feeling smashed and twisted, Mary emitted a gasp of shock as the Doctor dragged her along. The world transformed abruptly into a patchwork of pain and dancing dark. It screamed and raged and Mary lost all reasoned thought to a furious adrenaline kick that thrust her headlong through the seething insanity.

She sensed in some detached way the explosions around her, as if she were both in and out of her body as they bolted. The physical jolts became integrated into the roaring blasts of her blood crashing like a tidal torrent.

Then there was only the flight. The last response of the human mammal. It consumed her. Whipped her back to primordial time. Stripped her of all social complexity and returned her to the state of the beast.

Only the flight.

A chasm opened. Took her down. Belted her into instant submission and the fire of the chase momentarily died. Reasoned thought took up residence again and she realised they'd stumbled into an unmanned trench. Briggs lay nearby, winded but struggling to get his bearings. The Doctor scrambled to his knees and threw himself against the battered boards that formed the wall of the trench, eyes flashing in the surreal grey light. He was everywhere at once. Checking their position, cover, weapons, fitness and strength.

As Briggs scrambled shakily to his feet, the Doctor gestured to an abandoned machine-gun post nearby, then scurried on his hands and knees towards a stack of sandbags while Briggs fought a losing battle with the intricacies of the gun's loading mechanism.

Another blast collapsed the boards where the Doctor had been crouched only seconds before, and Mary scurried like a rat through the sludge to help Briggs with the gun. Together they managed to get the thing firing, pulsing a storm of bullets into the void, keeping their heads low and completely blind to the effect they were having. It just felt good to be fighting back.

Mary saw the Doctor rip open a sandbag and appear dismayed when a pile of soil fell out. He tried another, only to find that stuffed with soil as well. He looked about in panic, then scrabbled over to a battered fire bucket that hung on a wooden peg nearby. Grasping the bucket, he dashed back and proceeded to pour out its contents carefully into the mud.

A crash of thunder by her ear knocked Mary sideways and dazed her momentarily. Her face was wet and she reached up in dread to find it was just mud. There was a scuffling nearby, and the gun was yanked out of her grasp as Briggs spun it to let loose a volley to her back. She heard a body thump heavily into the mud.

'Here!' the Doctor was yelling. 'Over here. Quickly. Get into the circle.'

When she looked, he'd created a circle of sand in the mud. Briggs was already halfway there, and another scuffling behind her sent Mary in hot pursuit. They slammed together into the Doctor and he slapped his arms around them.

'*Vos attestor,*' the Doctor screamed. '*Per mandatum Domini!*'

The howling hell fell still. As if the Doctor had thrown a magic switch, an eerie, echoing quiet instantly permeated the air. There was only the sound of their own racing breath. The rest was silence.

A squad of corpse soldiers stood on the rim of the trench, guns poised, glancing between themselves indecisively.

'*Vos contestor,*' the Doctor yelled, his voice strong and sure, '*ne zeletis, quem soletis vos vexare, homini, ut compareatis et post discedatis, et cum desperatis chaos incolatis!*'

The guns were lowered. The soldiers stood in meek surrender

like a line of prisoners of war. Mary became aware of the Doctor's hoarse breathing in her ear. There was a moment of tense uncertainty, then he allowed himself a gargantuan sigh of relief.

'I think I got their attention,' he said.

'So what do we do now?' asked Briggs.

The Doctor seemed unsure. 'I could try to bargain with them.'

'You can't *talk* to them,' Mary told him in alarm.

'Why not?'

'Well...' she floundered. You can't leave us, she thought. They'll shoot you down, then come after us and we won't survive without you –

'You can't *trust* them,' declared Briggs.

'But we can't stand here for ever,' the Doctor pointed out.

Then the motion started. A stirring in the mud beside the circle. The sludge began to curl and boil, and a blunt shape emerged beside them, rising into the air until it towered eight feet tall, a grotesque parody of a man. It reminded Mary of the huge clay forms that Banham used in his therapy. As she watched in awe and horror, the face took on vague areas of shadow that became nightmare eyes and a twisted mouth. Then it leaned closer as if peering at them in their pathetic little ring of sand.

'*Per mandatum Domini!*' the Doctor began, this time his voice less sure.

The twist of shadow that represented the thing's mouth spread into a definite smile and it shook its head slowly at the Doctor.

'*Vos contestor,*' the Doctor continued, the uncertainty in his voice now plain to hear, '*per mandatum Domini...*'

The creature reached in and gently stroked the side of Mary's cheek. A cold, damp touch that left a gritty grey stain.

The Doctor fell silent.

A tense moment followed, before the thing grasped Mary by the throat and lifted her bodily off her feet. She gasped for breath that wouldn't come, felt the searing spasms of agony leap around her spine as her legs thrashed convulsively beneath her. Eyes bulged. Ears roared. Hands grasped. Darkness came.

They were scrabbling about downstairs, moving furniture and slamming doors. Iris and Bill Cromby listened fearfully together in the dark of the bedroom as they considered their options.

Apart from the wardrobe, there was nowhere to hide. There were several dead men, and Cromby's shotgun held only two cartridges. To reload meant precious seconds' work and in that time they would be dead.

Cromby crept over to the window while Iris crouched in the dark by the door. They were second-storey and the drop was sheer.

Then she heard the stairs grumble as something thumped its way up. She gave Bill an anguished look and he gazed back from the window. As Bill reached slowly for the eiderdown, Iris shook her head in consternation. There were sounds of movement just outside the door.

No way out.

They were going to die.

The Doctor launched himself out of the circle, collapsed into the mud with a splash, rolled and instantly was back on his feet, dashing for the machine gun that Briggs and Mary had manned just a short time before. The dead men on the banking swung their weapons to cover him, but the Doctor was too fast. Grasping the gun, he yanked it from its cradle and turned it on the creature.

The clay thing dropped Mary and turned to face the Doctor. While Briggs frantically tried to get the dazed Mary back into the circle without disturbing the mound of sand, the Doctor and the creature faced each other in a moment of stand-off. The Doctor gritted his teeth, gun firm in his grasp, but the shots didn't come.

With a slow squelching and sucking, the thing began to recede into the mud, sinking steadily until nothing remained.

Gasping with relief, Briggs waved the Doctor over, but to his amazement the Doctor refused to budge. He sat in the mud, surrounded by corpse-soldiers with their rifles raised, and simply gazed about at the ground with gaping eyes.

Rubbing her bruised throat, Mary watched as the ground started to heave again, this time around the Doctor himself. He began to submerge and, as he thrashed, the mud took him slowly but steadily. Mary watched him sink until he was completely immersed. The splashing stopped. Then so did the boiling beneath the surface.

The machine gun sat upturned in the mud, but the Doctor was gone.

The bedroom door crashed open and a dead man stepped inside. The room was apparently empty, but there was a wardrobe that would make a good hiding place in the shadows. The dead man tried the door but found it locked and the key had been removed. It was about to force the door when something arrested its attention. A sound from outside in the yard. The sound of giant doors opening.

Dashing to the window, the dead man looked out in time to see a lumbering shadow vanishing into the barn and closing the door again with a clatter. There was a makeshift rope of end-to-end blankets hanging from the window ledge and it led down to ground level.

With a fixed grin on its death's-head face, the corpse soldier turned and left the room with a limping quick-march.

When it had gone, after a short hiatus, the wardrobe rattled and a high-pitched whisper came from inside.

'Bill? Bill! William Cromby! Let me out!'

Silence.

'Bill?'

* * *

With the Doctor gone, Briggs and Mary huddled together and gaped at the surrounding soldiers clambering down into the trench, seemingly intent on concluding their mission of massacre.

There were a dozen or more, dead men all, smashed and torn and decaying. They sauntered across to the circle. Briggs watched one of them level a mud-spattered Lee Enfield and take casual aim at Mary from a few short paces. The rifle went off with a flash and an echoing crack, and Briggs felt Mary convulse in his grasp.

But Mary didn't crumple. Her tight grip on his arm remained, and he looked down to see her gazing in confusion at him.

'They can't harm us,' Briggs laughed. 'Not if we stay in the circle. They can't touch us in here.'

More of the dead men took aim and fired, a barrage of bullets and shrieking ricochets. Briggs automatically closed his eyes, but after a moment of sustained chaos, he peeped to find the dead men gradually giving up.

One of them came up close and studied the sand piled around them to form the delicate circle. It raised a pistol, took a lazy shot at the sand, and Briggs saw a puff of dust and grit fly up. Another shot sent more grit flying, and another. The others joined in, all of them taking careful aim now and firing in unison at the precise spot on the perimeter of the circle. It was infuriatingly slow, but the sand was yielding with relentless erosion.

One of the dead men grasped the machine gun from the mud where the Doctor had dropped it, and took aim. The gun roared into action, shots spraying everywhere as it jerked and bounced with recoil. Briggs and Mary cringed together, Mary covering her ears from the rattle and racket. Gradually the shots grew more controlled, and finally Briggs could see that the sand was erupting into the air in little wisps of smoke. The integrity of the circle was collapsing now with a swiftness they could see. After only a minute, there was an incision like a tiny ravine, and precious little sand left to sustain the circle unbroken. Finally the last grains were blasted and the gunfire ceased, leaving a resounding silence in its wake.

The soldier with the machine gun dropped it into the mud and stepped over slowly, removing a pistol from its holster. Releasing the safety catch, it swung the pistol into the circle and took a pot shot. The mud inside the circle erupted with a faint *glug* as the shot echoed around them.

Mary glimpsed a fearful fleshless grin and the next thing she knew the dead men were rushing in.

They scurried across the yard with lightning speed, rushing shadows like lightplay on a rolling river. Merging with the darkness in front of the barn door, they fell into silence and stillness. Shouldering arms, they waited and listened. There was movement inside the door. A scuffling.

Black holes-for-eyes watched warily as the leader grasped the door and –

The doors exploded outwards with a cacophony of sound and motion. Giant black shapes burst through the dark and the dead men were scattered. Guns clattered. Bones cracked. The turmoil receded with a furious clapping of hooves, and a fragile calm returned.

Checking their guns and equipment, the dead men gathered together. One of them remained prostrate on the floor, its chest and head crumbled to dirt under the onslaught from the horses. The others stood round momentarily before regrouping at the barn door.

Now the place looked empty, full of dark and secrets. The dead men stepped inside and began to search methodically.

The world went mad with furious activity. It became instantly a series of disjointed images that reminded Mary of the time she'd been at the cinema watching the *Battle of the Ancre* and the projector had broken down. Ruptured scenes jigged about in front of her in a frenzy of black and white and grey. Her arms were jerked up her back with a ferocity that made her yelp in pain. She was manhandled through the slime until she came to rest at one end of the short stretch of trench. Unable to move for cold hands gripping her wrists, Mary watched Briggs being tied to an outcrop of wood that had been blasted by the bombardment. Under unspoken command, a pack of dead men lined up nearby and Mary watched them check their weapons.

She found Briggs's eyes vacant of fear. He seemed entirely resigned to death, and stood with his chest thrust out, facing them proudly. Mary struggled against the grip on her wrists.

There was a pause as the men raised their rifles. A summary execution. A single insignificant pulse in the blizzard of bullets that was war. Mary cried out in rage and despair at the waste –

Take aim…

Briggs was a *good* man. An *old* man. A life spent in the service of others. He didn't deserve to die like this in a nightmare world gone mad –

Fire!

One of the dead men clambered up the ladder to the hayloft, leaving the others to search the lower barn for Cromby. As it rose into the darkness, vigilant for attack, it found only shadow and the musk of hay and straw. No movement. No sign of life. Nobody breathing.

It stepped up into the loft, rifle poised, and as it began to move slowly into the shadow it felt the rope across its ankle. There was a sudden *whoosh* of movement like a swooping bird of prey. The dead man looked up and the last thing it saw was the rushing, rope-bound fork that swiped its head from its shoulders.

The body toppled back and tumbled through the loft hatch, crashing to the ground below and erupting into a burst of dusty death. The others gathered round, then gazed up into the darkness above.

In silent unison, they made their move up the ladder.

As the firing squad opened fire, the trench in front of Briggs exploded and a tower of mud surged high into the air. The force of the blast threw the soldiers back, and Mary felt the grip on her wrists released. The ground swooped up and she suffered another jarring crash.

The turmoil subsided but, when she looked up, she found a mountain of mud filling the space that used to be trench. The mountain surged and slurped as it gradually took form, finally resolving itself into the indistinct shape of a man, this time twenty feet tall. Mary glimpsed great tree-trunk arms and a giant, seething face, features raging and changing as she looked. A cleft opened up where the thing's mouth should have been and a baleful roar emerged, a wail from the depths of the earth that rang out in the strange land.

Immediately all hell was let loose. The air screeched. The world shuddered. Mud splashed. Already-dead bodies scrambled about the trench seeking cover. Some of them exploded while they ran, bodies blowing apart and slopping into the mud. Mary dived into the circle, frenziedly patting the disrupted piles of sand back into place. She hunched alone amid the turmoil, bringing up her knees and trying to curl into a tight ball against the onslaught.

Midair bursts lit up the dark-grey sky with flashes of fierce white light. The sky seemed to tear open in several places at once. Bodies were launched through the air. They landed in muddled heaps of arms and legs and trunks, dark holes gazing out of severed, flesh-tattered skulls.

A pair of dead men nearby wrestled with bayonets, slicing each other with savage ferocity. A third man blasted one of them into oblivion. The survivor made a salute of thanks, then it too was destroyed by the same assailant in a spectacular eruption of spraying viscera.

Mary tried to avoid registering the horrific detail of the carnage, but the split-second images were embedded in her brain like shrapnel.

The giant mud shape wailed and roared. It seemed to be half submerged in the ground, the top half of its torso thrashing wildly.

Suddenly Mary saw Briggs on the other side of the trench, wrenching his wrists out of ragged ropes. He dashed towards her, hands outstretched. She screamed his name but the sound came out all wrong. Her voice yet not her voice. Briggs launched himself into the air and the motion slowed to a dead stop. He hung suspended, eyes wide, hands grasping. Frozen.

Hot blood roared through Mary's ears. She had the fleeting idea that she was suffering some kind of complete mental collapse. Too much happening. Too much noise. Too much death and destruction.

Too much…

The frozen picture of the world began to spin, a swirling motion that made her feel dizzy and sick. The ground gave way and suddenly she was tumbling. Surging grey. Devastating nausea. Dark and light mingled. Falling. Spinning. Dark and darker.

Too much…

Chaos crushed her.

Blackness rushed in and there was nothing at all –

They moved warily through the hayloft, alert to every nuance of the night. Rifles ready, they fanned out into a search pattern. When they reached the far end of the loft, they discovered the open pitch-door with the hoist-beam above it, and the hanging rope that dropped to the ground below. The rope was swinging slightly, despite that fact that there wasn't even a whisper of breeze.

A silent signal sent them all scrambling to the loft hatch and back down into the barn.

The suffocating black cleared sluggishly and Mary found herself sprawled in the mud. The place was dark, cold and still. At first, she thought she was still in the netherworld, but reality sank its slow white fangs into her when she heard Briggs groaning nearby. She dragged herself up to see him rising shakily to his feet. His face was as silver-pale as his hair, and he looked as if he'd been dragged kicking and screaming through the middle of a battlefield.

'Are you all right?' he asked.

'I think so,' Mary said, trying to gather her thoughts and moving warily to avoid disturbing any broken bones she might have sustained.

They were back in Banham's clay room, and now the door was ajar and creamy light drizzled in from the corridor. The candles had blown out but she could smell the smoke and see the still-glowing red tips in the dark.

Gazing into the dense gloom, Mary became aware of a third body sprawled on the floor nearby. Scrabbling through the clay, she found the Doctor lying motionless. She leaned over and checked for a heartbeat, only to find a curiously chugging pulse that bumped from side to side as if he had a heart as wide as his whole chest. She bent closer and felt his warm breath emerging on her cheek.

'This is becoming a habit,' he whispered softly in her ear.

Mary jumped out of her skin, fell back and landed in the clay with an undignified squelch.

'I'm sorry,' the Doctor announced, pulling himself upright. 'Did I startle you?'

'I thought you were…'

'What?'

She shook her head in a muddle.

'What happened?' Briggs demanded, offering the Doctor a hand.

'I fought the Demon with its own weapon,' he said. 'The power of the psyche.' He tapped his forehead. 'Turned the Forces on themselves and tied them in knots. That's the trouble with war, you see. Too much friendly fire. After a while you don't know *who* the enemy is.'

'It's an insane pastime for the human race,' Briggs said reflectively, and Mary regarded him with a look of new respect.

The Doctor paced over and picked up the book from inside the chalk circle, turning it thoughtfully in his hands. Shoving it under his arm, he turned to them with a bright smile.

'I think we could all do with a nice hot bath,' he announced.

'I hope not together,' Mary said.

'I could do with a cup o' tea,' said Briggs.

As they stepped to the door the Doctor stopped abruptly, and Mary became aware of a faint slurping sound behind them. They turned together to see the darkness in motion. The ceiling bulged in, forming an immense face. Dark eyes snapped open even before the face had finished emerging.

'It's Banham,' Mary gasped.

The Doctor pushed them on their way, not for one second taking his eyes off the vastly bloated shape appearing in the ceiling.

'Get this place evacuated,' he told them, snatching open the book and squinting into it in the dark.

Mary and Briggs lingered in the doorway.

'*Now!*' the Doctor yelled.

As Mary bulldozed Briggs down the corridor towards the exit, she looked back to see the door slam shut behind them. The sound of it reverberated down the corridor with ghastly finality.

Down in the barn, the dead men made their way swiftly to the door, but when they swung it open to plunge outside, the air was filled with a double explosion that sent them reeling.

They collapsed back, stunned and disarrayed. The leader scrambled on its belly to peer out into the night, and saw the shotgun tied to the cart just outside the door, jury-rigged with ropes and sticks to go off when the door was opened.

Yellow teeth ground and a snarl curled into the lame excuse for a face. It surveyed the damage caused by the wide-angle spray from the shot, and saw that it now had only two men left that were any use. The others had sustained too much damage to be able to function. Tattered limbs and rags for hands are useless even to undead soldiers.

With a furious signal to the other two, the leader brought them together by the door and they planned their strategy. As they were about to leave, the dark broke into a fissured thing that swam about them in a tangle of slants and whispers.

One of the dead men collapsed before the last two knew what had hit them, and as the next one dropped, the leader finally saw the great hulking shape of William Cromby wielding a scythe like some barbarian Grim Reaper.

Shouldering its gun, the leader blasted a hole in the dark. But the rifle was yanked from its grasp, hurled into the distance and rattled across the floor in the pitch black.

Commotion followed. Hand-to-hand engagement. The scythe clattered to the floor and the two warriors connected in a very personal skirmish.

Cromby spent long hard days in the fields. He was a hulking chunk of farm machinery. Never stopped. Never flagged. The thought had occurred to him that if these things were dead already, then they wouldn't tire either, and close combat probably wasn't such a good idea despite his undoubted strength. There were only confused impressions of his opponent in the dark. A flash of bone, a spray of fluid, a blaze of pain. He lashed out a left hook that connected with solid bone and there was a loud crack that may have been the thing's skull or his own knuckles. He felt bones suddenly squeezing into his throat. Felt his windpipe crush. Swung up his arms but his bad shoulder suddenly gave with a blinding white flash of pain and the next thing he knew the dead man had the scythe.

It swept through the air above them and –

The rolling lands in front of Hawkswick Hall were full of waiting people. As Briggs watched, Mary emerged from the main entrance with the last clutch of men, some in pyjamas, some in uniform. They made their way briskly out into the night. The one good thing about abandoning a military hospital, Briggs supposed, was that the evacuation was always going to go with military precision and speed. It had taken less than ten minutes to get the entire place empty, and with the exception of a couple of men who were known for their night-time skulking off, everyone was now present and correct.

There was subdued confusion about the evacuation, and people were looking in bewilderment for rising flames or billowing smoke. But the night sky was clear black, sprinkled liberally with pinprick stars, and there wasn't the slightest hint of any disaster, unfolding or pending.

When the explosion came, Mary was only yards from the house. The force of it flung her into the grass, and Briggs watched the roof of the east wing blow itself high into the dark night sky.

The blast was a single clap that slammed shattered slates and roof joists into the night. They came down with a clatter around the house, and the gathered crowd stampeded, dashing for cover, crying out in pain or panic as they went.

Briggs pushed his way through the scattering flow to Mary, and reached her in the echoing aftermath of the explosion. As he lifted her, they looked together back at the Hall. From the east wing, they could see a wide band of dark matter rising like thick smoke into the sky. The darkness gathered above, blotting the stars and making the clear sky nebulous. Then it began to spread swiftly and descend.

The subsequent storm broke instantly. Thunder and lightning and blasting gales.

Briggs covered his eyes, listened to the shrieking wind, and could swear he heard the squeal of human voices mingled with it. A choir of suffering. Howls and cries fused with the wailing gale. There was the unmistakable sound of shells whistling through the air. He uncovered his face and saw black shapes in the storm. Clawing hands. Gleaming eyes. Hideous phantoms whipped up in the tempest. Rotting faces with ragged flesh drawn impossibly long in the distorting substance that was storm and something more.

– the dead man raised the scythe with a quick-slick motion that set the dark dazzling. Cromby drew his hands up over his face and waited for the crash of the blade.

The scythe crashed instead to the ground, and Cromby moved his hands in time to see the dead man arch and buckle in some strange torment. It was whisked into a small formless storm above Cromby, and in no time at all it had been whipped up into the rafters of the barn.

Cromby watched in amazement as the tiny hurricane raced about the roof space battering the boards until –

– moments later the gale blew itself out, receding into the night in all directions with a wave of rustling trees that settled promptly back to rest.

The summer night returned to normal and the sound and fury seemed suddenly a thing imagined. Clambering to her feet along with the men around her, Mary took in the moonlit lawns littered with debris. People were beginning to emerge from their cover, some with fresh wounds from the soaring slate.

Mary and Briggs looked at one another in dread and they spoke together.

'The Doctor!'

Being fitter and faster than Briggs, Mary was the first to enter the basement, but she clattered to a halt when she realised the extent of the damage. The building was demolished, and there was a view now of the sky through the ruptured space where there should have been ceiling and walls. The upper levels having collapsed through, it was almost impossible to see a way to the clay-room door. When Briggs arrived, they proceeded frantically together to clear a path, shouting as they went.

It took minutes to reach the room, and they found the door already smashed open by fallen beams. Scrabbling over the timbers and rubble, Mary made her way to the middle of the room. The fallen masonry was daubed here with clay, and splashes of the stuff covered everything. The place was a mass of angles and lines, black shapes and areas of dim obscurity. She came to a precarious halt and gazed into the convoluted shadows. There was nothing discernible except mangled light and dark. Mary sensed a rising hysteria gushing up from deep inside. When she spoke again it was a fearful whisper that emerged.

'Doctor?'

No reply.

'Doctor!'

She listened for the slightest sign of life, but heard only silence. Then, abruptly, there was movement in the gloom. A shape lifted itself out of the rubble, crashing to its feet in the dark, and Mary's heart leapt. It was a thing long dead, spattered in shadows and clay, hair on end and wild eyes staring. The thing spoke.

'It's only me,' it said softly. 'I'm fine.'

'Doctor!'

More laughter than word. Mary felt the relief rush through her like a crashing wave, and held out her hand for the Doctor to grab. As they picked their way back through the rubble towards Briggs, Mary felt the Doctor's slimy wet hand and hoped it was clay and nothing more critical.

'Is it really all over now?' she asked.

'I think it really is this time,' the Doctor told her.

'You destroyed the Dark Force?'

He shook his head. 'It can't be destroyed,' he told her grimly. 'It's an elemental force of nature. All I've done is dissipate it again. It should be too weak now to cause any more real damage.'

When they reached the corridor, Briggs was waiting to help carry him back. But, with Mary on one side and Briggs on the other, Mary wondered just who was supporting whom.

They made their way outside and the Doctor stopped unexpectedly, gazing up into the clear night sky, lost in secret thought. Mary observed him closely. There was perhaps a hint of sadness in those sparkling eyes. They were full of stars and wonder, but they also contained something else that was hard to define. There were things inside that head of his that Mary could only begin to guess at, and she knew now that she would never be allowed in.

'Did I hear someone suggest a good hot bath?' the Doctor asked, still staring into the Milky Way, his voice a million million miles away.

Epilogues

I

The Reverend Clarence Forster woke early to one of God's own mornings. There was a particular beauty contained in this sunrise, and it lifted Forster's spirit to witness such a splendid, serene view from the door of the church over the cemetery. One of God's many gifts to the world was morning. Forster could not imagine a world without the glory of daybreak. A world that orbited its star without turning on its axis could have been a tragedy that man might never have realised. The magic of morning was to the Reverend Forster another clear sign of God's signature in creation.

Down at the bottom of the cemetery was a tumbledown wall, and slumped on the wall was a figure. Although he was turned away, Forster could see that he was reading what appeared to be a letter. The Doctor folded the paper and slipped it into his pocket. Forster may have been mistaken in the idea that the Doctor wiped his eye.

Although the Doctor had shown some degree of disrespect, Forster was not a man to harbour a grudge. It was such a beautiful morning, he thought he might share it with the stranger, and with this idea in mind he began to make his way to the end of the graveyard.

To the accompaniment of the dawn chorus, with its voices higher than the sky, Forster strolled among the headstones and reflected upon the peace and tranquillity that might be found in this small corner of time and space. Many of the headstones in this part of the cemetery were now hundreds of years old, marked with lichen and overgrown with wild grass. Forster knelt to view one of the headstones from a new perspective, and from here he noticed the long slender stalks of the poppies that grew out of the grass. They reached heavenward, their smiling flowers kissed by the sun. From the earth we rise, to the soil we return, and from our material remains springs new life. And thus the melodies play, one after another, many in unison, to God's own orchestration.

As he rose to his feet and continued on his way down the grassy path, Forster was puzzled to find the wall empty and the Doctor gone. Quickening his step, Forster reached the wall and peered over in each direction, only to find the fields beyond quite empty. For a hundred yards or more in each direction, there was no exit from the field, and Forster was certain that the Doctor could not possibly have travelled so far so fast on foot as to avoid being viewed. Left where the Doctor had been sitting was a small bundle of poppies that were bound at their stalks with string.

Baffled, Forster gazed back into the cemetery to see if the Doctor had crossed him on another path, but all he saw was headstones. Then he noticed the cross fixed to the very top of the steeple, and realised abruptly how immaculate it looked, reflecting the golden sunlight in a blaze of superlative glory.

II

Mary woke to a silent house. Her bedside clock told her that it was almost a quarter past nine, and she jumped up in bed with a start. She had never in her recollection slept so very late. What on Earth would the Doctor think?

As she sat in the silence, listening to the house, she realised suddenly that the Doctor was no longer present to think anything about how late she had slept. The house was empty, apart from one lonely soul. That soul had never felt lonely. It had always been a vibrant thing, cheerful in solitude, without the need for company. Now, curiously, however, she sensed a new isolation inside herself.

The feeling of aloneness was a peculiar one. She missed her brother intensely. She missed her father when he was absent for so long. But now there was a new void. Another domain of desertion. Another private pain. She had prepared for his leaving, and she had left him a note in readiness. She hoped he would find it concealed among the other curious slips of paper he carried around in his pocket. Had he remained, she would have removed it this morning, but now she was satisfied that she had taken the opportunity to write it in the night.

Not bothering to get dressed, Mary went downstairs and stood for a moment in the middle of the lounge. It seemed a little larger now than it did only a couple of days ago. A little more empty. The fire had gone out and the room, facing west, felt cold.

She noticed that the photograph of David had been moved. It was left at an angle amongst the others. She stepped over and looked behind it, expecting to see a note from the Doctor, but there was none.

With a sigh, she went into the kitchen, and in the sunlight in the middle of the table she found the small vase of flowers. Sweet peas and snapdragons. A vase of vivid colour. A parting gesture.

From one who had gone for ever.

III

Constable Albert Briggs woke to an oratorio of thrushes. It was nearly ten o'clock but he lay there motionless. After all that had happened to him over the last few days, he was loath to set foot out of his bed today.

Instead, he lay with his memories. Half-dream notions that he could hear Effie breathing gently at his side, hear her stirring from sleep, feel the bed sink as she turned to lean over and kiss him good morning.

Half-dream notions.

Through the curtains, thick with dust, he could see that the sun was already high in the sky. Really ought to shake a leg, he thought. Drag himself from his nice warm den to face the world. There was a report to write on the events of the last few days. God alone knew what he as going to put in the thing. Maybe he ought to let Mary Minett have a look at it with him. Maybe he could write an introductory bit, about a page of preamble, number it 'page one of six', and then say he'd lost the rest. Maybe.

He shambled downstairs in his socks and nightgown, and as he shuffled across the little kitchen, he noticed a folded sheet of paper on the mat in front of the door. The paper was a note from the Doctor written in a scrolling, perfectly formed hand.

Dear Constable Briggs,

I have arranged for the collection of my box to be undertaken by Messrs. Bracket and Flockton of Grimston Removals. They will pick up the box around midday today and transport it under my instructions. I would be very grateful if you could please furnish them with any assistance they require.

It has been a very great privilege for me to work with such a diligent and helpful local officer, and I offer you my earnest thanks for your help in resolving this particular case.

I wish you all the very best regards.

Sincerely,

The Doctor.

Briggs folded the paper and placed it on the table, thinking it might come in useful later when he feigned loss of his report. He could always refer any enquirers on to the good Doctor at the Ministry of…

Which ministry, exactly, did he say he was from? Perhaps Mary Minett knew. Not important at the moment, he thought. The important thing right this minute was to get that kettle on!

IV

Iris Cromby had never in her life been in bed at this ridiculous hour of the day. There was so much to do, so much work on the land still to organise. The mangelwurzels weren't going to just jump out of the ground and come running into the barn of their own accord. And the barley wasn't going to get itself in this year. And now, with the stables gone up in smoke, the barn needed some work on it before the horses could be given a proper temporary home…

The bedroom door clattered open and Bill Cromby stood there with a giant tray. He lumbered over and set the tray on the bedside cabinet next to Iris. She was amazed to see a pot of steaming tea and an entire loaf of bread sliced like doorsteps, toasted, and dripping in butter and thick layers of lumpy strawberry jam. There was half a slab of cheese on a separate plate and this too was cut into great wedges that were more suitable for rats than mice, Iris thought.

'Breakfast in bed,' Cromby announced proudly.

'William Cromby! Yer old romantic!' she grinned.

He gave her a bashful smile and shoved the tray a bit nearer as she shuffled up in bed. He watched her take the tray and plonk it on her knees, before heading back for the door. Iris watched him, puzzled, and stared again at the mountain of food on the tray.

'Where are you goin'?' she asked.

'Goin' to bring mine up now,' he said.

V

Mary's letter

22nd August 1918

My Dear Doctor,

I do not know what makes people choose the partners they choose. Perhaps it is God, or Fate. I suspect it is something in our biology we simply have no inkling of as yet. I am sure medical science has a great many wonders still to uncover. Perhaps it is the same gift that animals possess when they sense our fear or love. There are subtleties to the human heart we do not comprehend.

Of course, I believe in God. But I also believe we choose our own way in the world, and that we are responsible for our own mistakes. God has no hand in our errors of judgement. We are all mortal and feckless. Sometimes we take the wrong track. He watches over us as we go, but I do not think He necessarily puts gates in our path. I suspect He wants us to learn the hard way, to experience the pain: the chagrin of failure, the distress of having made a mistake. Perhaps these are the things that make us strong. Perhaps they fortify our soul and prepare it for entry to Heaven. It is not for us to know in this world.

I cannot believe you were blind to my intentions. I do not believe for all your strengths and complexities of nature you have an Achilles' heel in Love. I know you are a passionate man. You have your reasons for leaving. I will never know what they were. But I think you know what you awoke in me, and I will never forget it. I will never forget you.

I wish you luck in your travels. I hope when you are a very old man of a hundred and ten, you finally do meet your friend in St Louis in the year of our Lord, two thousand and one.

   Yours truly,

   Mary Minett.

VI

Short extracts from *The Medic*, issue 294, dated 13 October 1993. The article was addressed to the British medical profession, and compared known epidemics and their relative severity…

…The Influenza Epidemic of 1918–19, also referred to as the Spanish Influenza Epidemic, was the most severe outbreak of this century. In terms of the total number of fatalities, it was possibly the most devastating epidemic in human history…

…The outbreak would more accurately be called a pandemic, since it affected populations worldwide…

…The severity and speed of transmission of the virus mark this episode as highly unusual…

…the virus mutated into a more lethal strain and a second more severe form emerged in August 1918. In this strain, pneumonia developed with surprising rapidity and death came ordinarily after only two days from the symptoms presenting. About half the deaths were among 20-to-40-year-olds, marking out an unusual pattern for this kind of virus…

…Outbreaks occurred in almost every part of the world. In India at least 12,500,000 deaths occurred. The United States of America suffered approximately 550,000 deaths…

…A total estimated 30 million people died throughout all populated areas of the world…

…The cause of the extreme virulence of this outbreak remains a mystery to modern science…

Who on Earth is Steve Emmerson?

Steve Emmerson is the alias of an author who writes a large number of bestselling novels under a whole range of pseudonyms, all of which are household names.

Besides this, he runs an international conglomerate whose capital assets exceed the value of the gross domestic wealth of many small countries. He has homes in the Seychelles, Lanzarote and the French Riviera. He owns the world's largest private collection of Ferraris and Porsches.

At 25 years old, a staggeringly handsome man, Steve Emmerson is quite possibly the world's most eligible bachelor. He controls his magnificent empire from a cupboard under the stairs in his mum's council house in South Croydon, and never, ever, ever tells lies.

Ever.

Acknowledgements

A number of people deserve thanks for helping me write this book:

Jac Rayner and Steve Cole. For their astonishing enthusiasm when I sent in my original, completely different, idea. TWTWTW!

Justin Richards. For helping develop my initial premise to make it a real *Doctor Who* story. And for all the other nudges in the right direction along the way.

Major Paul Laycock. For his eager assistance with the technical detail connected with the military side of this book. Please note that any mistakes are not down to Paul's misinformation, but my misunderstanding.

Jane Moore for reading and commenting in such minute detail, and for discovering the embarrassing mystakes in my first draft. Susan O'Neill for spending so much of her time with Mary, Briggs, Cromby et al. Peter Holmes for help horological. Chris Shaw for help on the farm.

Books galore! I used too many to list here, but particular thanks for clarity and inspiration must go to: Christopher Martin's *English Life in the First World War* (1974) (ISBN 85340 417 8), Arthur Banks's *A Military Atlas of the First World War* (1975) (ISBN 2435 32008 4), Marie Hartley and Joan Ingilby's *Yorkshire Village* (1953/1979) (ISBN 0 460 04425 7).

Last, but certainly not least, my wife Shirley for her tireless encouragement and assiduous and diligent checking of my drafts.

This book is not by Steve Emmerson. It's by a whole lot of people. That charlatan Emmerson just put his name to it.

THE MONTHLY TELEPRESS
The official BBC Doctor Who Books e-newsletter

News – competitions – interviews – and more!

Subscribe today at
http://www.e-groups.com/group/Telepress

PRESENTING

DOCTOR WHO

AN ALL-NEW AUDIO DRAMA

Big Finish Productions is proud to present all-new *Doctor Who* adventures on audio!

Featuring original music and sound-effects, these full-cast plays are available on double cassette in high street stores, and on limited-edition double CD from all good specialist stores, or via mail order.

Available from September 2000
THE FIRES OF VULCAN

A four-part story by Steve Lyons.
Starring **Sylvester McCoy** as the Doctor
and **Bonnie Langford** as Mel.

Two thousand years ago, a cataclysmic volcanic eruption wiped the Roman city of Pompeii from the face of the Earth. It also buried the Doctor's TARDIS...

Arriving in Pompeii one day before the disaster, the Doctor and Mel find themselves separated from their ship and entangled in local politics. With time running out, they fight to escape from the shadow of Mount Vesuvius. But how can they succeed when history itself is working against them?

If you wish to order the CD version, please photocopy this form or provide all the details on paper. Delivery within 28 days of release.
Send to: PO Box 1127, Maidenhead, Berkshire. SL6 3LN.
Big Finish Hotline 01628 828283.

Please send me [ ] copies of *The Fires of Vulcan*
each @ £13.99 (£15.50 non-UK orders) Prices inclusive of postage and packing.
Payment can be accepted by credit card or by personal cheques, payable to Big Finish
Productions Ltd.
Name...
Address...
....
Postcode...
VISA/Mastercard number ....
Expiry date...
Signature..

Other stories featuring the Seventh Doctor still available include:

THE GENOCIDE MACHINE   THE FEARMONGER

For more details visit our website at
http://www.doctorwho.co.uk